WEDNESDAY'S CHILD

Raymond Bliss was born in Leicester and educated at Kibworth Beauchamp Grammar School, and trained as an articled clerk in accountancy. His early life was spend in the Midlands, but in the mid-1980s he moved with his second wife to Cornwall when he took on a new career as a postmaster, and he still does some locum management work today.

Creative writing has always been in Raymond's blood, and as a young teenage boy he was writing a regular school classroom magazine. During his years in business in the Midlands, he was regularly quoted in the national and local press.

He is also a keen bridge player, having won numerous trophies, and has represented Cornwall in league competitions.

Raymond Bliss

WEDNESDAY'S CHILD

Olympia Publishers
London

www.olympiapublishers.com
OLYMPIA PAPERBACK EDITION

A CIP catalogue record for this title is
available from the British Library.

ISBN: 978-1-84897-495-1

(Olympia Publishers is part of Ashwell Publishing Ltd)

First Published in 2015

Olympia Publishers
60 Cannon Street
London
EC4N 6NP

Printed in Great Britain

For my loving children; Debbie, David and Ian and precious grandchildren; Andy, Tom, Vicki, Sammi, Ollie, Philippa, Esme and Eddie

ACKNOWLEDGEMENTS

Monday's Child is fair of face,
Tuesday's child is full of grace,
Wednesday's child is full of woe,
Thursday's child has far to go,
Friday's child is loving and giving,
Saturday's child must work for a living,
But the child that is born on the Sabbath day,
Is fair and wise and good they say.

I must thank my mother for the title idea of this novel because as a child she was always quoting this little poem, the origin of which is unknown to me.

My son David's short stint working on the buses helped with a lot of the information regarding bus drivers' duties. Other transport information was sourced with my grateful thanks from the West Midland Transport Museum, Eastern Counties Omnibus Society, D F Roberts of the Crosville Archive Trust.

My grateful thanks also to Ian, Nikkie and Ros and the Wisbech Society that all contributed amendments. My proofreading friend, Debbie, who corrected all my many mistakes.

Thanks also to the Olympia Publishing team and, of course, that information highway, the internet.

Finally, I must thank Olenka Maria Dicu, who gave me considerable encouragement to get this story published.

CHAPTER ONE

Wendy Marshall stood looking at her image in the full length mirror that was on the inside of the wardrobe door in her mother's bedroom. Her discarded dressing gown and A-cup bra lay haphazardly on the faded rose pink bedspread, her knickers at her feet where she had stepped out of them. She was not naked. She was wearing a towel, wrapped turban style over her head to dry her wet hair after her bath.

At twelve years old she was at an impressionable and inquisitive age. Self-conscious about her looks, she believed others saw her as a skinny, unattractive and plain looking girl that no boy would look at twice. She felt she had small breasts for her age and wondered why she couldn't have a figure like her best friend Anne's.

She envied how grown up Anne looked at her thirteenth birthday tea party the previous Sunday, when it was the first of March 1953, in a pussy-bow blouse, pencil skirt and adorned with some of her sister's make-up. Her coal black hair was out of the schoolgirl pleats and in a long ponytail that went halfway down her back. Would she be as big as Anne and hopefully filling a bigger bra when she was thirteen?

It was at her best friend's house earlier that Thursday afternoon when her headache started, caused by trying her first cigarette. The first puff she had harmlessly blown out. With the second very small puff she had copied Anne and inhaled a little, but the third she fully inhaled and it almost choked her. Her uncontrollable coughing caused some hot ash to scorch a hole in the sleeve of her blouse that she had hidden from her mother's prying eyes beneath her blazer. Alone in the house a Beechams powder and a soothing bath had helped relieve her self-inflicted headache. Her mother, a school dinner lady, was out celebrating a work colleague's birthday and she was supposedly child minding her ten-year-old brother Michael. He had made her task considerably easier by taking some of his Dinky toys to play with his friend Gregory who lived next door but one.

She studied her profile. At five foot four inches she was already the same height as her mother and the third tallest in her school class, despite being one of the youngest. When she breathed in and held her breath it made her developing bust look bigger. Rubbing her hand against the glass she searched for the mark she had made the previous week but it was undetectable. She looked in the mirror again and felt sure her size had increased.

Turning slightly she gently patted her bum that seemed to be getting bigger. She turned again to confront her full image in the mirror. Her hips seemed to be wider. Just over six stone in weight, she hoped she was not going to go from skinny to fat. What would she look like in July when it was her thirteenth birthday?

She removed the towel and brushed her damp, naturally wavy, rich chestnut hair. Inherited from her mother, it was the one feature on her body that she was proud of. It had earned her some derogatory nicknames in the past like conker top and carrot head but also earned her the compliment of having hair like the film star Rita Hayworth. She was about to use some of her mother's lipstick until she saw the reflection of the alarm clock in the mirror. It was almost eight thirty and the time when Michael was due back.

She was fully dressed and listening to the wireless when Michael came in twelve minutes later. *'It's Cheerful Charlie Chester'*, let's listen to that before I go to bed?'

Wendy stirred after a short but deep sleep, wondering what had troubled her. The flimsy curtains, drawn across the window at the bottom of her bed, did not stop the moonlight from making everything visible. The door leading to Michael's room, directly above the kitchen, was wedged in the frame. It was warped and had never closed properly. She could hear her brother's noisy breathing as he slept, not quite snoring; more like the sound of a dulled pant of a dog.

She heard it again, laughter and the sound of a man's voice. She sniffed, puzzled by what she could smell. She slipped on her dressing gown, wondering if she should investigate, but her fears eased when she heard her mother's voice that sounded in jovial mood.

At the bottom of the staircase Wendy gently pushed the door that opened into the back room, that her mother always called the parlour. She was greeted by a man sitting at the table with his back to the kitchen eating a plate of egg and chips, left-handed by the way he was holding his cutlery. He was wearing a soiled vest, exposing arms that were black with body hair. His bushy eyebrows almost met at the bridge of his nose. His jowl cheeks reminded her of a bloodhound and she could tell his thinning black hair was layered down with Brylcreem.

Her mother appeared at the doorway leading to the kitchen wearing a cleavage-revealing underskirt and carrying two cups of steaming tea. 'Wendy, what are you doing up?'

'I – I heard,' she mumbled, rubbing the sleep from her eyes.

'I expect we woke her, Doris,' the man said; his dark brown eyes focused wantonly on Wendy. 'I'm Sid,' he said boastfully, 'and you must be Doris's little girl, although I didn't expect you to be this big and beautiful.'

Wendy did not appreciate his smarmy compliment or the manner of his voice that suggested she should know who he was.

'Sid kindly walked me 'ome,' her mother said as she put the teacups on the table.

'Thanks, Doris, that was a lovely meal that was,' Sid said as he took his cup of tea, 'and this'll swill it down nicely.' He belched as he moved his plump figure to a fireside armchair. 'Pardon me,' he grunted.

After a sip of tea Doris felt an explanation was due to clear the air. 'Jarvis's chip shop was shut so he came in to let me cook 'im some supper.'

She then noticed that her daughter's face was still drained of colour. 'You still look a bit pasty, let me get you a cup of tea.'

Wendy swiftly followed her mother into the kitchen, catching the strong whiff of alcohol on her breath as she moved close to her side. 'You're not dressed,' she whispered sternly.

Her mother winked at her. 'I 'ad to get me best frock off in case fat splashed over it.'

She handed the cup to Wendy and returned to the parlour. Wendy followed. Sid was poking at the fire in the grate trying to bring some more life from the dying embers. Tea was the last thing Wendy wanted but she felt she would have to drink it to give her an excuse for not returning to her bedroom.

'Sid works on the buses,' Doris said to break the strained silence.

'That's right I'm a driver,' he said, scratching his dimpled chin. 'Here, did I tell you I was nearly caught up in all them bad floods last month? I was driving the five, the route through the Broads to Yarmouth, only the day before it all happened. It weren't half bad round there.'

'Those floods were terrible everywhere,' Doris said, 'worst in living memory.'

Wendy was feeling cold and wanted to get back to the warmth of her bed, not listen to the two grown-ups exchanging stories about the tragic floods that swept across the East Coast at the beginning of the previous month of February.

Tragedy had been no stranger in her young life. She had been born at the beginning of the war; a cruel war that had robbed her of her father seven weeks before her birth. She had only sketchy memories of her first stepfather, George Silverwood. He was another war victim, being killed in Northern France in June 1944, sixteen months after his son Michael was born and six weeks before her fourth birthday. Stan Woodman was the only father she had known. Her mother married for the third time at the end of the war and for six years her childhood was as normal as any other working class family in a tiny cottage in Biggleswade. They had moved to Norwich last autumn, when Stan found the house where she now lived, but her excitement had turned to devastation a few weeks later when he was killed in a road accident.

Her tea was almost stone cold by the time she became aware of Sid's imminent departure. 'Look at the time,' he said. 'I've got to get home to me boy.'

'I've met the boy I'd love to marry,' Wendy said dreamily to Anne on Monday morning. Her mood was as bright as the sunshine as they set off on their daily routine walk to Blyth School; a girls' grammar school that was a short distance away.

Anne liked Wendy's genuine forthrightness, so unlike some of the other bitchy girls in their class, and admired her candid, get on with life attitude that was not put off by adversity. She admired Wendy's beauty almost to the point of jealousy; her soft porcelain complexion, pencil thin eyebrows, long lashes over eyes that were the colour of the sky on a summer day and delicate small lips. Once her bust developed on her lithe body she would have a queue of boys wanting to marry her.

'Who is it then?'

'His name's Graham Rawlins and he's really handsome.'

Wendy had been expecting Sid's boy to be some young hoodlum about Michael's age or younger, so was delighted when he turned out to be a really dishy youth, with mousy hair over hazel eyes in an innocent sort of face. Lean-fleshed, he was taller than his father despite only being fourteen. He was quiet, polite and courteous. She could hardly take her starry eyes off him when he sat opposite her at the dining table in a Fair Isle pullover that was at least one size too big. Her heart had raced when he sat next to her, smelling of carbolic soap, during a family game of Ludo in the afternoon. It had been the high point of her weekend when she had expected it to be horrible and boring. The low point had been on Saturday morning.

She was in the usual queue at the butcher's, armed with ration book and shopping basket, with Michael in tow in one of his why moods. Her mother's thrice repeated words were embedded in her mind. "Make sure it's a nice lean piece o' beef, not all fat and gristle, no more than three shillings and ask Mr Hodges to put it in the book." It was for Sunday and she was not looking forward to seeing Sid again or meeting his hoodlum boy.

She was not interested in the conversation of the two ladies standing immediately in front of them about the recent death of Stalin. The conversation being spoken in lower tones by two in front of them was more intriguing, "daughter only fourteen".

'Why do we have to buy milk checks at the Co-op?'

'To pay the milkman,' Wendy replied hurriedly as she overheard "having a baby".

'Why can't you just give him the money?'

'It's absolutely disgraceful,' was the final snippet she heard as the two women reached the front of the queue and a smiling Mr Hodges.

Wendy answered her inquisitive brother. 'If you gave him the money Mam wouldn't be able to get the divi.'

Back home, her angry mother challenged Wendy the moment she walked through the door into a steamy kitchen. 'Have you been smoking?'

'No, Mam.'

'You're a liar, Wendy,' said Doris, confronting her with the burn hole in her blouse that she had just washed. 'What can't speak can't lie.'

'It was at Anne's; one of her sisters caught my arm.'

'Damn and blast it my girl, 'ow many times have I told you not to lie? No pocket money for you this week until you learn to tell the truth.' It was hardly punishment. Often she did not get her two-shilling pocket money when her mother was strapped for cash.

Recalling Graham's age put a less enthusiastic tone in her voice. 'The trouble is he's almost two years older than me so I don't expect he'll want to take me out.'

'That would be cradle snatching,' giggled Anne.

'I expect so,' a deflated Wendy was forced to agree. Locked in her daydreams she almost bumped into the milkman who was stubbing out a cigarette with his boot.

'Does he smoke?' Anne asked.

'He didn't yesterday and that's another thing; I'm never going to have another cigarette.'

'You'll soon change your mind. Both my sisters have said that and now they both smoke like chimneys. My brother Jimmy goes through twenty Park Drive a day and both my parents smoke. Flipping heck! You'll find more smoke in our house than at Thorpe Railway Station!'

'Well I shan't,' Wendy replied emphatically. 'It made me so sodding ill you would not believe it. Besides I thought…um,' she paused, wafting her hand over the two small bulges in her school uniform, 'doesn't it stop your growth?'

Anne laughed. 'Flipping heck! It's not stopped me growing.' She breathed in and pushed out her chest to demonstrate her point. 'Look at Judith Nethercott,' continued Anne, nodding towards the larger of two girls walking ahead of them. 'She smokes at least a couple of packets of Players Weights a week and look at her, tits as big as coconuts.'

'Sid'll get a big tax refund.'

'That's no reason to get married, Mam, and you know it.'

Wendy was agitated. Everything was moving quicker than an express train. Only ten days had elapsed since Sid had moved in as a lodger the previous Thursday. On that day she had rushed home from school in the pouring rain to find Sid painting Michael's bedroom. His was the small bedroom above the kitchen. She discovered that his bed was in her room, situated directly above the parlour.

'Just for tonight, love,' Doris had said as she put her hands comfortingly on her daughter's shoulders. 'Sid's doing up the back room for you.'

'Me?' said a flabbergasted Wendy, 'but that's Michael's room.'

'Not any more it ain't,' said Michael, having climbed the stairs from the bathroom where he had changed out of his rain sodden clothes. His walnut brown hair, usually untidy and straggly, was still wet and looked like an upturned mop. 'Me and Graham are having your room.'

It had stunned Wendy. Only a week had elapsed since that night she had first seen Sid and here he was moving in as a lodger. Moreover, only four months had elapsed since Stan was buried. It quite deflated her spirits after she had run home excitedly to tell her mother that she was going to take part in a school pageant to celebrate the Coronation.

Doris cringed. Wendy was just like her father. He would not have approved of the speed of events but needs must. A tax refund, due to Sid if he married before the fifth of April, was not to be sniffed at and an extra wage coming into the house would further ease her stretched finances. She detested being on her own and despised living in a house without a man.

Sid was no Ted Marshall. Wendy's father had been love at first sight. She remembered her first date at the Beckton Park open-air swimming pool in Plaistow on a very hot Saturday in June 1935.

Remembered the over the moon feeling of her first passionate kiss in Sweetnams Cinema in Rathbone Street, she never ever called it by the correct name of Sweetingham's. Remembered her wedding day in October 1938 when she was so proud at becoming Mrs Marshall she felt on top of the world. Remembered the day it was cold enough to freeze the Thames in January 1940 when she hugged and kissed him goodbye, little knowing that it was for the very last time. She still craved for him, still missed him and still hated the war for taking him from her. Hated the bombs and the gypsy lifestyle that had been forced upon her by constantly moving from lodgings to lodgings.

George Silverwood, a soldier that was older by eleven years, had married her immediately she found herself pregnant with Michael and had accepted her young daughter as if she was his own. For over two years she had a settled life, living in a terraced house in Hitchin before disaster struck again. She could not believe how cruelly life was treating her when the telegram arrived reporting his death; forcing her back to the perpetual struggle of managing on a war widow's pension. Forced to move again she found a cottage in nearby Biggleswade.

Deep in debt, she was days away from being evicted from her home when she met Stan Woodman. She bumped into him during the May celebrations at Ickwell Green when they were watching the maypole dancing. The attraction was as instantaneous as the striking of a match. They were holding hands as they watched the crowning of the May Queen. That evening he walked back to Biggleswade with them, often with Wendy sitting on his shoulders and other times pushing Michael in his pushchair. He was kind, hardworking and good with both her kids, but for reasons unbeknown to her she was unable to reward him with a child of his own. Yet again life was sadistically brutal to her. She was widowed for a third time last November when his lorry skidded on some black ice and crashed into a tree.

She was almost in tears when she became aware of her daughter's cold stare. 'The vicar 'as only just been able to squeeze us in.' Truthful though it was it was all she could think to say.

Barely reasons for committing yourself to a wedding, thought Wendy but the ceremony took place the following Saturday at one fifteen.

Wendy adored her outfit. Mother had bought her some new underwear at Marks & Spencer on Tuesday afternoon and the following day the railway parcel van had delivered a lovely camel coloured skirt with matching jacket. It hugged her body, giving her some curves so that she felt very grown up. The curve of her small bosom was exaggerated with a pair of ankle socks to fill out her bra and she was wearing a girdle and her first ever pair of nylon stockings. Apart from clothes for school they were the first new garments she had had for ages. She just hoped her mother was not going to send them back on Monday. It would not be the first time.

There was no wedding dress. Her mother was wearing a similar two-piece outfit in an ivory shade from the same catalogue.

Doris Eva Woodman looked a picture as she said, "I will" to becoming Mrs Rawlins; hair immaculately permed, a taut complexion keeping her fresh and young looking and the ivory suit, which she had tailored to a perfect fit, revealed her voluptuous figure. Standing outside after the wedding service, mother and daughter with their matching chestnut hair looked like sisters; Wendy five years older than her true age and Doris ten years younger than her thirty-five years.

The house was packed out. Neighbours, dinner ladies and bus drivers with their respective spouses were crowded into all the downstairs rooms of their house in Rosewood Road. There had been no time and no money for a reception to be anywhere else. The sandwiches that Wendy had been preparing all morning while her mother was at the hairdresser's were being devoured quicker than a flock of vultures could strip a decaying carcass.

There was only one relative, Aunt Ethel, who had travelled from Peterborough by service buses that had taken nearly five hours the day before. She had the same dark features as her brother Sid and the same dimpled chin. She was almost as plump and her black hair was severely swept back into a bun, which with her beak nose gave her a witch-like appearance.

Wendy had been forced to give up her tiny bedroom and suffer the indignity of having to sleep in the same bed as Michael in the boys' room. She had worn her longest ankle length nightdress and kept on the largest pair of navy knickers that she had. As she spotted Graham inching his way towards her she smiled with the wicked thought of sleeping in the same bed as him. Only one more night and things would be back to normal.

'Fancy a walk to get some air?' Graham's words were music to her ears. Watching adults drink themselves into a stupor in smoke filled rooms was not for her.

'How does it feel to have an older brother?' Graham asked as they sauntered down the hill towards Angel Road.

Wendy had not thought of Graham as being a stepbrother nor had she even entertained the idea of his father being her latest stepfather. She had only thought of Sid as "him" or "that man" and she doubted she would ever call him by a relative name like "Dad" or "Father".

'I honestly hadn't thought about it.'

They reached the junction and Graham held her hand briefly while they crossed the Angel Road, giving her a warm feeling inside her body. She had given up all hope of a romantic liaison between them even before the marriage making them family ruled it impossible, but she still admired him.

'What about you, how do I measure up as a stepsister?'

'Okay.'

'Okay,' Wendy repeated. 'That's not very flattering. Does the thought of having a sister bother you?'

They reached the entrance to Waterloo Park. They both turned and walked through the gateway as if their journey had been pre-planned.

'I didn't mean it to sound like that. I've had a sister before you know.'

'Have you? So your dad's been married before.' It was a fact that she had learned for the first time. Either her mother did not know or had not thought to tell her. 'What happened to them?'

'They were killed in an accident.'

'Oh that's really awful. I had a stepfather that was killed in a road accident. When did it happen?'

'It was a long time ago. I was only eight. Dad met me out of school and took me to Aunt Ethel's. When I asked where Mum was he got very angry and said, "she's gone and taken that girl with her". Later Aunt Ethel told me Mum and Gwyneth, that was my sister's name, had been knocked down by a motor car.'

'How old was your sister?'

'She was actually a half-sister and four years older than me. My mother had been married to a coal miner who was killed in some colliery accident in the nineteen thirties.'

Absorbed by their conversation they had reached the play area. Wendy sat on a vacant swing and automatically he gently pushed her.

'We're a right mixed lot aren't we? My name's Graham Rawlins, your name's Wendy Marshall, your brother's Michael Silverwood and this morning your mother was Doris Woodman.'

Pushing Wendy from behind, Graham could not see the smile that beamed across her face. If only she had been given a penny every time she had to explain about their names. 'Your dad is Mam's fourth husband. My dad, Ted Marshall, was her first and I think the one she was most in love with but he was killed at Dunkirk before I was born.'

The person he was most in love with was this gorgeous girl he was pushing on a swing. As Wendy continued her explanation his mind drifted back to the time they first met. Looking across the Sunday lunch table he was instantly smitten by her good looks, her cheerful smile, her dazzling blue eyes and her beautiful chestnut hair that now almost touched his face as she swung to and fro. He had mixed emotions about the wedding. Wendy was a person he wanted as a girlfriend not as a sister. She was at the centre of his dreams, his desires and his fantasies. Last night he hardly slept a wink, content to listen to her breathing. How he wished he could be Michael and sharing his bed with her. Suddenly he was aware of the silence.

'Were you listening?' asked Wendy.

He was too embarrassed to admit his thoughts so he said the first words that came into his head. 'You make this Mr Woodman sound like a nice bloke.'

'He was. He was a driver like your dad, but he drove lorries for British Road Services. We used to live in Biggleswade but Dad; I mean Stan Woodman, put in for a transfer so we could be near the seaside and have a house with three bedrooms and a proper bathroom, even though it is next door to the kitchen and not an upstairs one.'

'Were you fond of him?'

'Yes he was very kind. He used to bring us things. I remember once, when everything was short, he brought a big bag of cherries from a load that he had delivered to a canning factory in Sheffield. Made my belly ache something rotten for a couple of days. He used to take us in his lorry in the school holidays. The first time me and Michael saw the sea was when he took us to Brighton. Best years of my life they were.'

'How long ago was his accident?'

'Last November.' Wendy sensed that Graham was surprised because he stopped pushing the swing. 'Hardly four months ago and she's met and married your dad.'

The gentle pushing continued. 'Didn't your mum have any kids with Stan Woodman?'

Wendy was embarrassed. Graham was older so he probably knew more about these things than she did. She only knew from Anne, who had gleaned information from her sisters, that girls had babies growing in their stomachs. She avoided the question by changing the subject.

'Are you going to give me a good push on this swing or carry on rocking me like a baby in a cradle?'

CHAPTER TWO

A slice of the tax refund was spent as a deposit on a new Ferguson television set. It was given pride of place on top of the sideboard in the front room and on the first night the whole family sat and watched the black and white images appear on the nine inch screen.

Michael was lying on his stomach on the fireside rug and watching intently. 'It's amazing, but how do we get the pictures?'

'The signals are picked up by the aerial,' Graham explained. He was sitting at the end of the settee nearest to the sideboard. 'That H-shaped metal thing they stuck on the chimney this afternoon.'

Wendy was feeling flushed, sandwiched on the settee between him and her mother but it was not due to the heat in the room where a blazing fire was giving off a cosy warmth. Her right side, from her knee to her shoulder, was touching Graham and every small movement in his body made her tummy wobble.

'I'll 'ave to get a licence,' said Doris. 'I wonder how much that will be.'

'Two pounds,' said Sid, joining in the family conversation, sitting in the armchair with his back to the window. 'That's what my mate Edgar said. He got a telly last month when he came up on the pools.' He supped at his beer that Graham had fetched earlier from the off licence counter at the Lord Rosewood public house.

'I 'aven't got two pounds to spare.'

Throughout her various marriages Doris had always had to scrimp, save and live on credit. When she got paid on Friday virtually all her money, together with the housekeeping Sid contributed, went on paying the rent, her weekly instalment on the club catalogue, paying Mr Hodges the butcher and paying as much of the weekly food bill at Mrs Thompson's shop as she could.

Sid took his wallet from his back pocket and pulled out a pound note. 'Take this,' he said, 'the other half will have to come out of the housekeeping.'

Doris slipped the note into her apron pocket. 'I think I might manage now but I may 'ave to borrow ten bob before the end of the week. Anyway, it's nice to have it before the Coronation. I'll be the envy of all the girls at work.' She smiled smugly.

She was not smiling, and she had to ask for more than ten bob, on Friday when she discovered the payments on the television meant she had to find an extra twelve shillings and nine pence per week. It caused the first marital tiff that can only be described as a blazing row between Sid and Doris.

On the first Saturday in May it seemed to Wendy that every Eastern Counties bus driver that was not working was crammed into the front room. It was Cup Final day and somewhere in the room Graham and Michael were watching the match between Blackpool and Bolton on the television.

Wendy heard the shouts as she sat sewing a button on her school blouse in the living room. 'What was that?' she asked Graham as he raced through to the kitchen for a drink of water.

'Bolton have just scored.'

At that precise moment there was a knock at the back door. He opened it and shouted that it was Anne before rushing back to the front room.

'Flipping heck, he's in a bit of a hurry isn't he?'

'He's watching the football on the television,' Wendy said as Anne sat in the opposite fireside chair. She checked the button was secure, neatly folded the garment and placed it with the sewing box on the table. 'Besides he's making the most of his freedom because he starts a job next week working all day Saturday for some bloke on the market.'

'As long as it wasn't me he was running away from. He's very dishy, I can see why you wanted to marry him'

'Can't do that now that he's my brother,' Wendy responded.

'I overheard my sisters whispering this morning.' Anne was all smiles, obviously excited by the news she was about to divulge. 'You remember I told you Marian went to Hemsby with her boyfriend last Sunday?' Wendy vaguely recalled a conversation about her sister on the topic as they walked home from school earlier in the week. 'Well when they found themselves alone in the dunes their feelings got a bit out of control. So after a lot of kissing and petting, off came her knickers and bang went her virginity!'

Wendy vaguely understood and chuckled while a giggly Anne continued with her story. 'It was hard not to laugh how she described it to Jane.' She pitched her voice a little higher to imitate her sister, '"pain in my fanny and sand in my arse", were the very exact words she used.'

'That doesn't sound very romantic.'

'No it doesn't. Flipping heck! I'm not going to lose my virginity in no shitty sand dunes. Mine will be romantic with a nice boy that I love, in a proper bed and with soft music on the gramophone like

28

in the films.' Anne paused from talking when they heard more noise coming from the front room. There had either been another goal or a near miss.

'I then heard them whispering about being pregnant,' Anne continued unashamedly. 'Marian reckons you can't get pregnant the first time but Jane said you could. So she's going to have an anxious wait to see if she starts on time.'

Wendy was getting lost understanding the conversation, 'Starts what?'

'Her period,' Anne boasted. 'You know whether you're having a baby or not by your periods. If you stop having them it's because you've got a baby growing in your stomach.'

Their conversation ended abruptly when Michael suddenly appeared. 'Dad said can you go and get 'im some fags.' He tossed a half-crown piece at Wendy and vanished back to the front room.

The next Saturday the house was peaceably quiet when Graham walked through the back door. 'Where is everybody?'

'Your dad's working, Mam's out with Mrs Sutton from next door but one and Michael's out playing with Gregory.' Wendy put down the school copy of Thomas Hardy's *Far From the Madding Crowd* she was reading. 'How did you get on?'

'I liked it. Mr Chadwick was pleased and I got paid ten shillings.'

'Ten shillings! That's really super. What are you going to do with it?'

'I've already spent some of it.' He took a small crumpled package from his pocket and passed it to Wendy.

It contained a sleeveless cream cotton tee-shirt that brought a cheek-to-cheek smile to her face. 'It's lovely,' she said as she got up from the fireside chair to line it up against her body. 'I thought I'd get you something, except I'm not very good at getting girls' things so I hope it fits.'

'I'm sure it will, thank you,' she said softly and planted a delicate kiss on his cheek.

'Don't go all soft on me,' he said as he touched his cheek as if Wendy had smudged it. 'I've bought Michael a Dinky bus; do you think he'll like it?'

'He'll love it. Now let me get you something to eat, a sandwich or something hot?'

'I think I'll have some bread and jam.'

Wendy went through to the kitchen and Graham followed her to the door. 'I'm afraid it's still the homemade apple and blackberry.'

'And margarine I suppose.'

'Mam can't afford anything else,' Wendy replied as she scanned the kitchen cabinet for ideas. 'There's a sausage. Let me fry it with an egg and some bread.' She did not wait for an answer as she lit the stove and reached for the frying pan.

Dithering in the doorway he watched his stepsister for a minute before finding the courage to speak. 'There's an amusement fair on near the cattle market, do you fancy going to it later?'

Wendy turned to face him. 'Aren't you going to the Firs Stadium to see the Speedway with your mates?'

'I haven't arranged anything because I wasn't sure how I'd feel after working, but if you don't want to go it…'

'I'd love to go,' Wendy interrupted. She would normally be going out with Anne but she had a "date" at the Capitol Cinema. The huge smile that beamed across her face expressed the happiness she felt. Perhaps some of her classmates would see her with this handsome boy and be envious, not realizing he was her brother. 'It will give me a chance to wear the tee-shirt.'

Michael came waltzing in ten minutes later leaving the back door wide open as his eyes focused on the Dinky bus. 'Is that mine?'

'It's a present Graham's brought you,' said Wendy sitting by his side at the table with the empty plate in front of them. 'So let's hear a big thank you and then you can shut the sodding door.'

'Thanks, Graham, it's super,' but as he went to kick the door closed he almost bumped into Sid returning from work.

He made straight for his favourite fireside chair with the back to the window and noticed Michael clutching his Dinky double deck bus as if it was made of gold.

'Let's 'ave a look at what you got there?'

'Graham bought me it,' he said as he handed it to Sid to look at.

Sid looked at the green and cream coloured bus. 'It's a Bristol K-type,' he said, 'that's what I drive most of the time. Tell you what, I'll take it down to the depot on Monday and see if my mate in the body shop will paint it red. I'll even see if he can put a number on it here.'

Michael could see that Sid had his finger on the route indicator position at the front of the model bus. 'Number eighty-nine like the one that runs at the top of the street?'

'Yes,' Sid confirmed as he stooped down to untie his boots.

During the next three weeks things in the city of Norwich built up towards the Coronation. Union Jacks fluttered everywhere, bunting was put up in the streets and shop windows were predominantly red, white and blue featuring pictures of the Queen. There were souvenir packs of everything from tea caddies to tins of biscuits, from paper bags to linen tablecloths. Even Graham had brown paper bags on the market stall displaying a picture of the Queen. By the end of the month everywhere and everybody was gripped by a fever towards the forthcoming event.

Wendy was busy trying to learn her lines for the forthcoming school pageant depicting the life of the country during the reigns of all sixteen monarchs that ruled between the two Queen Elizabeths. Her particular part was to play Queen Anne who ruled at the beginning of the eighteenth century. Doris was busy with her sewing, making the period costume from crinoline material that Graham had somehow managed to obtain as a gift from his market employer.

Doris had been taught her sewing skills by her mother as a young girl and had used her expertise profitably over the years; making and mending dresses, making and altering curtains, and repairing and patching clothes. In the dark days of the war when Wendy was young it was often the only income that kept food on the table and clothes on their backs. The dress she lovingly laboured over for her daughter was brown in colour, figure hugging around the waist before flowing outwards over a large bustle in the style of the period. The sleeves were white cotton as was the waistband and front neckpiece that had sequins sewn on to it.

Apart from the pageant, Wendy was also taking part in a carnival parade that was taking place in the city the day before the Coronation. The father of the girl playing King George II was Stan's old boss at the BRS depot and he had entered a float on the same theme.

'You were fantastic,' Graham enthused as the family returned from watching the pageant. Only Sid was absent, as he was unable to swap his driving shift.

Doris put her hand around her daughter's shoulder and hugged her. 'I don't think I 'ave ever been more proud of you than I was tonight and in front of the Lord Mayor too.'

'I reckon the flag event was certainly the best part of the whole night,' said Graham.

The scene written depicted the Act of Union of 1707, a major event during Queen Anne's reign, uniting England and Scotland. In the sketch Anne acted the part of Sarah Churchill and Susan Leach, the tallest girl in the class, played her husband the Duke of Marlborough. It ended with a tableau to symbolize the occasion, played out like a scene from a silent movie.

The adept fingers of Mrs Dwyer, the music teacher, dancing on the piano keyboard provided the background music of Handel's *Largo*. Without speaking, Anne and Susan produced the national flag of Scotland using an easel, a blackboard covered with material and cut out fabric shaped like Saint Andrew's cross. The arrangement was then repeated on a second easel to create Saint George's cross. Cued by Mrs Dwyer, the red plus sign of the English flag was then placed over the white cross of the Scottish flag.

At that point Wendy moved majestically to the front of the stage and the music stopped, ending the silent film routine.

'This was the birth of the Union Jack flag, brought about by the Act of Union,' Wendy had shouted to the audience. 'It was almost a hundred years later before Ireland became part of Great Britain.' She paused to allow the final arrangement to take place. A narrow red cross was brought on to the stage by Susan and positioned corner to corner on the easel.

'The Union Jack,' shouted Wendy, 'the flag of Great Britain and her empire.'

'How did they get the material to stick together?' Michael asked. 'Were they using glue?'

'No the material was like baize and bonded together like the old flannel graphs we used to see at that Sunday school in Biggleswade.'

The elation of her two pageant performances was dampened during the parade through the streets of Norwich in the bucketing rain. She was on an open truck and by the time the procession reached Riverside Road her hair was saturated, the white cotton sections of her dress were transparent and the out-flowing skirt was wet and limp, but Wendy's spirits were high. She waved enthusiastically when she saw her family gathered in front of the gas works.

Meal times in Doris's household were determined by the Eastern Counties work schedules rather than regular standard times. It was a sunny June evening and, being Wednesday, Michael was at the church boys' club. Doris had just opened the oven door to check the cottage pie was browning nicely when her husband charged in like a raging bull.

'Where's Graham?' he shouted.

'Whatever is the matter, Sid?'

'He's been pinching fags from that shop in Magdalen Road, the bloody little thief.'

Wendy could hear the commotion and the sound of movement upstairs as she sat in the armchair in the front room revising for the next day's Biology exam.

Graham, having descended the stairs two at a time, appeared at the doorway. 'What is it, Dad?'

Sid darted towards him. 'Front room,' he yelled as he started to unbuckle his belt. He had always worn a belt and braces so that his uniform trousers remained in place when he gripped the buckle tightly in his left hand.

'Get out,' he ordered Wendy as he pushed Graham and sent him sprawling over the arm of the settee. 'I'll teach you not to pinch fags.'

Having gathered up her school books she had only reached the doorway when he lashed Graham across his back. She was horrified and closed her eyes tightly for a moment as if she felt the pain of Graham's agonizing scream.

'No, Dad, it wasn't me,' he shrieked, his voice high-pitched, portraying his fear.

Doris had moved to stand by Wendy in the doorway and was wincing helplessly with her hands on her mouth.

'Bloody liar, you were caught red-handed,' Sid yelled in his rage as he whipped another stroke of his belt across Graham.

'No, please God, no,' Graham tearfully wailed before another stroke flayed his buttocks.

Wendy had seen too much. She turned to the comfort of her mother's arms. Graham's screaming was as painful to her as a dentist's drill on a raw nerve.

'Get upstairs and stay there.'

Five minutes later Wendy sat silently at the dining table, tense and afraid, listening to a calmer Sid talking to her mother.

'I'd only just left the pub, having nipped in for a quick pint, when this irate man came out of his shop and ranted on about Graham stealing two packets of cigarettes.'

As Sid paused to eat, Wendy looked across the table at the empty chair and strangely quiet place set for Graham. It was unfamiliar and eerie.

'The only way I could shut 'im up was to tell 'im I'd get Graham to call in first thing tomorrow and pay for them. Senior Service, dearest bloody fags in that mangy old shop.'

At the end of her meal Wendy thought of an excuse to leave. 'Mam, I need to pop round to Anne's to check something for my exam tomorrow.'

Wendy had never liked Sid and after what she had just witnessed that dislike had turned to loathing hatred. Agitated by it all she walked to the top of the street, thought about turning right when she reached the Post Office, but as that would take her past the shop in Magdalen Road, she turned left and walked up St. Clements Hill instead. By the time she had walked down Chamberlin Road and along Angel Road she had calmed down.

It was as she was passing the Lord Rosewood close to her home that she thought of something positive she could do to help Graham. At the off-licence counter of the pub she spent the last pennies of her pocket money on a packet of crisps.

Returning home, Wendy walked through the back door, used by friends and neighbours alike as the main entrance to their house, to find the kitchen deserted. She moved through the ever-open door into the parlour and sat on one of the red marl fireside chairs, either side of the tiled fireplace. Behind her was the window overlooking the back yard and behind the other chair the door leading on to the staircase was closed. The way to the front room, where she could hear Sid arguing with her mother over the sound of the television, was through an alcove directly opposite the doorway from the kitchen.

'Bloody 'ell it weren't that hard,' she heard Sid yell. He was a violent evil man and she hoped her mother's anger voiced opposition to the thrashing he had given to Graham.

Having no wish to advertise her presence she removed her shoes and tiptoed to the staircase where she opened the door quietly and climbed the stairs as silently as a ghost. She nudged open the door to find Graham lying on his stomach on top of his bed in his underwear. 'Can I come in for a moment?'

'Not if it's to gloat,' he said, his voice muffled by the pillow.

'It's not.' She moved closer and handed him the packet of crisps. 'I've brought you these.'

'Thanks,' he mumbled.

Seeing the bloodstains on his vest and pants where the belt had flayed him filled her with compassion. 'I expect you're really sore, would you like me to put some ointment on?'

'It's stinging like mad do you think it would help?'

'Mam always put some on me whenever I fell over and grazed myself.'

Wendy quietly went downstairs to get the cream that was kept in a cabinet in the bathroom. When she returned Graham was leaning on his side and tucking in to the crisps. She sat on the edge of Michael's empty bed to face him.

'I didn't pinch any fags from that miserable old man,' Graham explained between mouthfuls. 'I went in to the shop to get a copy of the *Speedway News* when those two Bilson brothers charged past and sent me flying. That silly old twat of a shopkeeper thought I was with them and that I'd fallen trying to rush out.'

'Why didn't you tell your Dad that?'

'He wasn't exactly in a listening mood was he?'

Wendy seethed with anger. She detested her stepfather's actions when she assumed Graham was guilty, but now she knew that he was innocent she was absolutely outraged and it showed in her fiery voice. 'Did you tell the man in the shop it was the Bilsons?'

'No. I didn't want to snitch on them,' Graham said calmly. 'Mind you I might have if I'd have known this was going to happen.'

'Your father's a monstrous sod, how could he do this to you?'

'He's done it before.' Graham stopped talking as they both heard Sid bawling his head off about money. He crumpled the empty crisp bag in his hands and reverted to lying on his stomach. 'And when he loses his temper I expect he'll do it again.'

Wendy moved to a position behind Graham and squatted on the edge of his bed. 'Can you lift your vest up or shall I?'

Graham raised himself, took his vest completely off and then returned to lie on his stomach.

She winced almost to the point of tears when she saw the ugliness of the wheals forming on his back.

'This may hurt a bit.' She delicately dabbed some cream on his back and then stopped immediately when he shuddered.

'No you're not hurting, it was just very cold,' he explained.

Wendy continued deftly, gently, slowly kneading the cream into his blistered skin. She did not realize how nice she would feel, quivering agreeably as if she was being gently tickled with a feather but not quite to the point that she would convulse in a fit of giggling. After spending as long as she could she said: 'There you are, is that better?'

'It feels a lot better.' Graham had never imagined that pain could turn to pleasure so quickly. He did not want his sister's fingers working their massaging magic to end and tried to sound casual. 'I don't suppose you want to do anymore?'

Wendy also tried to sound very casual, 'I will if you want me to.'

She was elated and felt all sorts of sensations in her body as she watched Graham ease down his underpants to expose his wounds.

'Oh you poor thing, no wonder you're lying on your stomach.' Two angry red lines, looking like tramlines across his buttocks denoted the marks caused by the belting.

She spread the ointment on the flayed abrasions and felt him wince when she touched a particularly bad sore. 'I hope I'm not hurting you?' she asked as she continued very slowly with the delicacy of an antique dealer handling priceless porcelain.

'No it's nice and soothing.' But it was more than that. The feeling was utterly sensational. He closed his eyes; happy that by laying on his stomach his erection was hidden from Wendy.

As she worked quietly, like a nurse on a bed sore patient, she felt these strange sensations in her body. The pit of her stomach felt tight, her vagina felt hot and tingly and the nipples on her developing breasts were stiff, erect and itchy. She had never felt anything like this before and wondered what part of her growing up she had now reached. Whatever it was it felt nice, but she did not think she would tell Anne about it.

She had almost finished smoothing the cream over Graham's buttocks when she heard the back door slam and the voice of Michael announcing he was home.

Graham quickly hoisted up his pants and Wendy stood abruptly as though somebody had stuck a pin in her backside. She opened the adjoining door and entered her bedroom as she heard Michael whistling as he climbed the stairs.

CHAPTER THREE

By the end of the week things were getting close to normal. Graham was almost able to sit properly without feeling any pain from his thrashing. Wendy was just about speaking to Sid, but only when she had to. The bruising that appeared on the right cheek of Doris's face on Thursday morning had virtually gone. 'Oh it's nothing,' her mother had said when challenged by Wendy. 'It was that silly top door on the kitchen cabinet that caught me.'

'Where is everyone?' Graham asked as he arrived home from his Saturday job on the market.

'Wendy will be back in a minute,' Doris said, concentrating on darning some socks in the comfort of the fireside chair. 'She's been watching the Wimbledon tennis on TV but 'as just popped down to Thompson's to get some potted beef for tea. Michael's gone with your Dad on the buses.' Her sewing finished, she looked up and her curiosity was aroused when she noticed he was carrying a small package under his arm. 'What 'ave you got there?'

'Oh nothing much,' Graham shrugged. 'Just something off the stall I thought Wendy might like.'

'What might I like?' Wendy asked as she came charging in at the end of Graham's reply.

'These,' Graham said and handed the poorly wrapped package to Wendy who eagerly ripped off the paper to find a pair of slacks.

'They're supposed to be all the rage in America. Do you like them?'

'Thanks they're really super but,' she stopped abruptly from asking why he had brought them when she saw him wink at her. 'I'll pop up to my room and try them on.'

As Wendy raced up the stairs Doris got up and put a friendly hand on Graham's shoulder. 'You're very good to her.'

Before Graham could give any acknowledgement Michael came racing in. 'Guess what,' he said exuberantly. 'I've been on the number twenty-five with Dad all the way to Blakeney and back. It was a Bristol single decker type LL number 712 and Fred the conductor let me do some tickets.'

Wendy looked three years older when she returned wearing the new navy blue slacks that hugged her body and did justice to her slender legs. 'How do I look?'

'You look great,' Graham replied, looking up from the newspaper he was reading in the other fireside chair.

Her mother's proud eyes looked at her from the doorway leading to the kitchen. 'You look nice in them but they look a bit tight, are they too small?'

'No, Mam, they're supposed to fit tight,' Wendy replied and then lifted her blouse and put her thumb on the inside of the slacks to show a normal gap.

Graham's eyes nearly popped out of his head at the sight of Wendy's slender waistline. Great, he thought to himself, was not nearly sufficient to describe her; fantastic, stunning, ravishing came closer.

Wendy watched as her mother went back into the kitchen in readiness to prepare tea and noticed it was the top left door of the

41

kitchen cabinet her mother opened as was customary because the hinge on the right door was broken and remained permanently closed. The opening door would have hit the left side of her face. The bruise to the right side of her face that appeared on Thursday morning was obviously caused by something else and Wendy did not need to be a super sleuth to guess that it was the left hand of Sid.

Friday twenty-fourth of July arrived and Wendy reached a new milestone in her life when she became a teenager. She came down to the parlour, eager and optimistic, to be greeted with a less than harmonious rendering of "Happy Birthday".

'I hope it's a nice one,' said Graham as she sat at the breakfast table opposite him.

'Here you are, Sis,' said Michael, handing her a parcel with a card tucked under the string.

'It's from all us, Wendy, happy birthday,' said Doris as she placed a cereal dish on the table for her daughter.

'Thank you,' Wendy said as she looked at the drawing of a red double deck bus on the front of the card.

'I did the card,' Michael said.

'I never would have guessed,' Wendy mocked as she read the greetings on the inside signed by Mam, Dad, Graham and Michael.

'Aren't you going to undo the parcel?' Graham asked.

Wendy untied the bow and pulled back the brown paper to find her present protected with corrugated paper that she excitedly parted. It was a short sleeve, calf length summer dress in a blue petal and green leaf pattern on white cotton.

'Do you like it? Graham got the belt and material and I made the dress,' Doris explained.

'Yes, thank you, it's really super; I'll go and try it on.'

Upstairs Wendy quickly shed her dressing gown and nightdress and slipped the new dress over her body. She raced into her mother's bedroom and turned first one way and then the other in front of the wardrobe mirror. She was speeding towards womanhood. The belt accentuated her narrow waistline making her developing bust look bigger. Her hips were curvy and her legs long and slender. Downstairs all agreed it was beautiful. She wondered if she should wear it on the planned trip to Yarmouth on Sunday but decided it would be more practical to wear the sleeveless tee-shirt with her navy slacks; previous gifts from Graham that she treasured.

'No you can't come with us,' Graham said loudly to a whinging Michael.

'Why not?'

'You're not old enough,' Wendy replied.

'Yes I am you silly cow,' Michael retorted loud and vindictively.

'Shut your mouth you cheeky little sod,' Wendy shouted back.

'You'll have to do as you're told for once,' Graham said sternly. 'You haven't any money so you'll just have to sit here with the spectators, like it or lump it.'

He turned his back on Michael and went with Wendy to put his roller skates on in readiness to try his hand on the rink they had found near to the Marine swimming pool.

The previous day Aunt Ethel had arrived from Peterborough. Graham had volunteered to sleep on the settee to save Wendy the embarrassment of sleeping with Michael. Having scared herself half to death watching the second episode of *The Quatermass Experiment* on the television, she had been relieved not to be sleeping alone in her room. In the middle of the hazy Sunday afternoon as the adults dozed in hired deck chairs to sleep off their lunchtime drinking, Graham, Wendy and Michael had wandered off to do their own thing.

'Did you like that?' Graham asked as they sat and changed their shoes after skating.

'It was great when I wasn't falling down. Thank you for treating me.'

'Who said anything about treating you?' Graham teased. 'Don't forget you start your paper round tomorrow. You'll be in the money at the end of the week.'

'I'm really looking forward to next Saturday. I'm going to get four and six a week so I can definitely pay you back.'

'Don't be silly, I was only joking.'

They moved out of the changing area but there was no sign of Michael in the spectators' seats. 'Where's he gone?'

Wendy scanned the vicinity with her hand shielding her eyes from the sun. 'Do you think he went back to the grown-ups?'

'I don't know, but if he hasn't and we do I'll get a right bollocking for losing him.'

'Let's have a look round, he can't have gone far,' Wendy suggested.

There was no sign of Michael in the immediate proximity of the skating rink. Wendy was outside the pier contemplating whether they should continue to walk towards the pleasure beach when a blue bus pulled up showing "One, Wellington Pier". The conductor was soon leaning over the bonnet winding the handle to alter the destination blind to read "Caister".

'I bet he's at the bus station,' Wendy said, thankful that the incident had caused the idea to come to her mind.

'He's mad on buses, it's certainly worth a try.'

'Can you remember where it is?'

Graham looked back along Marine Parade. 'Look there's the Windmill Theatre,' he said pointing in its direction. 'I'm sure we walked by that. It must be up a street past that.'

They held hands to stay together as they briskly walked by the holidaymakers meandering along the crowded promenade. 'Has he always been interested in buses?'

'No, when we lived at Biggleswade and Dad worked for British Road Services he used to collect depot numbers.'

'How did he do that?'

'I'm not sure but there were lots of depots and each had its own number, which was painted on the lorries. He spent hours in Shortmead Street watching out for BRS lorries using the A1.'

'He must be interested in all transport.'

'Aren't all you boys. He's mad about buses and you're mad about Speedway racing.'

They reached the Windmill and further down Devonshire Road, which ran alongside the theatre, they spotted a red bus. They raced the remaining short distance to find Michael sitting on a seat in a yard area where passengers boarded the vehicles.

An irate Graham shouted at Michael. 'You gormless twat, why did you run off?'

Wendy interrupted the argument that flared up between the boys. 'Graham, could you lend me a penny? I need to use the ladies.'

'Wendy,' Graham shouted as he rushed in the back door from his Saturday work at the end of September.

'Yes,' she responded placidly as she emerged from the bathroom with the sound of the toilet flushing.

'Are you interested in a Saturday morning waitress job?' He was panting from running and, between deep breaths, he explained that the café near his market stall had a vacancy. The girl that had held the job since July had consistently muddled up customers' orders and constantly dropped cutlery and crockery. When she failed to turn up that morning it was the last straw for Sandra the proprietor. 'If we go straight away Sandra will give you an interview.'

'I'll have to get changed.' Wendy was thrilled by the prospect and rushed past Graham still standing at the back door. 'I'll be two minutes,' she yelled as she flew up the stairs.

She was ten minutes but was transformed from a working Cinderella to a glowing princess. Her neat chestnut hair was brushed and backcombed without a hairgrip in sight. Foundation, eyeliner and lipstick, raided from her mother's makeup, had been sufficiently applied to give her face a warm and sensual look. She had borrowed the black court shoes and charcoal skirt from her mother's wardrobe. The crisp white blouse was her best school one that had been washed and ironed in readiness for Monday. She looked classy and capable and Graham was confident she would sail through the interview.

Twenty minutes later she was sitting in front of Sandra while Graham waited discreetly outside the café.

'You certainly look smarter than the last girl,' said Sandra who could not believe she was only thirteen. She was attractive and feminine and would be a real head turner in a couple of years' time. She would certainly attract more male customers into the café. By way of a simple test she made Wendy take down an order from the menu and was satisfied with the speed and legibility of the writing. 'Let's see how you get on making a milk shake.'

Wendy was fighting her taut nerves and followed Sandra's instructions, pouring milk and banana concentrate into a stainless steel jug then fixing it on the electric whisker displaying "Horlicks". It was perfect and she was allowed to drink it while Sandra outlined all the various aspects that the job entailed; the working routine, the washing up, the wages and the tips.

'Harry speaks very highly of your brother, so if you work as well as him the job's yours.'

'Oh thank you, thank you,' said Wendy, as excited as a child with a new toy.

It had started to rain when Wendy stepped outside and saw Graham sheltering in a shop doorway. Throwing her inhibitions to the wind she raced to him and embraced him so tightly onlookers would have thought they were long lost lovers. 'I've got it, I start next Saturday.' The jubilance in her voice matching the happiness she felt, she was completely oblivious to the rain that was soaking her.

Sid rushed into the barber's to escape the light rain to find three other men sitting and waiting for a haircut. 'Morning, Arthur.'

'Morning, Sid,' the barber acknowledged. 'Had a nice Christmas?'

'Lovely thanks,' Sid replied as he sat on the only remaining vacant chair. 'I didn't expect you to be this busy.'

'I reckon everybody put off coming before Christmas because they thought I would be busy but in fact I was very quiet for the whole week before,' he said as he started trimming a pensioner's hair. 'Are you doing anything special tomorrow night?'

'No I'm working.' Sid's roster would see him on the Dereham Road service and the nearest he would get to a pub on New Year's Eve would be turning his bus round at "The Oval".

The pensioner joined in the conversation. '1953 ain't been a bad year though 'as it? The Coronation, Stanley Matthews winning his first cup winners medal, England winning the ashes, Gordon Richards winning his first Derby and that Edmund Hilary conquering Everest.' It started a general discussion among the other waiting customers. Sid picked up the morning newspaper and started to read. It was going to be a long wait.

Wendy decided it was time to get up. She slipped on her dressing gown and new slippers, a Christmas present from her mother, and moved through the empty boys' room. Downstairs the wireless was playing *Housewife's Choice* with a request of *Singing in the rain*, very appropriate as drizzly rain was falling outside, but there was nobody to be found. She remembered her mother was going to do some cleaning at the Lord Rosewood, she presumed Sid was working, she guessed Michael was at Gregory's house and she knew Graham was helping Harry Chadwick on his market stall.

She wondered how cold it might be in the bathroom because an empty house was an ideal opportunity for a bath, with nobody banging on the door wanting to use the lavatory. The flames in the gas geyser took the chill out of the room and to ensure continuity of hot water Wendy went to the kitchen cabinet to get a shilling, which she slotted into the meter, located in the storage area under the stairs.

This Christmas had been different, Wendy meditated as she soaked in the bath water. She had financial independence. She remembered feeling rich on the first occasion she received the princely sum of four shillings and sixpence for doing her paper round before becoming positively wealthy with her second job as a waitress. It was work she enjoyed and Sandra seemed pleased with her. It added a new dimension to her young life. She smiled at the memory of buying her first lipstick when she was with Anne and the excitement it generated. But she never spent all her hard earned wages. She had regularly bought savings stamps at the Post Office and then opened a National Savings Bank account when the book was full.

Having her own means had allowed her to buy her mother a silk headscarf and a calendar so that she could include Sid when she wrote "Mam and Dad" on the tag. It had been easy to choose Michael's present, a Dinky toy model of a Maudsley observation coach that he was ecstatic about. Graham's present had been the most difficult. She had seen a book about Speedway that was affordable but in the end she had spent rather more than she intended on a long sleeve jumper that he could wear on the market to keep him warm during the winter.

She doused herself liberally with talcum powder before making her way to stand in front of the mirror in her mother's room. She started to sing along with the music she could hear from the wireless that was playing a request of *Diamonds are a girl's best friend* as she reflected how much her body had changed since the previous Christmas. She was growing up fast. Her firm breasts had developed and she had outgrown her first bra. Neither could she squeeze her hips into year old skirts or struggle to get them over her taut rounded bottom. Her wispy threads of pubic hair had spread and thickened. She was blossoming into womanhood yet she was still too young, too unknowledgeable, and too full of childlike innocence to understand. She was too engrossed in studying her image to notice that the bedroom door had quietly opened.

'What the hell are you doing?' Sid growled at her.

With the singing and the wireless Wendy had not heard him climb the stairs. She jumped when she heard his voice before quickly putting one hand in front of her vagina and her right arm across her bust in a vain attempt to cover her nakedness.

'I didn't hear you,' she murmured

'Flaunting yourself like a bloody harlot. Well I'll show you want happens when you bloody flaunt yourself.'

He moved into the bedroom and closed the door firmly behind him. Wendy backtracked until she was cornered on the opposite side of the bed from a leering Sid and the door. Suddenly the bedroom had become a jail cell from which there was no escape. Visions of Graham's thrashing and the abrasions he suffered flashed to mind as Sid started to unbuckle his belt. Frightened out of her wits she threw herself on to the bed and covered herself with her discarded dressing gown.

'Please don't belt me,' she begged mercifully.

Sid released the braces from off his shoulders to allow his trousers to fall to the floor. 'Now I'll show you what happens to bloody harlots.' He yanked her dressing gown away and lay beside her.

Petrified and bewildered her body was as still and rigid as a corpse. Only when his hand cupped her breast did she scream, but only for a moment before his same hand moved swiftly from her breast to her mouth to gag her.

'One more sound out of you and I'll belt you,' he said threateningly as Wendy remained motionless. He lifted his hand from her mouth.

Wendy bit her bottom lip and fearfully nodded.

He moved on top of her.

She could see his nicotine stained teeth, smell his stinking breath and feel the hardness of his penis pressed against her. She watched him spit on his fingertips before she closed her eyes, unable to witness any more of her living nightmare. She felt his fingers moisten her vagina. She could feel his hand guiding his penis and then she screamed with the pain of his penetration before his hand clamped over her mouth to silence her.

It seemed forever but it was soon over. She lay frightened and still as her stepfather dressed.

'This will be our secret,' he said pointing his finger threateningly at her before hoisting up his trousers. 'That means not saying a word to anyone,' he continued as he gathered his belt from the floor but instead of slotting it through his trouser loops he suddenly used it like a whip and lashed it across the empty half of the bed, missing Wendy by a whisker. 'Especially your mother, do you understand?'

Too terrified to talk she nodded. She was devastated. She felt as though life had been sucked from her, leaving her as fragile as an empty egg shell and just as vulnerable. Painful though the penetration was she feared a belting would be much worse.

CHAPTER FOUR

'Running about the 'ouse naked.'

Her mother's angry outburst started as soon as Wendy returned from her work at the café. It completely threw her. What lies had Sid been spreading?

She had endured three nights of poor sleep disturbed by horrifying nightmares. Three tormented days when she had agonized over telling her mother but the threat of a belting and the image of Graham's thrashing had been enough to silence her. And what could her mother do? Certainly not wind back the clock and stop it all happening. While silence was not golden it was better than a sodding beating.

'What if it 'ad been Graham that caught you?'

Wendy could not believe what she was hearing. Sid had bullied her into secrecy but had now fabricated a story to her mother making her the villain and him the hero. She moved quickly into the parlour, threw her coat on a fireside chair and turned to face her mother who had followed and was angrily ranting on.

'It's a wonder 'e didn't belt the living daylight out of you.'

It lit the fuse to her own rage and she exploded. 'Oh yes,' she yelled, 'He's bloody good at that. Look what the sodding monster did to Graham!'

'Graham was pinching fags, 'e deserved it.'

'Are you sure about that, Mam?'

'He was caught red-'anded.'

'Then why didn't they find the fags on him?'

'His mates ran off with them,' Doris quickly responded. 'If that shopkeeper had 'ave called the police then Graham would 'ave been in a lot more trouble.'

'The police would have proved Graham was innocent.'

'You kids are all the same, sticking up for each other. You've only got 'is word for it.'

'He still didn't deserve such a beating even if he had have done it.'

'It was just a good thrashing to put 'im right.'

'And the bruises that appear on your face from time to time, are they to put you right?'

'What bruises?' Doris flushed as she put her hand up to the right cheek of her face. 'Oh that's when that silly door on the kitchen cabinet opens too quickly and catches me unawares.'

'No, Mam,' Wendy said defiantly. 'You always open the top left door of the kitchen cabinet because the other sodding door is broken. That would hit the left side of your face and your bruises are always on your right side caused by a swipe from a left hand. Sid's the only left handed person in this house.'

'You cheeky little madam,' Doris yelled irately. 'You've never liked Sid.'

'No and I never will,' Wendy seethed, 'I detest him, he's a bloody bully and a sodding maniac that ought to be locked up.'

Doris slapped her hand across Wendy's face at the cutting remark. 'How dare you say that?'

Wendy was stunned and put her hand to her cheek to counter the sting. With tears welling she promptly pushed past her mother and headed towards the back door.

'Just you show some respect, my girl, or I'll throw you out of this 'ouse,' Doris yelled at her departing daughter.

'That'll suit me fine,' Wendy shouted before she slammed the door with a force that matched her anger.

Wendy shivered when she reached the top of the street and realized she had stormed out without her coat. It was a blustery day and she was only wearing her black waitress skirt, a white cotton blouse and an old cardigan. She pulled the cardigan tightly around her to try to keep warm, crossed the road and walked the length of Denmark Road.

She was completely innocent in this horrible sordid business so why had her mother made her feel guilty? She would not have been naked in her mother's room if she thought anybody else was in the house and certainly nothing less than a dressing gown, bra and knickers if she thought Sid was about. In point of fact since Wednesday morning she had taken to always getting fully dressed in her room, no longer appearing at the breakfast table in nightdress and dressing gown.

Absorbed in her anguished thoughts, she reached Mousehold Heath and instinctively followed one of the paths. She passed an elderly man walking his dog and ambled on until she spotted Judith Nethercott in the distance ahead of her. The company of the classroom chatterbox was the last thing she needed. She quickly veered off the path and ran behind some bushes, only to have the misfortune to stumble across a young couple, kissing and cuddling. Wendy apologized and hurried off.

What stuck in Wendy's mind was the quick glimpse of the boy's hand beneath the girl's jumper and over her boobs. When do you let a boy touch you? Sid had put his grubby hands over her and she had hated it. Would it have been different if it were somebody else? Somebody she liked? Should it have hurt so much? Was she pregnant? Had that sodding monster made a baby start to grow in her stomach? Questions, questions, but she had no answers. She wished she knew as much as Anne about these things.

Oblivious to the cold she stood staring at the panoramic view of Norwich. Stan had brought her to this viewpoint soon after they moved in, pointing out the Cathedral spire and explaining that it was the second highest in the country. She had loved Stan. He would have listened to her and comforted her. He would have knocked Sid's sodding head off. How she missed him. Why did he have to die so tragically?

Feeling very isolated and vulnerable she left the heath and walked up Mousehold Lane. Where could she go if she had to leave home? She knew her own father had a brother but they had not kept in touch and as far as she remembered he lived in Plymouth. She had never met him and apart from a vague recollection that he was in the Navy, she knew nothing about him. Not much to go on and Plymouth was the other side of the country.

There was no relative that she was aware of from her mother's second marriage and nobody that she could recall in all the years her Mam was with Stan. The funeral was very sparsely attended with a few drivers from British Road Services, some friends from Bedfordshire and someone described as an aunt who had travelled from Letchworth. Certainly nobody she could find in a hurry and certainly nobody she could go and live with at the drop of a hat.

She reached the Boundary Park greyhound racing arena that looked miserably forlorn under the grey sky. Very much the way Wendy felt. The green painted corrugated iron fencing that she leaned against reminded her of the Firs Stadium, home to Graham's beloved Speedway. Should she confide in Graham? She always had a soft spot for him and he had treated her well. He was so unlike his father in looks and character yet he was still his son and hardly likely to take her word against that of his own flesh and blood. Be that as it may right now she would love to be in his arms in a comforting hug.

The deserted stadium suddenly burst with life when two boys riding cycles, one an obvious shiny new Christmas present, came from around the back and screeched to a halt on the car park. Not being in the mood to having two young boys stare at her Wendy quickly moved on.

She ran for the protection of a bus shelter in Sprowston Road before the worst of the squally shower lashed down. It was just the way her luck was running when of all the buses in Norwich, the first one to draw up was a number ninety-one with Sid driving. He was all smiles and waved, but she turned her head away in disgust. Sid really was a wicked sod that had filled Doris's head with a pack of lies. Most of the time he was friendly enough but he had an uncontrollable temper, which caused him to belt his son and strike his wife. He could turn on the charm like water from a tap but Wendy always suspected it was false like a "smile please" for a photograph. Michael liked him, Graham tolerated him and her mother loved him. Wendy loathed him even before he sexually abused her.

Abused or belted? What a choice! Graham could not sit down properly for a week after his belting whereas the physical pain of

Sid's penetration had not lasted long. Her vagina had felt sore for most of that day but she thought that was due to her constantly washing and scrubbing herself.

As the rain eased she left the bus shelter for fear of seeing him again on a return trip. That sneering smile from the half cab of the bus had given Wendy a new determination. She was not going to let him get the better of her without a fight. She would return home and act like nothing had happened and Sidney Rawlins could go to hell.

Her resolve had waned by the time she reached home, creeping in as meek as a mouse. Graham was sitting on the stool at the kitchen cabinet finishing off a bacon sandwich. Michael was noisily playing with a Subbuteo football game with Gregory, completely occupying the dining table. Her mother was in the front room rushing a last minute request from Gloria Sutton, Gregory's older sister, to alter a skirt that was wanted for that night. Wendy was about to go upstairs when her mother called her. The argument was forgotten; being the same size, she wanted her to wear the skirt to see how it fitted.

'Are you okay?' Graham asked when Wendy was quiet and subdued at the tea table.

What should she say? That she felt sodding rotten because she had had a sodding rotten day caused by her sodding rotten stepfather? She looked across the table at Graham, smiling at her with his tender caring eyes. She could see Michael, sitting next to him, looking at her curiously and was aware that her mother's eyes were focused on her. She felt like Sylvia Peters on the television with everyone watching her, waiting for an answer. 'I've got a headache,' she replied, hoping that it was a plausible excuse for her strangely silent behaviour.

'I'll get you a Beechams powder,' Doris said.

'No it's all right, I think I'll go to bed after tea.' There was nothing on the television that interested her so there seemed little point in doing anything else. Although tame for a Saturday night she was hoping to get stuck into a "True Romance" magazine that Anne had given her.

'I thought you might like this,' said Graham as he entered Wendy's bedroom an hour later balancing a cup of tea and a slice of cake.

Wendy was still dressed, lying on her bed and trying to concentrate on the love story she was reading. 'Thanks, I'll have the tea, but I really can't eat anything.'

'How's the headache?'

'All right, was that the back door I heard a minute ago?'

Graham sat at the end of Wendy's bed. 'Mum's gone to work at the Rosewood. Michael's downstairs watching the television and I've got to stay with him but.'

'But you want to go out,' Wendy interrupted. She put her magazine down and met the imploring look in his eyes. 'Don't worry I'll come down. Are you going out with your mates?'

'Well, er, no.'

The hesitation said it all. 'You've got a date haven't you?' Although despondent, she forced a smile to match his beaming grin. 'I can't say I'm surprised. When I'm working in the café I see all the girls hanging around your market stall. Anybody I know?'

'I'm not sure. I don't think so.' Graham was not usually so reticent but equally he had not previously been out with any girls. 'Her name's Janice and I've got to go or else I'll be late.'

'Janice Prigmore,' Wendy called as Graham waltzed through his bedroom before rushing down the stairs. 'I really don't think she's your type,' she said softly and to her miserable jealous self.

Easter was late in 1954, Sunday falling on the eighteenth of April. It was very sunny but the aptly named showers had returned by Wednesday. Rain was lashing against the window when Wendy came down for a late breakfast to find her mother getting ready to go out. 'As soon as this shower stops I'm taking Michael into town to get 'im some new shoes for school. Be a treasure and do some ironing for me.'

Alone in the house she switched on the radio and with nothing better to do she tackled the ironing, made a lot easier now that they had purchased a new electric iron even if it was not completely paid for. She thought it strange that her mother was buying shoes from the town. Normally all the footwear came from the catalogue and was paid weekly like the iron. Sid was definitely working, doing middle shifts all week that meant he was away from the house during the day. She no longer assumed anything with regard to her stepfather and paid particular attention to the shifts he was working. She had avoided him like the plague even to the point of roaming the streets in atrocious weather rather than going home to a house where she suspected her stepfather was alone. Wednesday was Norwich market day so Graham was working at Harry Chadwick's stall, a regular occupation for him during school breaks.

It was after midday before she finished and as she unplugged the iron Sid entered and stood at the back door. For a moment Wendy stared in disbelief as if she was looking at a ghost. 'W-what are you doing here?'

'That's not a very nice welcome,' Sid replied with a smirking smile.

Wendy could feel the tension rising in her body like milk boiling up in a saucepan. Paralysed with fear she stood rooted in front of the kitchen cabinet. 'You should be working.'

'Even bus drivers get dinner breaks and I decided mine could be enjoyably spent with you, particularly as you've been avoiding me.'

She watched him turn the key to lock the back door and slip it into his pocket. 'Mam will be home in a minute.' Her voice was less than convincing, downhearted like a mouse trapped by a vicious tomcat with raunchy, wanton eyes.

'She won't. I gave her some money so she could go into town to buy Michael's shoes.'

She clenched her hands together tightly to try to control the trembling she felt in her body. 'You're a sodding maniac,' she shouted at him, 'and if you touch me I'll scream.'

She tried to dash past him to escape through the front door but he grabbed her arm in a vice like grip. 'And just who will 'ear you?'

She wriggled to try to free herself but it was no use. She was herded like a defenceless animal through the doorway and up the stairs.

'It will be better this time,' said Sid as he followed a shaking agitated Wendy up the stairs.

Wendy lay there degraded and humiliated, her nostrils filled with the smell of his breath and the aroma of stale cigarette smoke. After her stepfather climaxed he withdrew and she felt the last dregs of his hot tacky semen on her thigh as he rolled off of her.

Behind a locked bathroom door Wendy took off her clothes and gave herself a thorough strip wash. Even after three vigorous lathers of soap she still felt dirty and used.

Heavily burdened with shame, she remained in her room in fresh clothes until she heard the back door open. Apprehension gripped her as she listened to footsteps on the stairs. Anxiety caused her to shudder when she heard the adjoining boys' bedroom door open. Then sweet relief; it was Graham. Suddenly she was filled with this urge to be comforted and embraced by him. A strange paradox that the only person she desired was the son of the monster that caused her distress. He was so different. If only she could tell him.

Three weeks later Anne invited her for tea in return for Wendy having had her friend for tea the previous day. It was because her stepfather was working early shifts and Wendy did not want to risk being in the house alone with him.

'Turn it down,' yelled Mr Hitchens.

'Flipping heck, Dad doesn't appreciate good music.' Anne turned the volume down a mere fraction on the record player that was playing Johnnie Ray's *Such a Night* for the umpteenth time. She wore her hair in a ponytail, having long since dispensed with the pleats. During the last year she had grown in height so that she no longer looked quite so dumpy.

'You're really lucky to have a gramophone,' Wendy said as the music stopped.

'We'll have a rest to give Dad time to calm down.' Anne sat on the double bed she shared with Marian and indicated for Wendy to do the same. 'He's been in a right mood all day.'

'He seemed all right to me.'

'Didn't you notice how angry he was when he came in from work?'

'But that was something that had gone wrong,' Wendy defended. 'I didn't understand it all but if some shoe firm had delivered the wrong lasts then!'

'It was the wrong size wasn't it?' Anne interrupted.

'Whatever, but you can't blame him for being annoyed!'

'Flipping heck, he was more than annoyed, threatening to look for a new job and all that. Anyway you should have been here this morning when he saw the love bite on our Marian's neck. Flipping heck, the air was blue, mind you it was a whopper. Looked like a vampire had been at her instead of her boyfriend.'

'Have you ever had a love bite?'

Anne smiled, 'Not yet but I live in hope.'

It started a discussion on the merits of love bites that led to both girls practicing giving them using the top of their arms.

'See it was easy,' Anne said as she slipped her love bitten arm back into her jumper. 'Now let's listen to Johnnie *Cry Baby* Ray again.'

Wendy was listening to Johnnie Ray on the wireless just before the end of the summer term when Michael came in and announced in a very unconcerned attitude that he had failed the eleven plus exam.

'Not to worry,' said Doris, 'I'm sure you did your best.'

'I'm not worried. I want to be a bus driver like Dad when I grow up and you don't need to go to a posh grammar school for that.'

Wendy cringed when she heard Michael refer to Sid as Dad.

'That's right, my boy,' said Sid from his fireside chair having recently returned from working an early shift. 'I'll take you down the depot tomorrow. We've got one of those new Lodekka's coming in from the Lowestoft coach works.'

'Have you?' an excited Michael responded. 'Will I be able to go on it?'

'No promises but we'll see.'

CHAPTER FIVE

Wendy and Anne were forced to stop chatting when the noise from the loudspeakers on top of the slow passing car drowned their voices. May twenty-sixth was the day of the 1955 General Election and in the early evening the car was appealing for people to vote.

'That car looks the same as old man Summerfield's,' said Anne, talking about the only family in her street to own a motor car.

'That horrible Greasley bloke has just got an old car,' Wendy responded. 'That's the third one in our road.'

'I wish we had one but Dad can't drive and reckons there's plenty of buses.'

'I'm going to learn to drive as soon as I'm old enough.' It was said in casual conversation but it was something Wendy was determined to do.

They entered Waterloo Park and Anne lit up one of the cigarettes that she had cadged from her sister. 'I promised Roger Crowson I'd ask if you would like to go out with him,' she said as she exhaled smoke into the air.

Wendy was wearing a grey skirt that she had almost outgrown and a clingy turquoise jumper over a new bra. 'No, and if I did I would expect him to ask me himself.'

'He would have but he's ever so shy, gorgeous looking though. Why don't you want to go out with him?'

'Because I don't.'

'Flipping heck, you never want to go out with any boy. You've no end of admirers. I know that Donald Aspinall's been keen to go out with you for ages yet you always keep refusing him even though he raves about you.'

They reached a bench and sat down. In her more vulnerable moments Wendy had thought about confiding in Anne. 'I really don't want to,' she said, quietly knowing she could never divulge her reasons. She was nearly fifteen, looked older and did not appreciate how stunningly attractive she was. The abuse had continued every three months or so, but at least she knew she was not pregnant as her menstrual cycle had started earlier that day.

'The trouble with you is that you don't know when you're on to a good thing. I just wish some of them would ask me out.'

'They will, besides I thought you were going out with that Squiggy what's his name?'

'John Squires, we went to the pictures once but he never asked me again.'

'Well all I can say is that it's his loss.'

Anne stubbed out her cigarette and brushed away stray ash that had fallen on her pale green dress. 'Doesn't that Ivor Ambler do a paper round at your shop?'

'Yes I think he goes around Elm Grove Lane, why?'

'Well I heard he'd just finished with that Taylor girl he was seeing so I wondered if he might want to go out with me. Would you ask him?'

'Yes all right; I'll do my best.'

'Tell him I'll pay if he wants to take me to the pictures.'

Their conversation was interrupted by a playful scream and they both looked towards the swings where a girl was being pushed very high on a bench-type swing by her boyfriend.

'Flipping heck, that's the third boy I've seen Janice Prigmore with this week.'

'She's a terrible flirt. She hurt Graham when she dumped him but I'm glad. She was never right for him.'

'You know our Jimmy is going out with her older sister. I only hope that brother of mine knows what he's doing.'

'Graham goes out with Brenda Frost now. Took her to the Speedway last week.' Graham was the other reason why Wendy did not want to go out with another boy. Nobody measured up to him, even though he was her stepbrother.

They both heard another scream. 'Flipping heck!' said Anne pointing towards the swings. 'That stupid idiot almost fell off then. Serve her right if she did.'

A month later a forlorn looking Anne was waiting outside the café for Wendy to finish work. This was the saddest moment in the whole of her young life. She inhaled one last time on the cigarette before stubbing it under her foot as Wendy approached her.

'This is a surprise, what brings you here?'

'I've got some shitty, horrible news to tell you,' Anne responded and sighed heavily. 'You're not going to like it, I hate it myself.'

Wendy tried some light-hearted banter to try to cheer her up. 'Let me guess,' she smiled, 'you're expecting a baby?'

'No it's worse than that.'

Although she had made a joke of it Wendy could not believe anything could be worse than that. She could see that Anne had been crying by her woeful bloodshot eyes. 'What is it then?' There was urgency and concern in her question.

'We're leaving Norwich.'

For a moment nothing registered with Wendy. 'What do you mean?'

'Me, Mum, Dad and the whole family are moving. Dad's got this new job with a shoe firm in Leicester and we've all got to move up there.' Anne's despair turned to weeping.

Wendy also started to cry. 'Oh, Anne, that's awful news.'

The two girls embraced each other as they cried.

When Anne regained some control of her emotions she continued. 'Our Jane's determined to stay. Says she'll get married even if she has to elope to Gretna Green to do so. Marian's livid. She reckons she's going to stay whatever it takes, even if she has to get pregnant. There's only Jimmy who wants to go and that's because he's going to get a better job at the same factory as Dad. It's horrible, Wendy, what are we going to do?'

There were more tears. It was hard to accept but as Wendy started to come to terms with it she realized there was not a lot she or Anne could do.

The door slowly creaked open as Wendy went to push the newspaper through the letterbox. 'Come in,' a female voice shouted, 'in the back parlour.'

Mrs Bellamy was one of twenty new customers to Wendy, following a reorganization of her round by the newsagent. It made her very apprehensive as she entered the room to see an old lady, crippled with arthritis, sitting in a chair with a blanket draped over her legs.

'Oh what a pretty girl you are,' the lady said, revealing her Norfolk accent that lengthened the beginning and shortened the ends of her words. Edged with crow's feet, her warm and friendly olive eyes smiled endearingly at Wendy.

'Thank you,' said Wendy, blushing at the compliment as she handed her the copy of Friday's *Eastern Evening News*.

The silver haired old lady laid the newspaper on her lap and took a piece of notepaper and a ten shilling note from under the black telephone resting on a side table. 'Now, my dear, the man at your shop didn't think you would mind doing this for me.'

Wendy glanced at the small shopping list she was handed that started with the words "pay papers".

'I wonder if you would be kind enough to drop them in tomorrow with the paper?'

'I can do it tonight if you like,' said Wendy spontaneously. 'I've nearly finished my round.'

'No, my dear, tomorrow will be soon enough. I expect you want to see your boyfriend tonight.'

'I haven't got one.'

'Dear me! All the boys in Norwich must walk about with their eyes shut.'

The next evening Wendy rearranged the end of her paper round so that she finished at Mrs Bellamy's house. The lightweight shopping of writing pad, envelopes and confectionery was all bundled together in a brown paper bag.

'You are so kind,' Mrs Bellamy acknowledged. 'Have you got time to sit down for a minute?' She beckoned for Wendy to sit in the high back chair opposite her as she rummaged through the bag.

'There you are, my dear, these are for you,' she said as she took out a bag of humbugs and passed them to Wendy.

'No really, I couldn't,' Wendy said shaking her head. 'I didn't mind bringing your shopping; you don't have to give me anything.'

'You take them,' Mrs Bellamy insisted, 'or I shall have to throw them away. They are no use to me with my dentures.'

'Thanks.' Wendy took the sweets and placed them in her empty newspaper bag just as the striking clock on the mantelshelf sounded the first ding of six o'clock.

'Now, my dear, I want you to take this.' Mrs Bellamy held out two three-penny bits that she had found in her change.

'No I couldn't possibly.'

'You must or else I will not be able to ask you again.'

'Yes you can. I really don't mind.'

'Not unless you let me pay you because if you don't I will have to ask that girl next door and she will take my money without any qualms.'

Wendy suddenly realized that Janice Prigmore lived next door and she was near the top of her most disliked persons list. She had two-timed Graham on several occasions before denting his pride by dumping him. Wendy accepted the money and eased her conscience by making a nice cup of tea before sitting and chatting for another thirty minutes.

The sixteenth of August and the day Anne was leaving arrived all too quickly. There had been some compromising in the Hitchens family. Jane and Marian had been allowed to stay and lodgings had been found with a recently widowed young mother in Lakenham who badly needed the income tenants could provide.

'I'll write every day,' Anne shouted as the train pulled away from the city station with a loud hissing release of steam.

Wendy watched, wept and waved until it went out of sight behind some goods wagons in the sidings before wiping her tears on her handkerchief. She turned away and went out to Station Road to start the walk home feeling lonely and vulnerable.

She stopped outside Anne's old house in Eade Road. Seeing it empty, with the front window whitened over to stop people looking in, only brought about another flood of tears. What was happening to her? Everybody seemed to be getting on with life.

Michael was forever with Gregory or down at the bus depot. Graham was working. He had started in the purchasing office of agricultural merchants, Hodgson and Farrell, the day after Wendy's fifteenth birthday. He had finished school the previous week and had arrived home in high spirits with his cap in tatters from an end of school ritual. Although he was almost two years older than Wendy, because his birthday was the last day of September and Wendy's in July they were only one year apart academically.

She was still sad and teary-eyed when she reached home only to find her mother was very excited.

'I got that job,' she said, waving a letter in her hand.

Sid had persuaded Doris to apply for a vacancy in the cafeteria at the Surrey Street Bus Station, which meant she would work more hours with more pay and a share of the tips. Doris had always found the long holidays an advantage as a school dinner lady when the children were young, but now her family needs were different. She would still be free to work the odd busy evening at the Lord Rosewood as a barmaid and still be able to do any sewing work that came her way. With her extra wages and Graham's board money Doris could look forward to a period of affluence that she had never experienced before in all her life.

'Do you think you could 'elp me write a letter to the school to tell them I won't be coming back as a dinner lady?'

Wendy sat with her mother at the table and between them they composed a letter, which Wendy posted at the pillar-box at the top of the street on her way to the Post Office. She made a deposit in her savings account, mostly money she had received for her birthday and had not spent. Her thriftiness was something she had learned from Graham. Unlike her mother she always saved some of her money each week. She looked at her book as she left the shop to see her balance stood at twenty-one pounds, eight shillings and four pence.

It was a minute before six o'clock when Wendy reached Mrs Bellamy's house during her third week back at school. It was her final year and, being late September, there was an autumnal chill in the air from a gusty wind that was bending the conifers in the garden.

'I had a letter today from my friend Anne,' said Wendy after she settled herself in the chair opposite the old lady.

With Anne moving away, Graham being at work and her mother's new job, it made it harder for Wendy to avoid her stepfather. She had visited Mrs Bellamy a lot more, doing more of her shopping and helping with small chores around the house.

She had tried everything she could think of to stop his abuse. Once she thought about biting him so that it would leave a mark for her mother to see but apart from it being almost physically impossible, she could not even bear to touch his hairy skin with her mouth. It was beyond the bounds of possibility to fight him; he was twice her weight and she was terrified by his constant threat to belt her. She always felt totally degraded, having to tolerate her sweaty and smelly stepfather staying on her after his climax and always went straight down to the bathroom afterwards to wash herself thoroughly everywhere.

Mrs Bellamy sipped at her tea that Wendy, following her usual custom, had just made for her. 'Now, Wendy, let me think,' she paused, 'Anne's your friend that moved to Leicester?'

'Yes she is my best friend and I miss her terribly. I'd like to write back straight away but I don't think I'll have time tonight.'

'Whyever not? You have the whole evening in front of you.'

'I've got masses of homework to do. I tried to do some of it last night but Mam and Sid were arguing. Michael had his friend Gregory round and they were watching the television with the sound on full blast. Graham had this book on ballroom dancing and was trying to learn the waltz and quickstep. He kept interrupting to ask me to be his partner so he could practice.' She did not reveal that this was the only part of the evening she thoroughly enjoyed. 'And to cap it all, next door's dog barked all evening. It was bedlam, absolute bedlam. I had to give up, I couldn't concentrate.'

'Oh, Wendy, you poor thing. If you have problems like that why not do it here?'

'Here?'

'I have a bedroom that I converted to a study years ago that my son Ralph used when he was at school. I never go up there now so it would not bother me. Why not pop upstairs and have a look for yourself.'

Since arthritis rendered Mrs Bellamy crippled she had not used the upstairs rooms in her house, using the front lounge as her bedroom. Wendy found two neat and tidy guest rooms, kept that way by Mrs Bellamy's cleaner, and the smaller bedroom converted to an ideal study. There was a table supporting an Imperial typewriter, an electric fire for heating, and two of the walls were covered in bookcases to give it a library look.

'It's really fantastic,' shouted a thrilled Wendy. She looked at some of the books and found a complete history section, her favourite subject since playing Queen Anne in the school pageant.

Wendy took one last longing look at the room before descending the stairs where Mrs Bellamy was waiting in the hall, supporting herself on her crutches.

It's really lovely,' said Wendy enthusiastically. 'Can I start tonight?'

'Of course you can, my dear. Did you see the typewriter?'

'Yes, did your son use that?'

'Not much, it was mine.'

'Were you a secretary or something?'

'No,' Mrs Bellamy smiled. 'I used to write stories for women's magazines and a number for the *John Bull* magazine.'

'You used to write stories that were printed?' Wendy repeated, wide-eyed with astonishment as if the news was too incredible to be true. 'Don't you write anymore?'

'No I'm retired, furthermore my withered old hands prevent me.' With Mrs Bellamy resting on the crutches tucked under her arms she held out her deformed hands to demonstrate her point. 'You must use it to save it going rusty.'

'I don't know how to type.'

'You'll soon learn, it is ever so easy.'

'I'll type a letter to Anne once I've finished my homework.'

'You are a lovely girl, Wendy. You do so much for me and I am so glad that I can do something for you for a change.'

Wendy was so thrilled with it all she moved forward and gave Mrs Bellamy an affectionate kiss on her cheek. 'I'll go home for my tea now and then I'll come straight back.'

Two months later she excitedly pecked Graham an affectionate kiss on his cheek when he surprised her with a gift of blue denim jeans that had been all the rage since summer. They were tight fitting, particularly on her bum, and she loved them. She wore them for her second surprise when he took her to a special class teaching the new rock and roll dancing that he wanted to learn without his girlfriend Margaret knowing. He had been going out with the trainee shorthand typist at his work since shortly after starting there. To the almost continuous sound of Bill Haley and the Comets playing *Rock Around The Clock*, Wendy learned to jive.

Graham was amazed. Wendy was taking to rock and roll like a duck to water. He was pleased he had brought her and was wearing a contented smile as he visited the toilet during a break. He was still smiling with satisfaction when he heard two men enter in conversation that he could not help but overhear.

'Isn't that fabulous bird with the chestnut hair good?' he heard one say as he remained out of sight in a cubicle.

'Yes and she's got a real sexy arse as well.'

'And those gorgeous tits! God I wish she were my bird. I would just love the chance to dance with her.'

'I wouldn't get your hopes up, she seems wrapped with the guy she's with.'

What would Wendy have made of it if she had overheard them? That was a thought as Graham heard them leave before hearing the sound of water flushing the urinal. Should he tell her? He had noticed the covetous looks she was attracting from all the young men in the hall and was proud of it. Nobody knew she was his sister and, if he had anything to do with it, nobody would.

CHAPTER SIX

Wendy was shattered. The café had been as busy as she had ever known it, although being near to Christmas it was to be expected. She had queued everywhere in the afternoon when she had been shopping for Mrs. Bellamy. The queue at the greengrocers had been outside the shop, the Co-op wasn't much better and the chemist kept her waiting forty minutes to make up the old lady's prescription. The paper round took much longer but for a happier reason; customers kept opening their doors to give her a Christmas tip. She had been the last one to sit down for the meal; hot stew and dumplings.

'I was rostered on the Hellesdon route this morning and it was bloody murder,' Sid said sitting on the diagonally opposite side of the table to Wendy. 'Bloody bell never stopped ringing. I couldn't count how many times it went three times for full up, sometimes before I was out of Reepham Road. Earlham wasn't must better either. I don't know why people have to leave everything to the last minute.'

'It's not last minute, Sid,' Doris mumbled as she chewed on a piece of meat. 'It's only the seventeenth and there's still eight days to Christmas.'

'Hopefully next week I should be on the thirty-three county service during the afternoon and the Thorpe Road route at night.' Sid nudged Michael who was sitting on a stool at the end of the table. 'Here, Michael, fetch me some bread so as I can dip it in me stew.'

Wendy looked across the table at Graham who was gobbling down his tea and looking very smart in a sky blue, crew neck jumper. 'Are you going out tonight?'

He had a tiny piece of toilet paper stuck on his chin where he had nicked the end off of one of his spots while shaving. 'Yes, I'm meeting Margaret. We're going to the Haymarket to see *A kid for two farthings*.'

'That's a good film, I saw it last week.'

'Who's in it?' he mumbled with his mouth full of dumpling.

'Diana Dors but the real star is a cute little goat that a boy thinks is a unicorn.'

'Sounds a bit sloppy to me,' Graham replied as he finished eating, then promptly said goodbye to everyone and rushed out of the back door.

'You've still got some paper on your chin,' Wendy called out to him.

She watched Sid take out a packet of Woodbines and stopped eating when the smoke drifted across the table.

Her mother finished eating at the same time and put her hand on Michael's shoulder. 'I'll just have a fag then you can 'elp me wash up.'

'I can't I'm going out. Can't Wendy do it?'

'Wendy's been working hard all day.'

'But Mam,' Michael pleaded, 'Gregory's coming round in a minute and we're going carol singing.'

Wendy touched her mother's arm. 'I'll do it tonight, Mam, and he can do it tomorrow.'

In the middle of the washing up there was a knock at the back door. It was Len, one of the regulars at the Lord Rosewood. 'Sorry to bother you, Doris, but Jack was hoping you could come in and give him a hand behind the bar. He's ever so busy.'

'I'll just finish washing up and then I'll come.'

Sid appeared with a fresh cigarette in his mouth. 'I'll help Wendy wash up,' he said. 'You pop over straight away. I'll be over myself later on.'

Wendy's spirits deflated. In the space of ten minutes a full gathering of the family with safety in numbers had gone and she was alone in the house with her stepfather who had a wicked gleam in his eyes.

Michael and Gregory were singing carols outside houses in Sun Lane usually getting a few coppers or a three penny bit for their efforts. 'My hands are getting cold through holding this hymn book,' Michael complained after half an hour of singing. 'I'll run home and get some old gloves with the fingers cut out that Graham uses on the market.'

'And I'm hungry,' Gregory moaned. 'I'll come with you so while you're doing that I'll go and get a packet of crisps. I'll meet you outside my house in a couple of minutes.'

Nobody appeared to be around when Michael entered the kitchen despite the fact that most of the lights were on. As he moved quietly up the stairs in his gym shoes he could hear some unrecognizable noise that seemed to be coming from the back bedroom. He crept into the room he shared with Graham and started searching for the gloves. He heard it again, a sound like a grunt. It was definitely coming from Wendy's room. He moved silently to the warped door that was not closed properly and peeped through the aperture. Wendy was on her bed with hardly any clothes on and Sid was on top of her with his trousers round his ankles. What sort of game were they playing? His stepfather seemed to be bouncing on top of her and grunting as he did so. Michael had to stop watching or else he would be late for Gregory. He found the gloves and left the house as silently as he had entered it.

'Do you mind if we do not have a cup of tea tonight?' said Mrs Bellamy. 'As it is Christmas Eve tomorrow and my son will be here I think a small glass of port is in order. Do you think your parents would mind if you had a glass?'

'No they won't mind,' Wendy answered. 'They won't know anyway. Mam's working at the pub tonight and Sid's on late shifts.'

'It's in the sideboard,' Mrs Bellamy pointed in order for Wendy to retrieve the bottle.

Wendy poured two generous measures and sat in her usual chair opposite the old lady.

They both sipped at the port. 'This is really nice. I've had a sip of whisky before but I didn't like that, but this tastes fruitier and it's not so harsh on my throat.'

'That is because it's a fortified wine and not a spirit.' Mrs Bellamy watched Wendy down a large gulp; 'You must not drink it too fast, it's not lemonade.'

'I'm sorry but I suppose I was thirsty. I helped Mam pluck the cockerel before I started my paper round and I think some of the feather fluff must have got down my throat.'

Mrs Bellamy continued to delicately sip at her port long after Wendy had finished. She turned and took an envelope from the side table. 'Here you are Wendy,' she said. 'I have a card for you.'

Wendy took the card and thanked her before starting to open it. 'No you must not open it now,' Mrs Bellamy said. 'Wait until you get home.'

'All right,' Wendy acknowledged, 'but I'm sorry I haven't got you one.'

'I did not expect one.' She took another sip at her drink so that her glass was about a third full. 'But you can top up my drink if you would be so kind.'

'Certainly,' said Wendy as she reached for the glass, 'can I have another?'

'Yes but be careful that you do not get too tiddly.'

Wendy poured another two generous measures and handed Mrs Bellamy her glass. 'How are you getting on with the typewriter?'

'Oh I really love it. I expect you've heard me. I've learnt the keyboard like you suggested. I stuck little bits of paper on the keys so I couldn't see the letters then I kept typing that sentence about the quick brown fox and the lazy dog using all my fingers.'

'You will be writing stories next.'

'No I don't think so. I do type things I need for my schoolwork and I find it helps me to remember.'

When Wendy arrived home, armed with a gift-wrapped present from Mrs Bellamy, she found the back door was locked. As was the family practice she went to the coalhouse for the spare key. She knew Michael was at his boys' club party but where was Graham? Feeling in a happy intoxicated mood she sat at the table and opened her card to discover it contained a ten-shilling note. She smiled, pleased with Mrs Bellamy's generosity and wondered if her feeling of cheerfulness was due to the drink. It made her wonder what advocaat tasted like, surely her mother would not miss a drop if she had a small glass.

She had just finished drinking when a drunken Graham arrived home. 'Hello, Wensie, how are you?' he mumbled.

'Just look at the state of you,' she said disgustedly as he staggered in smelling like a brewery. 'I'll make you some black coffee.'

She poured a good measure of chicory liquid from the Camp bottle and heard Graham fumble with a chair in the parlour as he sat at the table. By the time the kettle had boiled and the coffee was made he was leaning on the table, resting his head in his arms.

'Nobody loves me,' he muttered.

Wendy put the black syrup-looking coffee in front of him and rested her hand on his shoulder. 'What are you mumbling about?'

'It's my pimples, they put everybody off,' he said as he lifted his head. 'Even Margaret ignored me at the works party. I know we only agreed to stop seeing each other after last Saturday but I thought we would still be friends.' He sipped at his coffee. 'Eh this is strong,' he winced as though he had tasted some foul tasting medicine.

'Don't you worry yourself about Margaret.'

'You should have seen her, Wendy; she was all over that Philip from the dispatch office. Rubbing it in she was.'

Wendy felt so much pity towards her stepbrother she could have wept but she edged herself into the chair beside him and placed her hand over his.

'He always has the girls swarming all over him. I wish that twat had spots like me.' He took another gulp at the coffee and burped. 'I feel a bit sick.'

'It's your own fault for drinking too much. You'd better change; you don't want to be sick all over your best clothes.'

Graham got up, wobbled a bit then used Wendy as a prop by throwing his arm around her shoulders.

'I'll help you upstairs,' she said putting her arm around the back of his waist to support him.

In the bedroom Wendy helped Graham struggle out of his suit before he flopped into a sitting position on his bed.

Seeing how pale he was she knelt in front of him. 'Shall I help you with your shirt?' At that moment Graham was sick, vomiting down his shirt and over her clothes.

'You dirty sod,' she shouted venomously and rushed into her own adjoining bedroom to take off her soiled sweater and skirt.

'I'm ever so sorry,' Graham apologized when she returned wearing her dressing gown over her bra and knickers.

'Get your shirt off and I'll go and wash them all out before they stain.'

Downstairs Wendy busily washed the offending clothes, stoked up the fire in the parlour and left them on the clothes-horse to dry. When she returned upstairs Graham, with more colour in his cheeks, was lying on top of his bed in his underwear.

'How do you feel now?'

'A lot better thanks.'

Wendy sat on the edge of his bed. 'Just warn me if you're going to be sick again.'

'I don't think I will be,' he said becoming magnetized by her cleavage.

Wendy could see some colour had returned to his cheeks and his speech was sounding more normal. 'You're looking a bit better.'

Graham's mind strayed back to the reason for his drinking after the snub he received. 'What upset me most about this afternoon was when she accused me of being a virgin and still wet behind the ears, and it was in front of that jumped up little twat.'

'Are you?' Wendy regretted asking the question as soon as the words were out of her mouth, but the advocaat and port were clouding her thinking.

'Yes,' he said and noticed she was looking down to avoid eye contact.

'Well that's something to be really proud of,' she said, trying to sound convincing.

'Are you?'

Wendy hesitated for too long and was aware of Graham grinning at her. 'You should save yourself until you meet the right person.'

The very thought of Wendy not being a virgin made Graham feel excited. Fortunately Wendy sat facing him with their hips touching so his arousal was hidden from her.

'How did it happen? How do you make love?'

Wendy was outraged. She slapped him across the face and stormed into her own room.

'What was that for?' Graham yelled as she went.

After a few minutes in her room Wendy began to feel guilty. Graham's questions had reminded her, all too vividly, of his father's abuse of her. She slapped him hard across the face because in that instant she was slapping Sid, holding him responsible for the sins of his father. It was wrong and her conscience bothered her. She liked Graham. She remembered the strange but wonderful feelings she had when she rubbed cream on his wounds. She often felt the urge to hug him comfortingly when he was hurt and upset, emotionally and physically. Now he was hurting because of

Margaret and it was not fair of her to cause him more pain. She had to apologize. She got up and pulled the adjoining door open.

'I'm sorry,' she started but then stopped abruptly. Graham was naked and aroused. She quickly closed the door and stood as still as a statue listening to the faint sound of Graham covering himself with the bedclothes.

'You shouldn't come barging in,' he shouted pitifully in his defence.

Wendy came back into his room. He was sitting up, his back propped against a pillow with the blankets covering up to his navel. He held his hands over his midriff. 'I'm really very sorry about that,' she said but the quick glimpse of his nakedness had fuelled feelings in her.

She sat down on his bed again, facing a blushing, embarrassed Graham. 'I shouldn't have slapped you, it wasn't fair.' She stretched out her hand and touched his face endearingly. 'I've not been with any boy but I do know about it because Anne and I used to talk about these things. I really do feel sorry for you and I feel angry at Margaret for hurting you.'

Her gentle fondling of his cheek caused a gap to open in her dressing gown so that Graham could see her bust and the movement caused by her breathing.

Wendy was conscious of his gaze and excited by it. Her head was becoming giddy with intoxicated naughty thoughts. She bent forward to tantalize him with a closer view and whispered in his ear. 'Would you like to see my boobs?'

Graham was stunned. Still embarrassed by her catching him masturbating he was now further mesmerized by her uninhibited question.

Wendy was happy beyond words. Her heart was going ten to the dozen, her stomach fluttering like a butterfly and she felt as though she had wet her knickers.

She stood and took off her dressing gown.

In ponderous unhurried movements she unfastened her bra, threw it into her room and sat closer to Graham.

His eyes were dancing with delight. If he was drunk he hoped he would never be sober. If he was dreaming he hoped he would never wake up.

She felt the nervous tremor in his hand as she took it and cupped it over her breast. An unanswered question was answered. The caress was nice when it was by someone you liked. She was elated. It was ecstasy. She leaned forward and kissed him on his lips.

Minutes later she stood again, switched off the light and in the darkness removed her knickers. 'Move over,' she said as she got into his bed by the side of him.

Soon Wendy experienced a new pleasure in her life, enjoying something for the first time that she had always previously vehemently detested.

The New Year arrived and by Monday the second of January 1956 life was back to normal in the Rosewood Road household. With everybody at work Wendy put some coal on the fire and then sat at the table to write a letter to Anne. After experimenting with two typewritten letters in the autumn, Wendy had reverted to handwriting her letters to her friend. Michael was still upstairs snoring away.

Although they still exchanged letters the timing was getting more spaced out. It was the beginning of December when she last wrote to her friend. At least it made it easier to start. She wrote about her one and only date with Donald Aspinall and how they went to the pictures. She thought that would please Anne. She did not put anything about Graham in the letter. That incident was a closed chapter in her life, as it appeared to be with Graham, either because he was too drunk to remember, too guilty about what happened or too ashamed that it took place. She knew it was not right but she was not ashamed. Could it be so wrong to be with her stepbrother willingly when her stepfather was constantly forcing himself upon her?

She posted the letter on the way to Mrs Bellamy's house. She had not seen much of her over Christmas because her son and daughter-in-law had travelled from Wisbech, where they were both teachers, to stay with her. Wendy opened the front door with the key she had been trusted with since she started doing her homework at the old lady's house.

'Hello, it's only me,' she called.

'Wait there a moment,' Mrs Bellamy called before appearing from the parlour in a new wheelchair. 'Well, Wendy, what do you think of this?'

'It's really lovely,' Wendy said as she approached her.

'My son, Ralph, purchased it for me for Christmas, it beats hobbling around on those old crutches.'

'I tell you what,' said Wendy, 'why don't I take you out for a little walk? The fresh air will do you good.' It was the first of many such walks and shopping trips that Wendy did for a very appreciative Mrs Bellamy.

CHAPTER SEVEN

'How late?' a very angry Doris shouted at her daughter.

Since Wendy had first started menstruating her mother had always kept sanitary towels in a cupboard near the bathroom and had become concerned that the stock had not diminished since Christmas. The confrontation began as soon as Wendy walked through the door from her morning's work at the café.

'Five weeks,' Wendy answered meekly.

'Damn and blast it, are you pregnant?'

'I don't know,' said Wendy truthfully, trying to suppress her tears while seeing the anger in her mother's eyes.

'Don't you go all soft on me. You must know if you've been with anyone, is it that Donald boy?'

'No he never touched me.'

Doris grabbed Wendy by her arms and shook her. 'Just tell me blast you, 'as somebody been with you or not?'

Despite often wanting to, she had never told her mother about Sid and now was certainly the wrong time. 'Nobody you know.'

She longed for comfort not confrontation. She wanted to cry not quarrel.

Doris slapped Wendy hard across her face. It stunned her for a moment before she rushed into the parlour, sat on a fireside chair and cried, not from the pain of the slap but to release all the pent up tensions of the last few weeks.

Doris fortified herself with a nip of gin before brewing a pot of tea, annoyed that she had not stayed calm as she vowed she would. Recriminations would have to come later. Right now her daughter needed her support.

A milder Doris gave Wendy a cup of tea and sat in the chair opposite. 'When did you last come on?'

'December the twelfth.'

'It's February the eleventh! Damn and blast it, Wendy, you could be two months pregnant!'

'Don't you think I've been worried about that?'

Doris coughed as though something was stuck in her throat but there was nothing and she soon stopped. 'Have you been sick at all?'

'I was the other morning and I have been before.'

'How long 'as it been going on?'

'About two weeks.'

'It's beginning to sound more and more like you're pregnant. I was about six weeks gone when I started being sick with both you and Michael.' Doris broke into more uncontrollable coughing and then swallowed the remains of her tea. 'You certainly are a Wednesday's child.'

'You've said that before, what do you mean?'

'You were born on a Wednesday. Wednesday's child is full of woe and you're certainly that. The shame you'll bring to this family. All these years I've worked 'ard to bring you up nice and decent and this is 'ow you repay me. Fifteen years old and pregnant! It's an utter disgrace; I'll never be able to face the neighbours again.'

As the realisation sank in, Doris continued to rant on, speaking her thoughts as they occurred to her. 'The boys mustn't know. You 'aven't told them 'ave you?' Doris did not give Wendy time to answer. 'I'll 'ave to tell Sid, goodness knows he'll probably belt the living daylight out of you.'

'I don't think so, Mam.'

'Don't you be so sure of that, he's not too choosy when it comes to dishing out punishment.'

Wendy was confident Sid would not touch her. She did not think he'd dare, not once he found out she was expecting his baby. 'Shall I have to go to the Doctor's?'

'Yes, I suppose – no, you can't go to Doctor Myers. Damn and blast it before we know it the whole bloody street would know. Let me think.' She paused and scratched her forehead. 'What a mess, what an absolute mess! You were regular with your periods weren't you?'

'Yes, Mam.' Wendy wondered what would happen to her and her baby, Sid's baby. What if it looked like him? She would not wish that on her unborn child but at least it would prove to her mother what a sodding bastard her husband was. She felt relieved now that her mother knew. It had been worth the bawling, the shaking and the slap across the face. It had been a constant worry to her since the middle of January, when she was a week late.

Sid was surprised to find that Doris was still up when he came home just before midnight. What is more, there was a glass of Scotch waiting for him on the table and the fire was giving a warming glow where it would usually have been dying embers.

'I want to talk to you, Sid, but before I do you must promise me you'll not lose your temper.'

'Look, Doris, I'm tired,' he said as he knocked back a swig of whisky and then retained the glass in his left hand. 'I'm not looking for any arguments at this time of night.'

'Keep your voice down the kids are all asleep upstairs,' Doris said quietly. 'You sit down a minute and for goodness sake stay calm.'

They both sat down in the fireside chairs facing each other. Sid swallowed the remainder of his whisky.

'I think Wendy's got 'erself into trouble,' Doris whispered.

'What sort of trouble? You mean at school?'

'No, Sid, not that kind of trouble. I think she's pregnant.'

Doris waited for the eruption of his violent temper but it never came. Sid sat in silence and stared at the fire. She noticed a few beads of sweat on his forehead before he wiped them away with his hand.

'She's over a month late and 'as been sick some mornings. I don't know what to do.'

'I need another drink.' He got up and poured the final remains of the whisky bottle into his glass. He usually drank beer but the Scotch, from a quarter bottle that Doris had bought specially that afternoon, was more than a good substitute.

'What's the bloody girl been saying then?' he asked as he returned to his chair.

'That's just it, she won't say anything.'

Doris was absolutely mystified as to how calmly he was taking it. She had dreaded telling him. She was horrified he would go straight up to Wendy's room and belt her so much that she would miscarry. Then the boys would have been awake and witnessed the commotion, but the worry was all in vain. He sat opposite gulping at his whisky.

'I think it must be that Aspinall boy. He's been the only boyfriend she's 'ad. We shall 'ave to go and see them, I think they live on the Mile Cross estate.'

'Now wait a minute,' Sid interrupted, 'we're not going to see anybody.'

'Well what are we going to do then?'

'I don't bloody know, can't she get rid of it?'

'You mean 'ave it adopted?'

'No you bloody fool, I mean get rid of it now! Isn't there something that can be done?'

Doris realized Sid was talking about an abortion. She did remember hearing something about drinking gin and lying in a hot bath when she worked as a dinner lady. It seemed a dreadful thing to do but the more she thought about it the more the idea of a forced miscarriage seemed the best solution.

Sid sat in his chair and lit a cigarette after Doris had gone to bed. What a shambles to come home to. He did not think for one minute that the Aspinall boy was responsible. What the hell would happen if Wendy's baby looked like him? It was a scary thought that made him decide to write to Ethel. She would know what to do.

Wendy was up early the next morning, very early for a Sunday because it was not yet seven o'clock, retching down the toilet with morning sickness.

Wendy sat in a chair at the table and swallowed a mouthful of neat gin straight from the bottle. It was unpleasant on her palate and hot at the back of her throat. 'It tastes horrible, Mam, how can you drink this stuff?'

A week had passed since Wendy's pregnancy had come to light. It was Sid's weekend off and he had taken the boys to the football match at Carrow Road to watch the Canaries play Walsall, leaving the whole of Saturday afternoon free for an attempted home abortion. The gas geyser was trickling water into the bath and there were three saucepans and a kettle full of hot water simmering on the gas stove, in reserve.

Her mother had explained that a hot bath and gin might terminate her pregnancy. At first Wendy had mixed feelings but when she remembered how she conceived; thought about Sid and the little monster she might give birth to; thought about the ridicule she would face at school, all maternal notions about having the baby were dispelled.

'Drink some more,' Doris urged as she stoked up the fire. The room was nice and warm with the doors leading to the front room and the stairs both shut to retain the heat.

'I can't now. I've got my paper round to do, even that swallow made me feel giddy.'

'Don't you worry about your paper round, the boys are going to do it tonight. It's all been arranged,' Doris said and pulled out the stool from under the table to sit next to Wendy. She gently touched her hand, 'Now drink some more gin.'

Wendy was finding the taste more acceptable. It was making her feel light-headed and relaxed in a could-not-care-less sort of way. She drank some more and then passed the bottle across the table for her mother to take a swig. After the next drink her head was fuzzy and she was feeling hot. She ought to take her cardigan off and started to fiddle with the top button while her mother bent down to untie her shoes.

'What are you doing? What's happening to me?' Her eyes were glazing and her speech was slurred. She tried undoing the second button but it kept moving. The whole room seemed to be going in and out of focus like somebody was meddling with the picture control on the television. Her mother took over her undressing as she sipped some more gin.

Doris struggled to get her to stand, loosened her skirt at the waist so that it dropped to the floor, quickly followed by her knickers.

'Look, Mam, I'm naked. Sid's sheen me naked.' Wendy ranted incoherently and stretched out both hands, palms outwards, in an invitational way.

After a lot of effort and complaints that the water was too hot Doris eventually managed to settle Wendy in the bath. Not being sure on how much water to run, she noticed the level finished above her daughter's navel.

Wendy leaned back against the end of the bath, shivering at first because it was like touching a slab of ice-cold marble and rested her arms along the top edges. The water was so hot she could see steam rising from it, making the little bathroom seem hazy and the flame of the geyser pilot light appeared to be flickering. Why was her mother watching her or was she using the lavatory? Somebody always wanted to use the lavatory when she was in the bath.

Doris used the toilet as a seat and looked at her daughter, a lovely young woman that was no longer a child. She had her father's amorous blue eyes. She was responsible for her daughter's rich chestnut hair, wavy and full-bodied, always brushed back from her face. If only Ted was alive, he would have been proud of the way his daughter looked and while Doris could not condone Wendy's condition, she could sympathize. She had such a magnificent nubile body, a saint from heaven would be tempted to make love to her.

It had been love at first sight when Doris first met Ted Marshall. She was seventeen when his family moved into the same street in Plaistow in which she lived. It was such a tragedy that he was killed before Wendy was born. She looked longingly at her daughter and almost envied her pregnancy. If she had let Ted have his wicked way with her at seventeen then he could have had a few happy years with his child.

Unexpectedly the irritation to her throat returned and Doris started coughing. It brought her reminiscences to an abrupt end and coerced her to action by gently pouring in the last saucepan of water.

'Can you feel anything?'

Wendy's speech was slow and disjointed. 'No what sh-should I feel?'

'Try pushing,' suggested Doris.

'What, p-push what?'

'I mean trying pushing as though you are forcing yourself to wee.'

Wendy obliged. She closed her eyes, pushed hard and then urinated in the bath water. 'Oops,' she smiled at her mother.

Doris studied the result but there was no blood. She retrieved the gin bottle from the table and gave it to Wendy to drink before kneeling on the floor at the side of the bath. She put her hand on Wendy's stomach, 'Try again,' she said and as her daughter pushed she applied pressure to her stomach.

Suddenly there were a few bubbles caused by Wendy breaking wind.

Doris got up and fetched the kettle of hot water and poured it into the bath. Wendy complained it was too hot as she leaned against the end of the bath with her forehead covered with sweat. She swallowed some more gin.

Doris took up her kneeling position and held Wendy's stomach. 'One last try,' she urged.

Wendy pushed hard and grunted noisily. Nothing happened until Doris released the pressure on her daughter's stomach and then she lurched forward and vomited.

Wendy was in the bathroom with morning sickness at twenty minutes to seven the next morning, which was nothing compared to the massive hangover she was suffering. Her nightdress-clad mother was in the doorway as soon as she turned round from the toilet.

'How are you feeling?' she asked with genuine concern.

'Rough, Mam, really rough, I'm never going through that again.'

'Come and sit down. I'll brew some tea and make you some toast; that's supposed to be good for morning sickness.'

Wendy walked slowly from the bathroom nursing the mother of all headaches to sit at the table. 'It didn't work did it?'

'No, my girl, I don't think it did.'

Wendy was not the centre of attention on Friday. That dubious honour fell to Graham.

'What do you mean you've given in your notice?' Doris asked angrily, sitting at the table by the side of Wendy who was just finishing her meal. Graham was sitting opposite with his elbows on the table, propping up his chin.

'The job's boring. First thing today I was sent to the cashier's office where I had to lick one hundred tuppenny postage stamps on these forms ready for them to make out receipts. When I got back to the purchasing office I was given this invoice for one ton of oyster grit. First I had to spend ten minutes searching for an order to see if we wanted the stuff and when I found it I had to write the number in this little box that had been stamped on the invoice. Then I had to find out if we had received them and as I couldn't find any dockets I had to go and ask the people in the Goods Inwards Office. This old twat took forever to look in this huge daybook and when he found the entry he signed his name in the appropriate space in the little box. Then I had to find out if the price charged was right and so it went on. I tell you, Mam, it's dead boring. It has been for weeks.'

'But what are you going to do for money?'

'Don't you worry about that, you'll get your board.' With that he took three crisp ten shilling notes from his pay packet and put them on the table. 'In six months' time I'll be called up to do my National Service and until then I'm going to live a little.'

An attentive Wendy had been fiddling with her knife and fork on her empty plate but Graham's last remark aroused her curiosity. 'You're not going to live off all that money you've saved?'

That made her mother twitch with curiosity. 'What money?'

'It's not much, Mam; a bit I've put by each week. Wendy has been putting it in the Post Office for me and I'm hoping to have enough to buy a motorbike with it. There's a Triumph for sale in Thorpe Hamlet and Harry Chadwick's said he'll take me on Sunday to go and have a look at it.'

'You're not having a motorbike, they're too dangerous.'

'Only the big ones, this is a Triumph Terrier with a one hundred and fifty cc overhead valve engine and a single cylinder, which won't make me a ton-up kid.'

Wendy stretched her hand across the table and placed it over Graham's. 'How are you going to afford to run it without a job?'

He liked her touch and smiled. 'I will have a job. I'm going to work for Harry Chadwick.'

'And just when was all this fixed up?' Doris asked.

'I went to see Harry on Wednesday in my lunch break. Didn't realize how much I missed the old stall until I stood there and served a couple of customers. Harry said he had missed me and if I'm prepared to get up early he'll employ me full time on the same money that I'm getting at Hodgson and Farrell. On top of that he'll pay for me to have driving lessons so that I can drive that old van of his. It will help him with his stalls at North Walsham and Stalham markets.'

CHAPTER EIGHT

Graham was rarely out of his bed before lunch on a Sunday but he was up bright and early on the fourth of March cleaning and polishing his newly acquired motorcycle. It had been a busy weekend for him, working his last day at the agricultural merchants on Friday and starting with Harry Chadwick at the crack of dawn on Saturday.

Despite only having a provisional driving licence Graham risked giving Wendy a pillion ride after lunch. At first Wendy held on to the little stanchion bar behind her seat but nearly fell off when Graham turned sharply left at the end of Norman Road.

'Hold on to me,' Graham shouted at her. She did. She moved so close and grabbed him so tightly around his waist it would have been impossible to get a fingernail between them. 'And lean with me and the bike when we go round a corner.'

He took her round the block a couple of times and then he did the same for Michael. As Wendy stood waiting, she started thinking about Michael. He did not seem as interested in the buses as he used to. He rarely went anywhere with Sid whereas he used to go with him at every opportunity. It must be something he was growing out of. He had asked Graham if he could go to the Speedway with him, perhaps he was getting more interested in that.

Graham hooted and they both waved as they went by for the first time. Michael was getting older. He was thirteen a fortnight ago and had been trying to get a paper round but there were no vacancies. Wendy had promised him her round when she left school in July.

'What about a lift to Mrs Bellamy's?' Wendy asked after Michael had dismounted from the machine. 'It's a nice afternoon, I'll see if she wants to go for a walk in the park.'

Wendy's morning sickness stopped as suddenly as it started two weeks before Easter. Although she had gone through the boys' room most mornings without disturbing them, there had been one occasion when the whole household was stirred abruptly from its slumber. Her nausea was particularly early one morning and as she made her way in the darkness to reach the stairs she tripped over some new boots that Graham had purchased as part of his motorcycle outfit. She fell in the direction of Graham's bed and threw her hands forward to break her fall, only for them to land directly over his genitals. He woke immediately, startled and screaming in agony with the pain in his scrotum, which in turn could not fail to wake Michael. His first sleepy thought was that there was a burglar and he started howling. Such a commotion soon woke Sid and Doris who came and switched the light on. Wendy was sprawled out on the bottom of Graham's bed; he was sitting up, white faced, with his hands clamped over his privates to protect them from further distress. Michael had hidden himself beneath the bedclothes in fear of his young life.

'Do you have to leave your sodding boots in the middle of the room?' Wendy shouted at Graham as she recovered herself. She did not wait for a reply. She rushed downstairs, hurtling past a bewildered Sid and Doris, to make the bathroom just in time.

It was a bright morning with a blue sky and fluffy cloud as Wendy and her mother got off the bus to go in search of the clinic. Wendy was as apprehensive as the morning she attended Blyth School for the first time, dreading the unknown that lay ahead of her.

Doris was similarly concerned as they found the street they were searching for just as the sun went behind a cloud. Sid's sister, Ethel, was the only family member informed of Wendy's condition, which had not exactly pleased Doris at the time. She had written to suggest a clinic in Peterborough that might be able to help. Doris had taken a couple of days off work to come with her daughter during the Easter school holidays.

Wendy felt she was trembling like a wobbly jelly by the time her mother knocked on the door of the terraced house that was two doors up from the corner shop. A round-faced, overweight lady, wearing a stained white smock opened the door and eyed her visitors like a security guard.

'You'd better come in off the street,' she said in an unwelcome tone and allowed her visitors to pass. She glanced up and down the street before closing the door. 'Wanted to see if any nosy neighbours were suddenly cleaning their windows or scrubbing their steps,' she said to explain her actions.

In the untidy front room Wendy and her mother were told to sit on a shabby settee and the lady moved round a table to sit with her back to the window. The clinic smelled like a disinfected toilet in a pub. Wallpaper was hanging off in one corner where a green patch of mould had formed. The table was littered with papers and an opened bottle of vodka was half hidden behind a pile of books. "Mrs C. Newman, Health Advisor" was displayed on a small sign.

'You up the duff then, duckie?'

The abrupt question, although casually spoken, stopped Wendy looking round the room. Her anxiety gave way to a feeling of intense dislike to the woman but she remained silent.

'We think so,' her mother answered.

Mrs Newman looked sternly at Wendy. 'When did you last come on?'

'December the twelfth.'

'Then I would think you're four months gone.' Mrs Newman picked up a metal instrument that was tubular, with a flat piece at each end, and moved round the table.

Wendy lifted her blouse as requested and felt the coldness of the instrument on her stomach. She caught the whiff of the woman's alcoholic breath when she lowered her head to put her ear to the other end. Wendy had never felt nor heard anything so she wondered what she was listening for.

Returning to her seat behind the desk the lady put her hands together and announced that Wendy was pregnant.

'Some boy took advantage of 'er against 'er will, is there anything you can do?'

'Now if we are talking about an abortion that will cost twenty-five quid payable in advance and another two quid a day for use of these premises.'

Doris was shaken by the amount of money involved. In her handbag was ten pounds that she had scraped together, hoping it would be enough. 'That's a lot of money.'

'Well, duckie, if you want something cheaper you will have to go somewhere else. There's them that will use the wire coat hanger method that is cheaper but it is unreliable and dangerous. You might think about drinking gin and a hot bath but it will be a waste of time. It could have worked in Victorian times when there was a toxin in the distilling that started an abortion, but it doesn't work today.'

Wendy did not need reminding of that unpleasant experience. 'So what does happen?'

'I use drugs and they are expensive. You would come here for a whole day. I would use a long needle to inject a salt solution in the uterus and remove some amniotic fluid. This will terminate the pregnancy and induce labour to expel the dead foetus.'

Wendy was finding the whole thing very repulsive. The Health Advisor, a made up title of self-importance, spoke as though she was quoting from a manual, which in all probability she was. 'Will it hurt?'

'Not very much, duckie, and considerably less than giving birth at full term.'

At that moment there was a loud scream that stopped Mrs Newman from continuing. Her hands twitched anxiously as she got up in readiness to leave the room. 'Excuse me,' she said and hurriedly left.

As the high-pitched screaming continued Wendy looked at her mother with some alarm. 'Do you think that's coming from a girl having an abortion?'

'I don't know,' her mother replied. 'Damn and blast it, this is turning into a right mess.'

'It sounds like absolute agony. I don't think I can go through with it.'

Doris was becoming less enthusiastic about it all. 'Let's go back and think about it.' She stood up and Wendy was only too pleased to follow her out of the so-called clinic.

That evening in the tiny parlour of Ethel's terraced house in Lincoln Road, Doris relayed everything that had happened.

'It was awful,' said Wendy. 'You should have heard the screaming, it was like in the films when somebody gets murdered.'

'It was a shame you didn't realize this might 'appen before you let that Aspinall boy 'ave his wicked way with you.'

'It wasn't Donald Aspinall, I was still on my period when I went out with him.'

Not wanting to argue in front of Ethel, Doris moved swiftly off the subject of blame. 'Twenty-five pounds for five minutes work, it would take me weeks to earn that sort of money.'

Ethel was visibly surprised by the amount. 'It's an absolute scandal.'

Doris began to think about the future without an abortion. 'I dread facing the neighbours when your bump starts showing.'

While Ethel had been prepared to contribute towards the cost there was no way she could find twenty-five pounds. Plan A had failed; it was time for plan B. 'Sidney thinks it would be best if Wendy stays with me when she starts to show. I live alone and I'm at work all day.'

Doris wondered when this idea had surfaced. Sid had not mentioned anything to her but as she thought about it she realized it would stop the neighbours' tongues wagging. 'Would you mind?'

'No, Sidney's the only family I've got. He's asked me if I can arrange for an adoption as well.'

Adoption! Doris was becoming more mystified by Sid's attitude and actions. At the beginning she imagined and feared he would literally belt Wendy until she miscarried. So why was he being so thoughtful and understanding? It was so unlike him and why hadn't he discussed these things with her?

Wendy thought Sid was being very cunning to have her out of the way when her pregnancy became obvious and how devious to have the baby adopted so that nobody would see that he was the father. She did not relish the prospect of living in Peterborough with her aunt but the alternative of being the centre of gossip and innuendo in Norwich was worse. She remembered the whispering in the butcher's when two women were talking about a young girl having a baby. She recalled how bulging Mrs Sanders, a lady from across the street, looked immediately before she gave birth.

'Do you think I'll show before I've finished my exams?'

'When do they finish?'

'Sometime in June.'

'With luck and one of my old corsets we'll be able to keep you from showing until then,' said Doris.

The old corset was not needed. Wendy remained in good health and "bump" free in the two months before her school exams started. Her mock exam results had been brilliant, attaining pass marks for seven out of the eight subjects she attempted, which earned justifiable praise from three of her teachers. She had worked hard. Mrs Bellamy's study and the books it contained had been a tremendous help.

It was close to the end of her first exam when she was reminded of her pregnancy with a jabbing dart in her womb caused by the baby kicking for the first time. As she left school in readiness to walk home she was surprised to find Graham waiting at the gate for her.

'Why are you here?' she said. 'And what are you grinning about?'

'Notice anything about the bike?' he said, pointing to the machine. 'The "L" plates are missing. I've passed my test.' To celebrate he took her for a ride in the countryside to Horstead, then along the Bure valley to Aylsham where he treated her to a milk shake before returning home.

By the time Wendy sat her last exam her waistline had expanded but fortunately not enough to reveal her condition. Walking home she had mixed feelings. She was sad because this was the time when she really missed Anne and the chats they enjoyed as they walked home from school. Sad because she could not go out and get a job or apply for either of two vacancies for junior typists that were posted on the school notice board. She was apprehensive because the next day would be her very last day at school before going to Peterborough and Aunt Ethel. She was apprehensive about being pregnant, alone and vulnerable to the unknown that lay ahead. She was pleased the examinations were finally over. She thought they had gone adequately enough and she hoped she had done as well as in the mocks but only time and the results expected in August would tell.

Wendy woke early on her sixteenth birthday and was downstairs before Aunt Ethel set off to catch the bus to work. Already the sun was shining and it looked like being another hot and sticky day. Since arriving in Peterborough her "bump" had blossomed out considerably. She was wearing a pink dress, one of only two maternity dresses that she possessed and both made by her mother before she left Norwich.

'Happy birthday! There are three letters for you in the post and here's a card from me,' said Aunt Ethel. She put her own mail in a drawer that was part of a built-in unit, occupying the recess between the chimney-breast and the wall, and dashed out to catch her bus.

Wendy looked at her cards; one from her mother and the family, one from Mrs Bellamy that contained a ten-shilling note and one post marked Leicester that was from Anne. Aunt Ethel's letter had intrigued her, for she had recognized Sid's left hand scrawl on the envelope. Curiosity got the better of her and when she peeped inside she discovered it contained a postal order for two pounds made out to Ethel. The drawer contained lots of letters and documents including her rent book and birth certificate. It was obviously the place where Aunt Ethel kept all her important papers.

Wendy kept busy by doing the chores around the house. It seemed only right as she was living rent-free. Aunt Ethel had no modern appliances, so clothes were washed by hand and then boiled in an old copper. There was no vacuum cleaner so that every room had to be swept and no electric iron, only a primitive metal one that had to be heated on the gas stove. As a birthday treat she had given herself a day off. She usually washed the back yard and scrubbed the front and back door steps on a Tuesday but they could wait until tomorrow. She had some new books from the library so she would sit out in the yard and read in the sunshine.

By midday, after her unborn baby had spent most of the morning kicking her, she had dozed off to be woken by a banging on the front door.

'Wendy, are you there?'

She froze midway to answering the door when she recognized Graham's voice. Whatever was he doing here? How could she possibly hide her bulging stomach from him? There was more banging and in her panic Wendy rushed up the stairs.

'What are you doing here?' she yelled from the bedroom window.

'Happy birthday,' he called back, 'are you going to let me in?'

'I'm in bed, I'm not very well but you can let yourself in round the back.'

Wendy quickly undressed and threw on her nightie. By the time she heard Graham climbing the stairs she was sitting in bed with the eiderdown arranged as best she could to camouflage her bump.

'Where's Aunt Ethel? I thought you were looking after her?'

'Yes I am,' said Wendy. 'She's had to go to the hospital for a check-up.' The fabrication put out by her mother and Sid was that Aunt Ethel had to have an operation and needed looking after during convalescence. Aunt Ethel's story was that her niece's husband was in Germany with the army and her fingers too swollen by her pregnancy to wear her wedding ring.

Graham squatted on the bed. 'What's the matter with you?'

'I've got a headache.' She nodded towards two packages that he had placed on the bed. 'Are they for me?'

'Yes, I wanted to bring Mam's present but she said I wasn't to come.'

'But you did.'

Graham smiled mischievously. 'I passed my driving test a fortnight ago and I asked Harry if I could borrow his van, but he wanted it today for Stalham market or we could have had a nice ride out somewhere.'

He watched Wendy undo her presents. The first package contained a pair of nylon stockings and the second a new nightdress. 'I hope you like them, Brenda helped me pick them.'

'Brenda?'

'I'm seeing Brenda Frost again. She came to the stall about three weeks ago and said she'd missed the Speedway so we agreed to go and we've been going out together since.' He watched Wendy hold the nightdress up by the shoulder straps. 'Are you going to try it on?'

'Not with you gawping at me I'm not.'

'Well if you want privacy I'll go and get out of this kit.' He went back downstairs to remove his motorcycle leathers.

'So far so good,' thought Wendy and to please Graham she changed into the new nightdress. It was short and flimsy and not the sort of thing she would have chosen.

'You look great,' said Graham when he returned and sat on the bed.

'You would say that, I expect you can see my boobs through it.'

The boyish grin said yes. 'Don't you like it then?'

'Yes it's really lovely,' Wendy lied; after all, what was one more fib compared to the whole charade she was living at that moment? 'I like your new hairstyle; how long have you had it?'

'About a couple of weeks.' Graham turned his head so Wendy could see the back of his hair. 'It's a DA, do you think it suits me?'

She reached out and stroked the back of his hair with her hand, going with the contours of the style. DA was abbreviated slang for duck's arse, which is exactly what the shape of the cut at the back resembled. She liked "Teddy boy" hairstyles. 'I hope you haven't gone the whole hog and bought a suit with wide shoulders, velvet lapels and drainpipe trousers.'

He was smiling when he returned his head to face her. 'Not yet!'

Graham stayed for two hours before Wendy feigned her headache was getting worse and she needed to sleep.

'Shouldn't I stay and say hello to Aunt Ethel?'

'She'll be hours at the hospital because they do all sorts of tests.'

With that Graham said goodbye and went out the same way he came in.

Wendy was relieved. She threw back the bedclothes and looked at her bulging pregnant state. 'How did you get away with it?'

At seven o'clock Wendy was waiting outside the telephone box in Lincoln Road in readiness to talk with her mother. It was a pre-arranged means of communication; her mother using the kiosk at the top of Rosewood Road to ring the kiosk within one hundred yards of Aunt Ethel's house.

The telephone rang and when Wendy answered she heard the operator say "press button A please caller". A moment later she was talking with her mother who was horrified to learn of Graham's visit.

'I told him not to.'

'It's all right, Mam, he doesn't know,' said Wendy who went on to explain.

Three minutes flew by. 'Happy birthday,' said Doris quickly after the operator asked her to put more money in the slot if she wanted to continue. 'I love you.'

Wendy brushed away a tear as she left the kiosk. She could not remember her mother ever saying that before.

CHAPTER NINE

A baby boy was born after nine hours of gruelling labour at eight o'clock on Sunday sixteenth September 1956. He was taken away before Wendy could see him so that she never knew if he looked like Sid. She was kept in the hospital another five days, tranquilized by day and sedated at night. Her ordeal had been painful and she had screamed very loudly every time she had been told to push during her final contractions.

The matron scorned her; never missing an opportunity to tell her how wicked she was for being young and unmarried. In contrast the nurses were full of kindness and compassion. One encouraged her to name the baby, which she did by calling him Stuart. Another talked with her about special mother and baby homes should Wendy want to keep her child. It only served to confuse her befuddled mind even more. She mentioned it to Aunt Ethel when she visited that evening, bringing a small box of Milk Tray.

'How could you manage?' her aunt said abruptly. 'These nurses should have better things to do than fill your head with such poppycock. Anyway it's too late because I've already completed the adoption arrangements.'

The next evening Aunt Ethel came with a formidable looking lady, supposedly taking care of the adoption, with some forms to sign. She signed where she was told without reading the contents.

She wanted to ask to see the baby just once and hold him in her arms just once, but she said nothing.

Doris arrived late at ten to eleven on Friday night. She had boarded the bus at Norwich at five minutes past six and then had to wait twenty minutes at Kings Lynn for the bus to Peterborough. She was tired yet anxious. She kissed Wendy on the cheek and hugged her with a crushing embrace like never before.

Baby talk was off the agenda as they settled in Ethel's parlour with a nightcap of cocoa. For Wendy it was the end of a dreadful week. Each day her mind had run riot with indecision, wanting to keep the baby one minute but not the next. Curious if she would make a good mother and wondering how much she could love him, before these thoughts were dashed from her head by visions of his looking like Sid. Sometimes she wanted to scream but the last thing she wanted was to talk about it.

Ethel was uncomfortable, worried that Doris or Wendy might ask about the adoption. It was not exactly run of the mill and the less they knew the better. She was ready to say the new parents would call him Stuart if the topic were raised. That would please Wendy and hopefully dispel more searching questions.

Doris's troubled conscience had re-asserted itself during the long journey. Why should she have cared what the neighbours thought? Perhaps she should have persuaded Sid to let them keep the baby. She wished she had been with her daughter at the birth. She should have come last Saturday and taken time off work. Racked with guilt, she had wept alone at the front of the bus, realizing that she would never see her grandson. Never be able to hold and cuddle him. She dared not risk asking about the baby for it would start her crying.

'I've got something for you,' she said to Wendy as she rummaged in her bag for a packet.

Knowing it was her exam results, Wendy stared at the envelope as though it contained something bad. When she opened it a few moments later she was delighted to find she had attained seven "O" level passes in the General Certificate of Education. 'I passed in seven subjects,' she said excitedly. It brought her some welcome joy to what had been a very bad week.

Wendy and Doris arrived home at a quarter past six on Saturday night, six hours after leaving Peterborough. It had been a slow, arduous journey with an hour and half wait at Kings Lynn, but like all the other bus trips it was free of charge as an employee's family concession. The only person in the house was Graham who was locked in the bathroom.

Wendy banged on the door. 'Hurry up I'm desperate to have a wee.'

Graham opened the door with a towel girded around his waist and a face white with shaving lather. He waited outside until he heard Wendy pull the chain and then re-entered to continue his shave.

Wendy remained in the bathroom. 'I presume you're seeing Brenda tonight?'

'We're going dancing,' he answered as he made the first long stroke with the razor down his cheek. 'Do you think Mam would mind if I invited her home for tea tomorrow?'

'I shouldn't think so but you'll have to ask, mind you I'm not sure if she's all that well.'

'What do you mean?'

'Not too loud,' warned Wendy aware that her mother might be just the other side of the bathroom door. She whispered, 'Her coughing isn't getting any better and she's gone a lot thinner. Has she been to the doctor's?'

'Not to my knowledge, do you think she should?'

'Last night we had to sleep together at Aunt Ethel's and twice during the night I heard her coughing real bad.'

'I don't think she'll go unless you drag her there, you know what she's like.' He finished shaving and went to wipe the residue soap on the towel until he realized he was wearing it. He turned to face Wendy, 'How does that look?'

She touched both his cheeks, 'Really smooth.' Despite what she had been through she could not resist yanking the towel from his waist, 'But you've missed a bit.' Nakedly embarrassed, he covered his private region with his hands as she dabbed his face before dropping the towel and walking out of the room.

On Monday morning Wendy was up bright and early to be in the youth employment office as it opened. She had to sit in a waiting room for six minutes before being ushered into an adjoining office.

Mrs Sawyer, a dark haired lady with two prominent incisor teeth giving her mouth a rabbit-like appearance, was her interviewer. 'Any idea what you would like to do?'

'I would like a typing job.'

'You have seven "O" levels,' said Mrs Sawyer looking at the certificate that Wendy had brought. 'You are far too qualified to work as a mere typist. Have you given any thought to a career or going to college?'

'No, I just want to get a job and earn some money so I can give my Mam some board.'

'What about banking or insurance or one of the professions? You could be articled to a solicitor or an accountant.'

'I've never been inside a bank so I don't think I could work in one.' Wendy hesitated, worried by the thought of not being able to find any work. 'Aren't there any vacancies for typists?'

Reluctantly, feeling Wendy was selling herself short, Mrs Sawyer looked through a card index and pulled one out. Perhaps all was not lost. 'There is a vacancy for a receptionist typist at Palmer and Moore, they are accountants with offices on Thorpe Road.'

Within a minute of Wendy's acknowledgement Mrs Sawyer was on the telephone arranging an interview for two o'clock that same afternoon.

Wendy was busy with the iron, pressing a blouse, when Graham walked through the back door in the middle of the afternoon. 'Guess what?' she said excitedly. 'I've got a job. I start on Wednesday as a receptionist with a firm of accountants.'

'Congratulations, so that's why you're ironing all your clothes.'

'I'm going to get two pounds and five shillings each week, how much do you think I'll have to give Mam?'

'About a pound I should think,' Graham paused looking at the sparkle in her eyes. 'I'm going to Yarmouth tomorrow, if you don't start till Wednesday do you fancy coming with me on the bike?'

Wendy was still sore from giving birth and sitting on a pillion seat was not something she relished but she did not want to refuse. Nor could she turn down the opportunity to have her arms locked around Graham during the journey. He was still the only boy that she had feelings for and in a week's time he would be going in the

Army for two years. 'Well as long as you stop at a shop that sells stockings. I need to get two pairs of Nylons for work.'

Wendy did not feel any pain on the motorcycle until they bounced over the level crossing at Caister. They stopped in Manor Road at the gateway of a camping site.

'Why have we come here?' Wendy said as she dismounted.

Graham propped the bike up on its stand. 'Harry Chadwick's got a caravan on this site and I wanted to find it. Hang on here, I won't be a minute.'

For the end of September it was a surprisingly warm day with the sun shining in a clear sky, but the buffeting wind of the forty-minute journey had chilled her to the bone. She jogged up and down in an effort to bring some warmth back into her body.

'Did you find it?'

'It's by the fence over there,' said Graham, pointing as he returned. 'Do you want to see it?'

Before Wendy could answer they both heard a clunk and turned sharply to see the nearby railway signal move downwards. Graham lifted the bike off its stand and pushed it towards a line of caravans.

'Why has Harry given you a key?' Wendy asked as she followed Graham into the caravan.

'He wants me to clean it out and leave it ready for the winter.'

'You cunning sod, is that why you've brought me?'

'No it's not, so don't get your knickers in a twist. Harry's lending me his van on Thursday so Brenda's coming with me because it's her half day.'

Wendy had known Brenda at school but as she was eighteen months older she was always in a different class. She had left last year to work at Garfields department store in London Street.

Brenda described her job as sales assistant over the Sunday tea table but Wendy thought it was probably some sort of junior sales girl. Still her mother had tried to impress, opening a tin of salmon for sandwiches and using butter instead of the usual margarine. She had used her best set of cups and saucers and the spread had been completed with tinned peaches and evaporated milk.

'All alone in this caravan with Brenda, I hope you're not going to do anything stupid.' What precisely would he get up to with her? Could he not have borrowed the van today so that she could have helped him? Why was she having these thoughts? Was she jealous?

'Are you jealous?'

Was he reading her mind? 'Of course not,' she lied.

'It beats me why you haven't got a boyfriend, after all it's not as though you are unattractive. In fact Brenda was telling me that her younger sister has been going out with that Don boy you dated once but she's going to dump him because he never stops raving about you.'

'I really haven't found anybody I want to go out with, now can we change the subject? I'm thirsty; is there anything to drink in this caravan?'

'We'll go to the Ship Inn. Harry said they serve a good pint in there so I'll treat you to a lemonade and see if they'll serve me this side of my eighteenth birthday.'

'All right then but if you can buy a beer you can treat me to a glass of port. That'll warm me through and celebrate my new job.'

Wendy was pacing up and down outside the offices of Palmer and Moore for over twenty minutes before a gentleman in a navy striped suit arrived at ten minutes to nine.

'Hello, I am Mr Cocker the office manager.' A small man, he smiled indifferently through thick-rimmed spectacles and fingered his pencil moustache.

'I'm Wendy Marshall, I've come to start to work as a typist receptionist.' She followed him into the building and was led into the reception room where she had waited for her interview.

'Wait in here and I will arrange for somebody to show you what's what.' He closed the door on Wendy and stood for a moment, pleasantly surprised by her attractiveness and the aroma of her perfume.

Once alone, she checked her hair and make-up in her compact mirror for the umpteenth time. It was nerves. She was anxious and her pulse was racing. She must stay calm. She looked around and decided it might impress if she read something from the limited choice of reading material available. She selected September's issue of the Investors Chronicle because it was smaller than the Financial Times and The Economist.

Ten minutes later she was introduced to Mrs Doreen Kyle who took her under her wing to introduce her to the other staff and show her what to do. An hour later her nerves were restored. She typed her first letter, a word-perfect request to the local branch of the National Provincial Bank to confirm balances for a client's end of year audit.

Having recounted her day to her mother to the point of exhaustion, Wendy was too excited to sit and watch the television so she decided to give Mrs Bellamy a spontaneous visit.

'The typewriters have extra long carriages so that you can type a double sheet of foolscap. It's for clients' accounts but I haven't done any of those yet,' said a stimulated Wendy. 'I typed three letters to three different banks,' she continued. 'There are two types of letterheads; one embossed, which we use for clients and one ordinary print, which is what I used.'

'It sounds as though you are enjoying it,' said Mrs Bellamy, refraining from sipping at the tea. It had almost become a ritual that Wendy brewed a pot of tea as soon as she arrived.

'Oh I am, Mrs Bellamy, I am. Mind you it took me a while to learn how to use the telephone switchboard. It's like a box with all these circles like eyes that wink at me when somebody is calling and then I have these plugs that I have to use to connect the different offices. I did get two muddled up this afternoon but Doreen still said I was very good. I was given a diary and I have to keep a record of all the time I spend on each of the clients. I have to record the name and the file number and do a timesheet at the end of each week. You know each of the partners keep their own set of clients and all Mr Palmer's clients start with odd numbers and all Mr Moore's with even numbers.'

'Tell me,' interrupted Mrs Bellamy, 'are there any nice young men working there?'

'They're nearly all men. There are seven articled clerks, four seniors', Mr Cocker the office manager and the two partners. There are only two other ladies; Doreen who is Mr Palmer's secretary and Mrs Preston who works for Mr Moore. There is another lady but she only works part time and I haven't met her yet.'

'How many of the articled clerks are dashing and debonair?'

'I haven't met them all because some were out of the office on audits. I was working with one this afternoon, David Rendle, he left school this summer the same as me.'

'I expect you brought a twinkle to his eye,' said Mrs Bellamy as she placed her empty cup on the table beside the chair.

'I know what you're driving at, but no. I did feel sorry for him because he seemed very conscious about the pimples on his face like our Graham had at his age.'

'I imagine it will not be long before someone asks you out. You are a very attractive young lady and you always dress so nicely.'

Wendy ignored the compliment. Ever since the first day they met Mrs Bellamy had always quizzed her about boyfriends but if she knew the real reason why she had spent the last three months in Peterborough she would be more understanding about her reluctance. She seized the opportunity to change the subject.

'Talking of clothes I will have to buy some two-piece suits for this winter. I've only got one to my name and I really can't wear that every day.'

'Now I can help you there; go and have a look in the wardrobe in the front bedroom, there are lots of clothes in there that I never wear. You are similar in size so take anything that you like that you think would fit.'

'You know I can't do that.'

'Why ever not? They will only finish up with the rag and bone man. Now run upstairs and have a look while I telephone Ralph.'

While she could hear Mrs Bellamy talking to her son, Wendy opened the wardrobe that was crammed full of lovely clothes, to be greeted with the camphor like smell of moth-balls. Not immediate fashion, but even to her unknowledgeable eye they were beautifully tailored and expensively purchased. She tried on an oatmeal coloured two-piece with a pleated skirt that was a perfect fit. There were three others that Wendy thought would be perfect for work.

She slipped into a full-length burgundy evening dress with spaghetti straps that puckered beneath her bust, highlighting her curvy figure.

She realized Mrs Bellamy had ended her telephone call and went downstairs. 'What do you think?' she asked as she twirled around in the evening dress.

She looked at her with admiration. 'You look beautiful, like Cinderella dressed for the ball.'

'It's a bit loose at the waist,' said Wendy, looking down and stroking her hands over her hips, 'but Mam will be able to alter the darts for me. You don't think it's too clingy?'

'Not on you it's not. You have the perfect figure for it.'

Wendy was too jubilant to sleep with the adrenalin pumping around her body like an express train. She kept reliving the day at work and the evening with Mrs Bellamy. She had brought back the two-piece suits, two calf length skirts, one lamb's wool jumper and a mink stole with a small black handbag that were accessories for the evening dress. A week ago she was miserable, depressed and drugged to sleep with the aid of pills. What a difference seven days had made.

A week later it was Michael's turn to be jubilant. He rushed in from his paper round two minutes after Wendy had got in from work.

'I've been picked to play for the school football team this Saturday.'

'That's nice,' said Doris taking a dish from the oven containing some faggots.

'I'm going to be playing right-half and I'm one of the youngest to ever play. Will you come and watch me, Mam?'

'Oh, Michael, I can't. I've got to work because Marlene's daughter is getting married. What about you, Wendy, can't you go and watch 'im?'

'I'm not interested in football.'

Michael looked disgustedly at his sister. 'I'm not interested in bloody typing but I have to listen to you prattling on about it.'

Doris hurriedly put his meal in front of him and then clipped his ear, 'None of that language in 'ere.'

Wendy had not appreciated just how much Michael had grown up while she had been away; his voice was breaking and he was sounding very adult. 'All right,' she said, 'if only to shut you up.'

Despite her lack of knowledge about football Wendy enjoyed the match more than she would have thought possible, particularly when Michael scored a goal with a thumping shot from outside the penalty area. It proved to be the winner, for a few minutes later the final whistle sounded and as she clapped from the touchline she saw three other girls run on the pitch to Michael. Two congratulated him with a pat on the back, as did some of his team, but one stayed with him as he made his way towards Wendy.

'What did you think then?' he said when he was close enough.

'You were very good but I am curious to know who your friend is?'

He introduced Lizzie, a girl with long red hair and freckles but well developed adolescently. 'We're going back to her place so I shan't be in until I've finished my paper round.'

CHAPTER TEN

'Have you been to the doctor's about your cough?' Wendy's voice was stern as she helped clear the crockery from the table. She frequently spent her lunch hour at the bus station café, giving her a few moments chat with her mother.

'It's the fags; I can't bother Doctor Myers about something so trivial.'

'It's not just the coughing, look how thin you're getting.'

'I'd sooner be thin than fat, now leave this for me to do, I don't want you staining your clothes.' With that she took the tray through to the kitchen.

That evening, Wendy attended her night school class at the City College where she had enrolled on a bookkeeping course after Mr Palmer suggested it might be useful. 'At least you will be able to know a debit from a credit,' he had said. With David Rendle attending the same class it was not as formidable as Wendy first feared.

'Do you think, um, you could do me a massive favour?' It was a stutter delivered by a shy David as they walked along Ipswich Road towards the hospital at the end of class.

'That depends on what it is.'

'I've got to go to Dad's cricket club dinner dance a week on Friday because he's the secretary and as it's a couples thing, um, I wonder if you would like to come with me?' It was a bit of a stumble but it was out.

Wendy's immediate instinct was to say no like she did with all boys' requests for a date, but then she remembered the burgundy dress and this would be the ideal opportunity to wear it.

'All right, but I can't dance very well.'

'Neither can I,' a happy David responded without stuttering.

Mr Palmer summoned Wendy as soon as she arrived at work the next morning. In a state of flummox she slowly climbed the stairs to his first floor office, wondering if she had done anything wrong.

'Good morning, Wendy,' he greeted her with a smile. Seeing she was rigid with tension he launched straight into his explanation. 'I am afraid we have a crisis on our hands. Doreen will not be coming into work for a while because she has broken her wrist in a fall, which leaves this huge problem of getting the accounts for Mawby Engineering typed.'

The relief that she was not being reprimanded for some misdemeanour was immeasurable and visual, as a smile replaced her sullen look. 'Would you like me to do them?'

'I was hoping you might say that. I had wondered about getting a temp in, but even if I could find one at such short notice I think I would sooner you do them. The standard of your work is very good and you are ready for something more challenging. I expect we shall soon have to review your pay.'

Mawby Engineering was a limited company requiring twelve sets of accounts in addition to office copies, so Wendy found herself typing on to wax-coated stencil paper for the first time. During the trading account she touched the wrong key and was mystified as to how to correct it or whether it had to be retyped. At that moment David walked in and between them they found a bottle of special correcting fluid that brushed over the incorrect word to provide a new wax coating. Wendy simply typed the correct word over the error before she became aware of David's fidgeting.

'Is everything all right?'

'Um, yes, um, that dinner dance is formal dress,' he mumbled. 'I've got to wear a dinner jacket with a bow tie and Dad wondered if you had, um, had an evening gown.'

Surely he or his father did not think she was going to turn up in a sweater and jeans or was there something more sinister behind his hesitant babblings. 'Yes, is there a problem?'

'No, um, that's fine, it's just that Dad, well my mother actually, said I had to make sure. I'm sorry I had to ask.'

Wendy's senses were picking up on his blushing discomfort. 'There's something more to this, what aren't you telling me?'

With his uneasiness detected, the confession came blurting out very quickly. 'Mum wanted me to take a daughter of one of her friends, a spoilt snob that lives in a big house in Drayton. When I told her I had asked you, she was livid but I don't care. If I can't take you I won't go.'

'So your Mam's hoping that I haven't got a dress to my name. Well I have and if you still want me to go I will. Now if you don't mind I have to get on with these accounts.'

It took most of the day and all of her sacrificed lunch hour, but the accounts were ready a full hour before the last post was collected from the post office at the corner of Rosary Road. David and Peter Stone, an articled clerk nineteen years of age, had checked every word and every figure for accuracy before the copies were duplicated on the Roneo in the front office. Wendy had typed twelve individual covers for each set that had finally been fixed together with two metal eyelets.

The next day Wendy had to master the Dictaphone; a tape machine on which Mr Palmer recorded the letters he wanted typing. Wendy's foot operated the play or stop pedals and the tape was heard through a set of headphones, leaving both her hands free to type. Typing her initials in the reference "WJP/WM" followed by the file number on embossed letterhead made her feel proud of what she had achieved in one month of working.

It was almost a month before the first letter arrived from Graham, which Doris ripped open eagerly and started to read. 'He thinks 'e's going to Catterick, where's that?'

Wendy was brushing her hair in the bathroom in readiness to go to work. 'I think it's up north somewhere.'

'With all this trouble in the world I worry about Graham,' Doris continued, 'what with this Suez crisis and something on the news last night about they might send troops into Egypt. Do you think they send them from Catterick?'

Wendy emerged from the bathroom and joined her mother in the parlour. 'You mustn't worry, Mam. Mrs Bellamy has a big map book, I'll pop round tonight and have a look, but if it is up north I shouldn't think he'll be going to Egypt.'

'There's all this trouble in Hungary with the Russians and all this talk of war; I do 'ope Graham doesn't 'ave to go and fight. 'Aven't the bloody wars taken too much from me already?'

Wendy shared the same fears as her mother but this was the time for consoling. 'There won't be a war. What else does he say in his letter?'

Doris focused on continuing to read the letter. 'He's in a billet with lots of other men and he'as to keep 'is boots polished until you can see your face in them.'

'That won't please him; he never liked cleaning his shoes,' interrupted Wendy.

'His 'air has been cut very short and he 'opes to get 'ome for forty-eight hours leave before he gets posted.'

'I don't think they would let him come home if they were going to send him to Egypt. Does he say anything about Brenda?'

'He's written to 'er. Asks if it will be all right to bring 'er 'ome for tea when he gets some leave.'

Wendy looked at the clock, 'I must dash or I'll miss my bus.' She kissed her mother delicately on the cheek and went out, stopping briefly for a moment as she closed the back door because she could hear her mother coughing.

On Friday November the second Wendy was having second thoughts about the dinner dance. Her mother had been teaching her the steps of the waltz and the quickstep but she still had misgivings about her dancing. Perhaps she should have let David's mother have her way, she certainly was not looking forward to meeting her.

It was a bad morning; she had woken late and had allowed insufficient time to remove the rollers from her hair. It went from bad to worse when she watched her bus go down the Angel Road without her. The next number ninety-two, the service Wendy used because it dropped her outside the office in Thorpe Road, was running late and seemed to take forever as journeys do when you are behindhand. When she raced through the front door of the office, nine minutes late, bad turned into a catastrophe when she bumped into Mr Palmer.

'Wendy, I was looking for you. Can I see you in my office for a moment?'

She tried to stay calm but her anxious heart was thumping like a traction engine. 'I'm really sorry I was late, but I missed my bus and the next one was late.'

Mr Palmer was impressed by the pure honest innocence of Wendy. He could fill a book with the excuses he had been given over the years by the late arrival of staff, yet here was one dedicated and very attractive young lady that simply told the truth. It was refreshing. 'I have not asked you in here because you are late, although I hope you will not make a habit of it.' Sensing she was flustered he smiled endearingly at her and beckoned with his hands for her to sit down. 'I wanted to talk to you about your wages,' he continued as Wendy settled in the chair. 'When you started with us it was assumed you would need day release to attend typing lessons but as this has proved unnecessary we feel it only fair to revise your pay to reflect the standard of your work. So Mr Moore and I have agreed to pay you three pounds each week and for that amount to be backdated.'

Suddenly the day was getting better! The dreaded ticking off and possible sack had turned into a huge pay rise. Wendy felt like shouting "whoopee", but instead settled for a big thank you. Before she was out of his room she had decided to spend some of the backdated pay on a pair of sling back shoes that she had been longing for. The shoes and the three tier imitation pearl choker that Mrs Bellamy had lent her would elegantly complete her outfit for the dance.

That evening Wendy rushed downstairs wearing her knee length dressing gown only to find that Michael had beaten her to the bathroom. She thumped on the door and shouted, 'You little sod, how long are you going to be in there?'

Michael unlocked the door and opened it a fraction. 'As long as it bloody takes and longer,' he retaliated before slamming the door in her face.

'Just don't stink the place out; I've got to have a bath after you've finished.' She turned round and leaned her back against the locked door. Feeling incensed she looked at the clock. David's parents were picking her up at half past seven and the last thing she wanted was to be late.

At that inopportune moment Sid walked in from work. Wendy pulled her dressing gown tightly over her chest to ensure that it was impossible to have the slightest glimpse of her cleavage.

'You needn't get any ideas,' she bellowed angrily at him.

Without saying a word he put his hands up as a gesture of submission, went straight into the parlour and sat down in his usual fireside chair.

Wendy was in sparring mood. She followed him as far as the doorway from the kitchen. 'If ever you try anything with me again I swear I'll kick you in the sodding ballocks.'

'I shan't, I'm sorry about what happened.'

'Sorry! And that makes it all right does it? Sorry about what? Sorry that you fucked me or sorry about the baby?'

'Both. Stone the bloody crows I never meant for either to happen.' Sid paused and scratched his chin. 'It was seeing you naked that triggered it.'

'You only saw me naked once, what about all the other times, what was your excuse then?'

'I don't know, I never wanted to. I suppose because it was so bloody good.' He sounded contrite, almost apologetic, before he continued in his usual vein. 'Bloody hell, girl, the only difference between you and that Marilyn Monroe is that she has blonde hair.' He stopped talking as they both heard the sound of the lavatory chain being pulled. 'Why do you think these bloody swanky people invited you to go tonight if it wasn't because you're a real beauty?'

Wendy did not answer but turned and went into the bathroom the moment Michael emerged and heard her mother arrive home a few minutes later.

'You look absolutely beautiful,' said Doris as Wendy emerged from the stairway, adorned in her evening gown with the mink stole over her shoulders and the imitation pearl choker embellishing her neck. Her chestnut hair was brushed and backcombed, a meagre amount of face powder gave sufficient colour to her cheeks and her lips were enriched with a touch of lipstick. She looked a radiant young woman and the scent of her perfume competed with the smell of Sid's cigarette.

At that moment there was the sound of a car horn outside. 'That'll be the Rendles,' said Wendy.

'It is if he drives a Humber Super Snipe,' Michael called from the front room.

'Damn and blast it, I wish I 'ad a camera; you look a proper picture,' her proud mother said. 'Just you go and enjoy yourself.'

She did. She observed everybody else in order to select the correct cutlery from the multitude of choice during the four-course dinner and sipped graciously at her glass of wine, blissfully unaware that she was turning the heads of every male present. It was during the speeches that she noticed Mr Rendle smiling lecherously at her and during the presentations that followed she became aware of his wife's aggrieved eyes looking daggers at her.

David was very smart in his formal dinner attire and with his facial spots camouflaged with cream he appeared older than the articled clerk from the office, but he had been right, he could not dance. Having had her toes trodden on a couple of times Wendy was gratified to be rescued by a young cricketer who was an expert dancer by comparison. He politely invited her to dance a quickstep to the music of "Zambesi", at the end of which the bandleader announced they would play a medley of rock and roll.

The young cricketer, who had informed Wendy his name was Robert, asked, 'would you like to continue?'

'Yes please, the jive is the only thing I can do.'

And jive they did, so well that they almost became an exhibition in the middle of the dance floor. After the medley she was bombarded with dance requests; some she accepted but not all because she felt it would be too discourteous not to spend some time sitting with David. If she accepted all the offers to buy her a drink she would have been totally inebriated; instead she rationed herself to two glasses of port mixed with lemonade. She also turned down numerous requests from handsome young men wanting to make a future date with her.

She was the belle of the ball. She could not remember an occasion she had enjoyed so much despite being given the cold shoulder by the Rendles as they drove home in the early hours of Saturday morning. She was tipsy and happy but well in control of her senses to observe Brenda Frost in the beam of the car lights. She was wrapped tightly round some young man like toffee paper, kissing frantically in a shop doorway in Wensum Street.

The following morning Wendy was awakened by the sound of her mother coughing a fraction after eleven o'clock. Still in ebullient mood from the previous night, she slipped her dressing gown over her nightdress and went downstairs.

'Mam, you're going to the surgery next week if I have to drag you there myself.'

Doris was rolling pastry for a meat pie she was preparing for dinner. 'You make too much fuss,' she said as she looked towards Wendy. 'I keep telling you, it's a smoker's cough.'

'Then why hasn't Sid got it?' Wendy sat in a chair to warm herself by the fire. 'It won't do any harm to have the doctor check it, so we'll go on Monday night.'

Doris left the kitchen and came and sat opposite Wendy. 'I suppose I'd better agree because I don't think you'll give me any peace until I do. Now tell me about last night, how did it go?'

Wendy did not need to be asked twice and launched excitedly into recounting the events of the previous night down to the last detail. She began by talking about the food, starting with the leek and potato soup and ending with the sherry trifle. She told her mother about every dance and whom she danced with and about Robert and how well they had danced during the jive together.

Doris smiled. Was Robert to be Wendy's new boyfriend, a future son-in-law? Refraining from comment she leaned forward to stoke some life into the fire, causing her to notice the letter on the mantelpiece. 'Oh I almost forgot, there's a letter for you. I think it's from Anne.'

Wendy reached up for the envelope and noticed a small wallet with the words "Premium Bonds" printed on it.

'Oh yes,' said Doris with her memory further jogged, 'I've been up the Post Office this morning and bought you three pounds worth of those new premium bonds.'

'Whatever for?'

'I wanted to. You've had a rough time, what with the baby and everything. You gave me that extra money out of your pay rise so I think you deserve it. Let's hope you're lucky.'

When her mother returned to the kitchen to finish the meat pie Wendy opened the envelope. 'Anne's got a job as a comptometer operator in the offices of the shoe factory where her dad and brother work,' she called out as she read the letter.

'Whatever is one of those?'

'We have one at work; it's like a massive adding machine that you can calculate on.' Wendy continued to read and call out bits of news from the letter. 'She's going out with this young man that works there but he's three years older than her. His name's Trevor, he's very handsome and he's taking her to the Knighton cinema, which is near where she lives.'

Doris finished her preparation and popped the meat pie in the oven before returning to her chair opposite Wendy.

'She's invited me to spend Christmas with her in Leicester,' Wendy said as she put the letter down on her lap.

CHAPTER ELEVEN

Wendy walked with her mother to the doctor's on bonfire night, their nostrils filled with the charcoal smell of damp wood burning on blazing fires. From all around they could hear the sound of exploding fireworks and see bursts of colour in the night sky. They made the surgery a minute before the door was closed at half past six.

Wendy was not interested in the fireworks when they returned forty minutes later. 'What did Doctor Myers say?'

'He thinks I've got bronchitis but he wants to send me to the 'ospital for tests.'

'What sort of tests?' Wendy asked as they passed two boys eagerly looking for somewhere to pin their Catherine Wheel.

'I've got to 'ave one of those barium meal X-rays. Blooming awful it is, a woman in the café was ranting on about it last week.'

Wendy had noticed her mother had been given a prescription when she came out of the consulting room and she asked what it was.

'Pills for bronchitis; penicillin I think because he asked me if I was allergic to it.'

'I hope you told him how bad your coughing has been and for how long.'

'I didn't 'ave to, he sounded me chest with 'is stethoscope. Blooming cold it was, it's a good job I put me clean bra on.'

'That nearly made us too late.' Close by, a rocket zoomed skywards before cascading into a variety of colourful sparks. 'When have you got to go to the hospital?'

'They'll send me an appointment. I expect I shall 'ave to take a day off work.'

'You have a malignant tumour on your right lung, Mrs Rawlins,' said Doctor Myers softly as he studied the report from the hospital. 'I am afraid that it has already spread.'

Doris had waited three weeks for her hospital appointment when various X-rays had been taken and then told to wait another week before seeing her doctor. White-faced, she sat like a young schoolgirl being admonished by her teacher. 'Can it be treated?'

'We can and will treat it with anti-cancer drugs but unfortunately it is far too advanced to do anything more than slow it down. Words that I hate having to say are that you should have consulted me a lot sooner; earlier detection would have given a better chance for treatment.'

'Am I going to die?' Deep down her own suspicions were being confirmed. She had tried to prepare for the worst but had hoped for the best. Her eyes watered as she tried to control her tears.

'I have never found an easy or comforting way to answer patients that ask that question even after fifteen years of general practice,' Doctor Myers said, nodding his head. 'I will prescribe some painkillers that will help.'

'How long?'

'Mrs Rawlins, I have been open and honest with you because I have always believed it is in the best interests of my patients, but that is one question I cannot answer. It depends on the reaction of the cancer to the drugs and how fast it has been spreading. I have known patients live two or three years when I would not have expected them to last more than a few months and I have known patients die after a few weeks when I would have expected them to last years. I am deeply sorry that there is nothing more I can do or say. I only wish there was.'

Doris wiped her eyes as Doctor Myers wrote out the prescription and in that instant she decided she would not tell her family. Ignorance is bliss. What they did not know they could not worry about.

There was a jolt as the nine thirty-five train pulled out of the city station on time and Wendy was on her way to Leicester to spend Christmas with Anne. She felt another jolt thirty-five minutes later when her carriage was attached to others at Melton Constable. At Fakenham an elderly couple joined Wendy in the compartment of the corridor carriage and sat diagonally opposite. There was a curt exchange of greetings before she proceeded to knit and he puffed on his pipe reading a book.

She was looking forward to seeing Anne again and grateful that Mr Palmer had allowed her two extra days off so that she could spend the whole week with her friend whom she had not seen for sixteen months.

A blanket of smoke from the engine obliterated her view of the flat Lincolnshire countryside as the train gathered speed on the single-track line after leaving Holbeach, where a young man in a "Teddy Boy" suit and his girlfriend had come in and sat opposite the old couple.

He reminded her of Graham who did manage to get a weekend's leave in the middle of November. Wendy smiled at the memory of seeing him in his khaki uniform with his hair cut short. It had been wonderful to see him even if it did almost cause a riot.

Wendy fought hard to control herself at the table when Graham brought Brenda to Sunday tea. She held her tongue for his sake and her family but not when she saw her alone outside the opticians in Castle Street the following Saturday.

'You're a two-timing two-faced sodding bitch,' she yelled at her, controlling herself sufficiently to avoid slapping her face.

At first Brenda Frost denied there was anybody other than Graham but then admitted it when she realized Wendy had seen her with him. 'So what? You needn't get bloody hoity-toity with me, I've seen your dad with that woman.'

For a moment Wendy was stunned by Brenda's accusation. 'You haven't seen my dad with anyone because he was killed in the war.'

'If you're going to be that bloody finicky,' Brenda screamed, 'your stepfather.'

'I couldn't sodding care if you'd seen him with every woman in Norwich,' Wendy screamed back at her.

'Perhaps not, but I bet your mother would.'

Brenda certainly knew how to stir it but Wendy ignored the remark and retaliated quickly. 'You've got to write to Graham and tell him what you've been up to or I will.'

'Fuck you,' she shouted and rushed off up the steps of Davey Place towards Castle Meadow and her bus stop.

Wendy recalled the squabble as if it was yesterday as the train slowed to an unscheduled stop at the Welland Bank Junction in Spalding and remembered the embarrassment when she realized how many pedestrians had witnessed their slanging match.

136

Sid was a balding, barrel-shaped, sodding bastard so she assumed "that woman" was a female bus conductor and that Brenda was just clutching at straws by suggesting otherwise. She could never understand what attracted her mother to him other than she hated being on her own and he was instantly available. Hardly reasons for a marriage, although it seemed to be working but how different it would be if her mother knew of his evil ways.

As the train lurched forward to be on the move again the young girl at Wendy's side sneezed and started to cough before leaning towards her boyfriend. Her mother's cough was not getting any better and Wendy was suspicious that it was something more than bronchitis. That night of the second visit to the doctor's she had come out of the consulting room with her face as white as pure snow.

'The 'ospital tests were a complete waste of time,' her mother had said, 'and I lost four hours of pay.'

When she got back to Norwich, Wendy decided she would go and see Doctor Myers and find out about this mysterious bronchitis that had troubled her mother for so long.

She stared out of the window when the train started to slow again and then noticed a red flatbed lorry waiting at a level crossing. It looked exactly like the one that Stan used to drive and she visualized him sitting in it with her at his side.

'Sodding trains,' he would have sworn.

It brought a smile to her face realizing that she would have said exactly the same thing. Stan had been the only "dad" she had known so it was understandable she was like him in other ways. He had been a very independent, straightforward man who faced up to problems head on, like the move from Biggleswade.

Unlike her mother, Stan had been a good manager of the family finances, which was another attribute that she had acquired from him. She was not as assertive as Stan, but during the last year she had certainly become more independent, due largely to having to spend three months away from home. She had grown wiser and she had grown physically, but would she be able to stop Sid if ever he tried anything again? An abuse-free year had passed since that last time; the incident before last Christmas when he had made her pregnant. Nothing had been attempted since, despite the fact there had been occasions when she had been alone in the house with him.

The elderly couple left the train at Bourne and the young girl snuggled up even closer to her boyfriend. They untangled themselves to depart at Saxby station and for the short four mile trip to Melton Mowbray, Wendy was alone. Two boisterous train spotters, about Michael's age, joined her for the final leg of her journey to Leicester.

'It were an Ivatt numbered 43065,' one said, as he wrote the number down in a notebook.

'Did you see what that shunter were?' asked the other boy that sat opposite Wendy, with tousled hair and short trousers. He sniffed loudly before wiping his nose on his cuff.

'It was a Duck Six 44231.'

Anne was on the platform to meet her when the train pulled into Leicester and they lovingly embraced each other. Wendy's first impression was that of a big bustling city when the two girls reached street level and the busy London Road. 'We'll wait here a minute,' said Anne as she stopped by a newspaper vendor shouting in an effort to sell the early additions of the Leicester Mercury. 'We can catch two buses; either the L8 Midland Red that goes from that stop,' continued Anne as she pointed, 'or a number 28 Corporation bus from up there.'

The Hitchens's house in Scott Street was similar to her own in Norwich. It was only when Anne took her to the bedroom above the parlour that they were sharing that Wendy noticed a difference. A narrow corridor led to the back bedroom, above the kitchen, used by Jimmy.

Having spent all afternoon chatting, the start of a full week of social pleasure began that night when they went to a dance in the church hall at Oadby. It was packed so that a full rendering of Rock and Roll was impossible. Like the cricket club ball, Wendy had no shortage of dance partners and neither did Anne for that matter.

They stayed until it finished with the National Anthem at midnight and caught a bus taking them through Wigston to Knighton. 'Buses don't run as late as this in Norwich,' Wendy said, as they settled themselves in a seat on the upper deck to allow Anne to smoke.

'This only runs on a Saturday night, that's why I came here. The girls at work told me about it.'

'Tickets please,' the conductor called as the bus stopped to let off some passengers.

'It's a shame your boyfriend couldn't come,' said Wendy once the bus was on the move.

'Trevor had to go to his gran's for the weekend but you'll meet him on Monday because we're all going to the Palais for the Christmas Eve dance.'

By the time they got off the bus it was raining, causing them to run down Knighton Fields Road. As they crossed Lord Byron Street, Anne stopped. 'Shit! I can't run in these shoes.'

They walked and they were both soaked to the skin when they reached Anne's house where everybody else was in bed. She brought out the clothes-horse from the cupboard under the stairs.

'If we put our things on here they'll be dry by morning,' Anne whispered as she positioned it around the fire grate. 'It's a back boiler that stays alight all night.'

Anne tucked her towel above her bust, sat down and lit a cigarette. 'I'll just have this before we go to bed,' she said softly as she blew exhaled smoke from her mouth.

She watched enviously as Wendy finished undressing. 'You've got a beautiful figure with curves in all the right places, I wish mine was like yours.'

Wendy tucked her towel under her arm, checked that it covered her crotch and sat down in a dining chair next to Anne. 'You have a lovely figure too,'

'I've not, I'm too big. You've got a figure like Marilyn Monroe and I'm 40-30-40!'

'That's an exaggeration,' Wendy grinned. 'You're a little fuller in the bust than me, that's all.'

'My bum's enormous, my stomach's fatter and to make matters worse I'm shorter than you. Look at my thighs,' she said as she patted one with her free hand, 'they're like tree trunks.'

'I bet Trevor never complains.'

'No he doesn't. I hope you like him, he's like a bean pole by the side of me but I love him.'

'How do you know when you're in love?'

Anne took the cigarette from her mouth and pursed her lips. She was about to give a silly reply but noticed from the imploring look in Wendy's eyes that she was deadly serious. She inhaled on her cigarette to think about her answer. 'I once asked our Marian that question and she said it felt like butterflies in her stomach but when I'm with Trevor it's more like a swarm of buzzing bees.' She paused to take a final drag on her cigarette before stubbing it in the ashtray. 'My heart starts pounding like the kick of a mule, my legs turn to jelly and I go all hot and juicy down there,' said Anne pointing to her crotch. 'I think and care about him all the time. Even tonight when I was dancing I was thinking about Trevor. I know I want to be with him forever. Most of all,' Anne smiled, 'I love him because he's got a car so we won't have this problem with the weather on Monday even if it pisses with rain.'

Wendy had never known a week of her life pass so quickly. Anne's clingy embrace on the platform was sad and tearful; such a contrast from her arrival when they had hugged each other with joyful excitement. The three fifteen departure was ten minutes late and a young couple who sat in the same compartment chatted more on the short trip to Melton Mowbray than all the passengers put together on the journey up.

It had been a wonderful week and she had done so much. Trevor was nice and seemed rapt over Anne despite her misgivings about her figure. She had dressed in her favourite burgundy gown for the dance at the Palais and was bombarded with dance requests. She was able to jive early on but when the band played her favourite "Heartbreak Hotel" the floor was too crowded to jive properly.

Wendy could never remember spending such a lazy Christmas Day. She and Anne slept until dinner time when Mrs Hitchens had wakened them. She even missed the washing up as it clashed with the time she had arranged to ring her mother, call box to call box. On Boxing Day Trevor had driven them to Bradgate Park where they walked up to Old John; an arch and tower. She did not feel as though she had climbed much of a hill, yet the view of Leicester was panoramic. It reminded her of the view of Norwich from Mousehold.

They went to the pictures twice; once on their own to the local Knighton cinema and once to the Picture House in the city centre. She did not care for Trevor's friend Barry who came with them but, for the sake of Anne and Trevor, she tolerated his egotistic behaviour. God's gift to women he was not, despite whatever he may have thought.

Anne's parents seemed pleased to have her stop with them; "come anytime" had been their parting words. The first thing she must do when she got back to Norwich was to write to Mr and Mrs Hitchens and thank them for their hospitality, perhaps send them a small gift.

The compartment door slid open and a young man in Royal Air Force uniform entered. 'Excuse me, would you mind if I sit in here?'

Sitting by the window and engrossed in her reminiscences, Wendy had not even realized the train had stopped at Bourne. 'No, not in the least.'

He threw his kitbag on the overhead luggage rack and sat at the other end of the bench seat. 'I have to sit the same way as the train is travelling or I feel sick.'

Wendy felt the jolt as the train pulled away from the station. 'Are you going home or back to your base?'

'I'm stationed at Coltishall. I normally hitch-hike but my mother gave me the money for the train fare so here I am.' He took out a silver cigarette case from his tunic pocket and offered one to Wendy, 'They're only Park Drive.'

'No thanks,' Wendy declined and, thinking how Graham had started to smoke since joining the army, she asked, 'Do all you National Servicemen smoke?'

He smiled, 'Helps to keep your sanity.'

She learned his name was Derek Ross, he was three months older than Graham and about the same height. His frizzy hair was brown, bordering on ginger, his face was gaunt like his body and he was easy to chat with as they steamed steadily eastwards in the gloomily lit carriage.

Wendy had warmed to him sufficiently to suggest he come home with her for a cup of tea before trying to thumb it to Coltishall. He lifted her case from the rack and carried it off the train where Doris and Michael were both waiting.

Later; much later than a cup of tea could have lasted, Wendy walked with Derek to the top of the street to catch the last bus to the aerodrome. He had stayed for three hours and it was far too late to thumb for a lift. They arranged to meet outside the Odeon the following Saturday as the bus trundled up Magdalen Road towards them.

It was a hurried arrangement and Wendy immediately started to have second thoughts as she walked back home. Was she doing the right thing? It was a date. He was nice, they had chatted a lot but he was not Graham. She shrugged. There was no way she could contact him to cancel it so the Odeon it was to be.

CHAPTER TWELVE

Wendy arrived home from work on Valentine's Day to find five cards waiting for her on the mantelshelf; four with local postmarks and one from Leicester. She could only think that the self-opinionated Barry had sent it so she ripped it open disgustedly, only to discover it was from Anne with the words, "I bet this is the only Valentine's card you get" jokingly written in it. It also contained a letter with news that her eldest sister, Jane was getting married on the second Saturday in March and the whole family would be coming to Norwich for the weekend.

She recognized the card sent by Donald Aspinall because he wrote exactly the same words as the previous year when it had been the only one she had received. Although it was signed "Guess who" she could identify David Rendle's writing on the third card.

The next card was from Derek. He had drawn the outline of a heart with an arrow piercing it, then written the words, "Roses are red, violets are blue, and you will never guess who loves you". She hoped the word "love" was just for the sake of rhyme rather than anything more serious. She liked Derek and looked forward to his company but she did not love him and knew she never would.

"To B squared" was another card sent as a joke by one or more of the clerks at the office. She smiled at the nickname. She wheedled it out of David as to why she was called B squared shortly before Christmas; he said it was for two letter Bs and was because she had a figure like Bridget Bardot, the French film star. She would get her own back tomorrow by teasing them that she had not received it.

'Ralph thinks I ought not to live on my own any longer. He is having the garage at his house in Wisbech converted to a bedroom for me so that I can go and live with him.'

It was too cold to take Mrs Bellamy out for a walk on Saturday so Wendy sat and gossiped with her. 'That will be really nice but I'll miss you.' The dear kind lady was like a grandmother to Wendy, a granny that she had never known.

Mrs Bellamy looked at Wendy with soft glazed eyes. 'And I will miss you.' She was very fond of her, deliberately treating her like the daughter she had craved for but never had.

A despondent chill of loneliness swept over Wendy. What was it about her that everybody she liked and wanted to be near kept moving away? First there was Anne, then Graham and now Mrs Bellamy. 'When is this likely to happen?'

'In a couple of months' time; Ralph wants me to move during the Easter school holidays. I have a man coming to value the house on Monday.'

'It's our Michael's birthday on Monday, he'll be fourteen.' Wendy's interruption was instinctive, but it served to steer their conversation in a different direction.

'I want you to have the typewriter and any of those books in the study that you would like because I am not going to be able to take them with me.'

It was a generous offer and Wendy knew better than to argue over accepting it but where would she put everything?

Michael had two two-shilling coins when he came in from his paper round that Mrs Bellamy had given him for his birthday, which made Wendy regret having told her.

'Is Mam still at work?' she said as she presented him with a pair of football shorts that he wanted.

'No, when I came home from school she was in bed. I don't think she's very well.'

She dashed upstairs to find her mother asleep but looking ghostly pale. Wendy had visited Doctor Myers early in January, but he had advised her to talk with her mother. This she had tried on lots of occasions but nothing was forthcoming except accusations of making a fuss over nothing. It did not look like nothing now.

Doris opened her eyes to see Wendy standing over the bed looking anxiously perplexed. 'It's only me bronchitis,' she said meekly. 'It got the better of me today.'

'You are going to get better aren't you, Mam?'

'Don't you fret about me, it's because it's been such a cold weekend.' She manoeuvred herself up to a sitting position as Wendy adjusted the pillows accordingly. 'Would you be a treasure and make me a nice cup of tea?'

Minutes later Wendy returned with a tray and handed her mother a sandwich filled with her favourite crab paste before pouring a cup of tea.

'Not much of a birthday for Michael, I should 'ave got up and made him a cake.'

'Don't you worry about him, Mam, he's in the bathroom getting ready to go out with Lizzie.' Wendy perched on the edge of the bed facing her mother. 'That girl is the best thing that's ever happened to him, I've never known him to keep himself so clean.'

'You kids grow up far too quickly. It doesn't seem five minutes since you were both babies in me arms and now Michael's got a girlfriend and you've started courting.'

'I'm not courting, Derek's just a friend.'

'Whatever you say,' said Doris as she slurped her tea.

Wendy did not want her mother getting any wrong ideas so she endeavoured to change the subject. 'Derek joked with me on Saturday, thought you must have liked "Peter Pan", because Wendy and Michael were children of the Darling family in the book; John is all we're missing.'

'You would 'ave been called John if you were a boy. Ted wanted that and I wanted to 'ave his name included so you would 'ave been christened John Edward.'

They both smiled at each other when they heard Michael's breaking voice singing *Why do fools fall in love?* as he came up the stairs to get to his bedroom to dress.

'What about Michael, who chose his name?'

'George and I both liked it. I did toy with the idea of Edward as a second name but I didn't think that would be very fair on 'is father so 'e was named Michael George.'

'So why am I called Wendy?'

'Because you were born on a Wednesday, your Dad wanted to call you Winifred but I hated that name. It reminded me of a fat old battleaxe that lived in our street when I was a girl and every time I 'ear the name I think of 'er. You were due to be born on a Tuesday and I suggested Grace because Tuesday's child is full of grace, but Ted didn't like that.'

'I'm glad he didn't, I would have hated to be called Grace.'

'We 'alf compromised on Julie after the month you were due to be born but Ted still liked Winifred. I was almost eight months gone when I 'eard he'd been killed at Dunkirk and I thought I ought to respect 'is wishes. Then when you came popping out on a Wednesday I choose Wendy. I still couldn't stand the name Winifred but Winnie, Wendy and Wednesday, they all sound about the same and I didn't think Ted would mind.'

Michael popped his head round the door to announce that he was off out to see Lizzie. 'Hope you soon feel better, Mam.'

Doris was no better when Wendy arrived home from her bookkeeping class on Wednesday night. She was still very pale, her eyes seemed to be sunken and her hair, her beautiful chestnut hair that Wendy had inherited, was unkempt and limp.

'Where's Sid? I thought it was his day off?'

'He's been 'ere fussing all day but I told 'im to go over to the "Rosewood" for a pint.'

Wendy leaned over and gently kissed her mother on her forehead. 'If you're no better in the morning I'm going to call Doctor Myers.'

'I'll be all right, besides you'll be at work.'

'No I won't. I spoke to Mr Palmer and he's let me have the next two days off because we're not very busy at the moment.'

The next morning Wendy was up early and had an apple with a cup of tea for breakfast. She tipped some cornflakes into a bowl as Sid appeared at the bottom of the stairs wearing a vest and trousers and scratching his chin.

'Is that for me?'

'No it's Michael's,' Wendy replied and knocked the ceiling with the broom handle to wake him. 'You can get your own sodding breakfast.'

He grunted before making his way to the bathroom for a shave. Half an hour later and Wendy had said goodbye to them both; Michael to school and Sid to the bus depot where he was working a "show up" shift that meant he was not rostered for any specific duty but had to be available in case a driver did not show up.

Wendy took her mother tea and toast on a tray. 'How are you this morning?'

'About the same,' Doris moved to a sitting position in the bed. It started her coughing and she quickly put her handkerchief to her mouth.

That was when Wendy noticed the stains. 'Are you coughing up blood?' She fired the question quickly, her voice full of concern, her eyes full of anxiety.

Doris quickly clenched her hand and crumbled the handkerchief to hide it from view, 'It's not much.'

'That does it,' said Wendy defiantly. 'I'm going straight up to the telephone box to call Doctor Myers.'

Despite weak protests from her mother, Wendy did just that. In the intervening two hours before Doctor Myers arrived at eleven fifty, she laboriously cleaned and tidied the house from top to bottom.

Wendy was tense and spoke softly as she led the doctor up the stairs. 'I'm sorry I had to call you out but my mam's been in bed all week.'

'Good morning, Mrs Rawlins,' he said when he entered the bedroom. 'I have come to have a look at you.'

Doris nodded and muttered a greeting to him before he turned to Wendy. 'I wonder, Miss Rawlins...'

'My name's Wendy Marshall,' she corrected, putting emphasis on her surname.

'I do beg your pardon.' He took his stethoscope from his bag and smiled at Wendy. 'I wonder if you would be so kind as to make a cup of tea while I examine your mother?'

He came downstairs minutes later carrying his black bag. Wendy was sitting at the table with her back to the kitchen having made the tea using her mother's best set of china crockery. She went straight to the point uppermost in her mind. 'Is my mother dying?'

'What has she told you?'

'That's the trouble, she hasn't told me anything. Keeps saying she's got bronchitis but I'm sure it is something more serious.'

'Right then, Wendy,' he said as he pulled out a chair and sat at the table opposite her. 'Your mother said I should tell you everything if you asked so shall we have that cup of tea?'

The doctor confirmed Wendy's worst fears, her mother was terminally ill with cancer that was very advanced. 'I have increased the dosage of the painkillers and I will arrange to have her go to hospital when I get back but I doubt it will be before tomorrow.'

Wendy was in shock. Her watery eyes were staring at her cup as both hands gently turned the saucer in a clockwise direction.

Doctor Myers found he was agreeing with her mother that Wendy was a sensible girl. Still, he would have preferred her to break the news to her daughter and much sooner. He wished he could have told Wendy when she visited the surgery in January but he had patient confidentiality to consider. He was impressed then, thinking how mature she was, but maturity did not soften the distress. He gently placed his hand over her wrist. 'Will you be all right?'

It broke her mesmerized stare and snapped her back to reality. She looked across at the doctor, 'Not tomorrow.' It was a pleading, not a command. 'It's Mam's birthday tomorrow and I think she would rather be here for that.'

He nodded his agreement and said that he would make arrangements for an ambulance for Saturday. When it was time to leave Wendy showed him to the back door.

'Your mother is quite right about you,' he said as he paused on the step. 'You are wise beyond your years. I would never have believed you are only sixteen.'

When the doctor had gone Wendy sat at the table and cried. She could have been a lot more supportive if her mother had have told her sooner. She wiped her eyes on her handkerchief and returned to the bedroom.

'How long have you known?'

'Not long, it was when I went to see about me 'ospital tests.' Her mother's voice was garbled as if she had a plum stone in her mouth.

'That was before Christmas. Why haven't you said anything before?'

'Cause I didn't want you worrying and I didn't want no fuss.' She paused and struggled to take deep breaths. 'You must promise not to say anything to Sid or Michael.'

'That wouldn't be right, Mam, they have to know and I'll have to write to Graham.'

Doris reached out and clasped her hand over Wendy's arm, but there was no firmness in the grip. 'Not yet, not until after me birthday, I don't think I could stand all the fuss. If you must tell them, then do it when I'm in the 'ospital.'

Wendy noticed her mother's voice was rasping and her speech was becoming slower but she agreed before leaving the room to allow her mother to sleep.

The next morning Wendy, red-eyed from spending most of the night weeping, packed Michael off to school in true motherly fashion and held her silence with Sid before he went to work. She took a breakfast tray to her mother, 'Happy birthday, Mam.'

Her mother looked drawn. She struggled to smile and struggled even harder to raise herself to a sitting position.

'Eat some breakfast, Mam, and then you can open your cards.'

While her mother crunched on a piece of toast Wendy noticed the birthday card from Sid standing on the top of the chest of drawers. By the side of it was a box of chocolates and a brooch that Wendy looked at after checking there was enough paraffin in the convector heater. It was typical of Sid; tacky and tasteless.

'I can't eat any more but it was ever so nice,' said Doris as she slowly reached out for the bottle of painkilling pills.

Wendy neatly arranged the cards by the side of Sid's after she had helped her mother open them. Apart from Michael's and her own the postman had delivered three more; one from Aunt Ethel, one from Graham and one signed by all her work colleagues at the cafeteria. When she showed her the present she had bought, an aqua green satin nightdress, her mother started to cry.

'Come on, Mam, don't cry, it's not that good a present.'

'It's beautiful and I don't deserve it,' she sobbed. 'I don't deserve to 'ave a daughter as good as you, damn and blast it, I've been such a wicked mother.'

152

'Don't talk daft, Mam,' said Wendy. She squatted on the edge of the bed by her side and put her arm comfortingly around her shoulder.

Two minutes ticked by as they comforted each other before Wendy could smell the unpleasant odour on her mother. 'I'll go and get a bowl and give you a nice wash so that you can try it on.'

Like a caring nurse, Wendy washed and dried her but could not fail to notice how thin and emaciated her mother looked. She had memories from the days of the old tin bath in the tiny parlour of the Biggleswade cottage when her mother had a lovely robust figure.

She put on the new nightdress and brushed her hair. 'There you are, Mam, you look like a new woman.' Wendy opened the wardrobe door to just the right angle for her mother to see her reflection in the mirror.

'Thank you, it's lovely.'

Wendy arranged the pillows and helped her mother to a sitting position. 'You're all ready to receive your birthday visitors now. I expect Mrs Sutton will be popping in soon.'

Doris stretched out her left hand and lightly grasped Wendy's arm when she sat on the edge of the bed close to her. 'Your Dad would 'ave been very proud of the way you've turned out.'

She sniffed to hold back the tears. 'I still miss 'im you know, even after all these years and after everything that's 'appened.' She took her hand away, sighed heavily and took as big a breath as she could manage. 'I 'ave some things that I want you to 'ave when I've gone. There are some letters from your father. They're in an old biscuit tin in the cupboard under the stairs. Sid doesn't know about it so don't let 'im see you. Yours and Michael's birth certificates are in there, as well as some other papers and some saving stamps. I took a leaf out of Graham's book when 'e bought that motorbike and started saving me tips.' She paused to breathe rapidly, almost panting like an athlete after a race. 'There's not much but I want you to 'ave them. They might come in 'andy if you want to get away, but you must promise not to look until after I die.'

'Well that will be ages yet,' Wendy smiled in order to cheer her mother up. 'I shall have forgotten all about it when that happens.'

Yet they both knew this was not true. Wendy felt a strange sense of foreboding as if her mother was trying to tidy up the loose ends of her life.

Doris felt a little better for telling her daughter but there was still one last hurdle to overcome, one gigantic obstacle that had played on her mind. She looked blandly at Wendy. 'What day is it? I lose all track of time.'

'It's Friday and not just any old Friday, it's your birthday.'

'I was born on a Friday, thirty-nine years ago to the day. They must 'ave got us mixed up.'

Wendy could see that her mother was on the verge of weeping again. 'What do you mean?'

'You should have been born on a Friday, "Friday's child is loving and giving" and I should 'ave been a Wednesday's Child because I'm full of woe.'

Wendy edged closer as Doris started to cry and embraced her. 'It's only an old poem, I'm sure it doesn't mean anything really.'

'I'm wicked and deserve to die for my wickedness,' Doris continued slowly, her head resting on Wendy's shoulder. 'I couldn't help falling for Sid. The first time I met him was when he stopped the bus I was running for so that I could get on. Then a few days later he came into the "Rosewood" when I was working and bought me a couple of drinks. I thought that was kind.'

Wendy listened as she cuddled her mother, stroking her hands over her back like she would a baby. But she was alarmed. She could feel her spine sticking out like she was a skeleton.

She could not listen to any more of her mother's reminiscences praising Sid. 'Kindness one minute does not excuse bullying the next.'

'I know and I've 'ad lots of time to think while I've been stuck up 'ere in me bed. I'm not afraid of dying 'cause I'm going to be with Ted but I am frightened for you. I love you, Wendy. You've brought a lot of joy to me 'eart and all I've done is filled you with sadness. But I need to know.'

Wendy did not understand and was mystified. 'Need to know what?'

'About the baby!' She paused and sighed, her breathing was laboured. 'It wasn't Donald Aspinall was it? He wasn't the father was 'e?'

Clutched together in their embrace their heads were on each other's shoulders but Wendy could feel her mother's body trembling. How she had dreamed, how she had clung on to the hope that one day she could tell her mother about Sid. Now did seem the right time but how much distress would it cause? How much harm could it do to her dying mother?

'It was...' She stopped abruptly.

'It's only me, shall I come up?' It was Mrs Sutton. Her intervention had rescued Wendy from confessing.

'Was it Sid?'

Wendy could hardly hear her mother's frail voice as Mrs Sutton called out again. 'Are you there, Doris?'

Wendy remained silent, hugging her mother with tears running down her cheeks.

'It was Sid.'

It was spoken as a whisper but Wendy just heard her mother's words. Did she know or was she guessing?

Wendy suddenly felt a strange limpness in her mother's body. She gently eased her down, 'You have a sleep it will do you good,' she said in a subdued voice and kissed her forehead. 'I'll tell Mrs Sutton to come back later.'

CHAPTER THIRTEEN

Doris Rawlins never woke again. At one minute after midday Wendy walked to the telephone box after having cried for a time in her mother's room. She rang the surgery and the bus depot before sending telegrams from the Post Office to Graham and Aunt Ethel.

Doctor Myers arrived first and confirmed her mother's death. He tried to console Wendy whose bloodshot eyes were exhausted of tears. 'Your mother is at peace and out of pain and that is something she has suffered for a very long time. Try to look upon it as a happy release.'

'She died on her birthday,' Wendy said softly, her comatose eyes staring as he wrote out the death certificate. 'It's so tragic yet in a strange sort of way I think it's what she wanted.'

The doctor wondered where her stepfather was. It was wrong to leave adult matters for such a young girl to cope with, even though this bright young girl had the maturity of somebody much older. He could think of patients twice her age that were far less capable of dealing with things. He wanted to wait but he had another urgent appointment so he asked if she would like him to make the funeral arrangements or leave it to her stepfather.

'I doubt Sid will know what to do, he's sodding useless. I think Mam had the Co-op when Stan was killed.' Speak of the devil thought Wendy as she heard Sid in the back yard.

She left the doctor to explain things to him and went out, walking down the street towards Michael's school.

They sat on a bench in Waterloo Park where she tearfully broke the news to him and then her not so little brother embraced her. She took comfort from the physical strength of a boy who was rapidly becoming a man as they both wept.

'At least it's an end to her suffering,' she murmured.

She was right. Sid was useless, for during the week she did the lion's share of the work with the funeral arrangements that Doctor Myers had implemented when he first contacted the Co-op on their behalf. She also made plans to escape his clutches for good.

She found the old biscuit tin on Monday when she was alone in the house and rummaged through the contents. The savings stamps amounted to thirteen pounds and fifteen shillings. She slowly shook her head, amazed that her mother had managed to save so much.

With her birth certificate was a wedding day photograph of her mother and father. She studied it for a long time and noticed she had inherited a lot of her father's features, but seeing his image for the first time filled her with emotion. Her eyes were very moist.

The telegram was still in the envelope that it had been delivered in. Wendy stared at the words "Missing believed killed in action". Her mother had always said he was killed but could there be doubt? No! It was 1957, he could not be missing for seventeen years.

She found seven letters sent while he was in the army and read them all several times. They were deeply moving, sometimes sensual and sometimes practical but always showing a loving concern for his wife and unborn child. She would never know why her mother had never shown them to her before.

She was thrilled at the information they contained. Her father had suddenly become a person that she knew. Knew his favourite colour and knew he hated beetroot, something she shared with him, a tiny inherited trait. Knew his lucky number, knew he was a football fan and a staunch supporter of West Ham United and knew he liked to play dominoes in the pub on Sunday lunchtime. Most of all she knew he would have loved her.

An image and a history was something precious she could relate to. That night with the photograph and letters under her pillow she had a good cry.

The funeral was on Friday. It was a blustery day and Wendy felt the chill of the wind as it swirled around the vast openness of the cemetery. She wept silently, flanked by her two brothers as her mother's coffin was lowered. Opposite, Sid was snivelling with his head on his strangely impassive sister's shoulder. Even at a time like this Wendy could not feel any compassion for the man.

She could hear Michael and Graham sobbing, but the only thing on her mind as she stared at the coffin was that her mother knew. "It was Sid." She could hear her mother's frail words reaching up to her from the grave. She wiped her watery eyes on her handkerchief and whispered, 'Goodbye, Mam.'

The next day things rapidly went back to normal. Thankfully Sid went back to work and Wendy helped Graham pack in readiness for his return to his barracks.

'Dad's got me a free bus ride to Kings Lynn and I'll thumb it from there.' He stood in his army uniform with Wendy in the kitchen. 'With a bit of luck, when I get on the A47 I might get to

Wansford in one go and it's usually quite easy getting lifts on the A1.'

Wendy threw her arms around his neck and hugged him. 'I do miss you.'

'Hey don't go all sentimental on me or I'll miss my bus,' he said as he comforted her. 'You will be okay won't you?'

She was deliberately silent for a minute, her tummy churning, thrilled with the pleasure of his embrace. 'I'll be all right and I'll write to you soon.' She was overwhelmed with a desire to kiss him full on the lips but he moved away to gather up his kit bag. Then he was gone.

Tearfully saddened by his departure she made a cup of chicory coffee and was sipping it when Michael appeared at the bottom of the stairs dressed in his football gear.

'Are you seeing Lizzie after your match?'

'Yeah, I'm going back to her place for dinner then we are going to watch the Canaries play. They're at home to Millwall.'

'Then why don't you both come here for tea after the match?'

'Okay,' Michael said unemotionally as he opened the back door.

'I'll make a cake,' Wendy shouted in his wake.

Michael was uppermost in her mind a week later as she sat on the coach taking her to Cambridge. They had been together for all fourteen years since his birth, through fights and squabbles, through thick and thin and through good times and bad. She did not like to leave him but surely no harm would come to him living with Sid.

She liked Lizzie and got on well with her at tea last Saturday. She was not as excited as Michael about the football but then nobody could be as excited as her brother when Norwich won. She was sensible, practical and pretty in a plain sort of way and very good with Michael who it was obvious she adored. Wendy hoped they would stay together.

She had been surprised by Mr Palmer's words when she had given in her notice. 'If things do not work out and you come back to Norwich there will always be a job for you here.' He had given her a glowing reference and not deducted any pay for the time she had taken off to look after her mother.

She moved to speak to the driver as they waited outside the Crown Hotel in Newmarket. 'Do you know if I can get a bus to Biggleswade when we get to Cambridge?'

'I don't know, my love, you'll have to ask when we get there.'

'It's just that my Dad thought I could,' she lied. 'You perhaps know him because he's a bus driver, Sid Rawlins?'

'Can't say that I do, love.'

It was planned deception by Wendy laying a false trail should Sid try to find her. When the coach arrived at the bus station in Drummer Street thirty minutes later, she took her suitcase and brown paper carrier bag and set off in search of the railway station. In doing so she passed a green bus that by a remarkable coincidence was displaying the number 175 Biggleswade on the destination blind. There was a hitch in her plans when the station, over a mile away, was further than she expected. By the time she arrived her arms were aching from carrying her bulging suitcase that felt like a ton weight. She recovered with a cup of tea and a currant bun as she waited almost an hour for her train.

She was alone in the dismal and dirty non-corridor carriage when the train departed with a noisy shudder and an angry hiss of steam. She had contrived this roundabout route instead of proceeding direct to Leicester from the city station to increase her chances of fleeing for good. It started when she went to the bus station to break the bad news to her mother's work colleagues. A coach to Cambridge where she could catch a bus to Biggleswade would throw him off the scent. At Thorpe railway station she had found out the times of trains from Cambridge to Leicester.

She had left a goodbye note for Michael telling him that she had to leave because she could not tolerate living with Sid and once she was settled she would write to him. In the note she left for Sid she had simply written, "Mam knew, you sodding bastard".

Two boys on their way home from school joined her in the compartment when the train stopped at Kimbolton. They sat at the other end of the upholstered bench seat and immediately started to talk about their plans for the weekend.

It went quite dark when black smoke encircled the carriage as the engine steamed through a deep cutting after leaving Raunds. Stan loved the dark. "Much safer on the roads at night 'cause you can see headlights around the corners," he used to say. His influence in her life was probably why she was one of the few girls in her school class that was not afraid of the dark, although one of the few memories she had of Michael's father was of him putting up blackout screens at the windows and explaining that darkness kept them safe from German bombers.

At Kettering, Wendy had to change trains before starting the final leg of her journey. She was looking forward to surprising Anne, having deliberately not written for fear that her friend might write back enabling Sid to discover her whereabouts.

She arrived in the middle of the rush hour and just managed to squeeze on a corporation bus, standing in the crowded lower deck. Calamity struck at the first stop in Queens Road when a passenger rushing to get off brushed heavily against her arm holding the brown paper carrier bag. It tore away from the string handles Wendy was holding and fell to the floor where the contents, all her underwear, spilled out.

More disaster awaited her when she reached Anne's house and nobody answered the door to her knocking. While she was contemplating what to do next an awful thought struck her at the same time as a lady appeared at a neighbouring door.

'There's nobody in, me duck, they've all gone to Norwich for a wedding.'

All her plans and scheming dashed by one stupid mistake of her forgetting that Jane's wedding was tomorrow, March the ninth. It was the second Saturday and it had not registered in Wendy's mind. Walking despairingly back to Welford Road she was annoyed at her own forgetfulness. She caught another bus to the station that was considerably less crowded than the earlier one. Peering out of the window of the Midland Red vehicle as it slowed for the last stop in University Road she spotted a sign in an upstairs window, "Secretary receptionist wanted". She rushed off the bus at the stop but it was to no avail as the offices exhibiting the sign were closed.

On the corner was the Park Hotel, and as she was still looking for somewhere to sleep, Wendy decided to investigate. 'How much is the cheapest room?'

The answer from the young receptionist came as a visible shock and she knew she could not possibly deplete her meagre funds by stopping in a hotel for three nights until Anne was back. As Wendy stooped to pick up her suitcase the young lady whispered to her, 'If you're looking for somewhere cheaper then try the YWCA.'

She followed the receptionist's directions the short distance to the young women's hostel in Granville Road. It was considerably cheaper and affordable thanks to the extra money her mother's savings stamps would give her.

Having decided to check if the vacancy advertising office was open on a Saturday morning, Wendy selected to wear a cream blouse and her oatmeal two-piece suit, but she had a problem. She had used a bathroom washbasin to wash all her bras and knickers that had embarrassingly fallen on the bus floor and now not one single item was dry. She had a clean suspender belt, a new pair of nylons and as long as she kept her jacket on she thought nobody would know that she was not wearing any underwear.

The door was still locked when she tried it at eight thirty so she set about her other urgent task of finding cheap accommodation. During her Saturday morning stints in the café she learned that one of the employees lived in a low rent bedsit in Unthank Road, which gave her the idea of looking for something similar in Leicester. She studied the small advertisements in the nearby newsagents and noted one address in Severn Street that seemed promising.

A few minutes after nine o'clock the outer door was open. A second glass-panelled door opened when she tried it but before proceeding she looked at some signs on the right hand wall. The top one read, "Pollard and West, Yarn Agents". Beneath, the next sign read "Henry Grant and Co. Incorporated Accountants" and below that was a sign headed with the word "Registered Office" followed by small list of company names.

Once through the door she found herself standing in a tiled hall not dissimilar to the offices of Palmer and Moore. She knocked and entered the first door on her right that was adjacent to the bottom of the stairs.

A man sat behind a table with three spools of yarn in front of him. 'You want Henry Grant, his offices are on the next floor,' he said casually after Wendy asked about the vacancy.

On the next floor Wendy stood on a square-shaped landing, illuminated by a single light bulb above her head and natural light from a window at the end of a narrow passage. The door on her left turned out to be a toilet. In front of her was a door marked "Private," by the side of which was a Grandfather clock. Along the passage leading to the window and access to the stairs to the next floor was a signal-type wall sign saying "Enquiries". There was no answer when she knocked and nobody in the room when she opened the door and peered in. A small waiting area was divided from the remainder of the messy office by a chest-high frosted glass and mahogany partition with the job advertising sign hanging in the large bay window.

She was wondering what to do next when she heard a thump that seemed to come from overhead. The landing on the second floor was identical to the one below. The only door that was open was the one on her left that was an extremely untidy and smelly kitchen. A locked door at the bottom of an enclosed stairway thwarted her entry to the next floor.

She returned to the door by the side of the Grandfather clock. Despite the loud ticking she could hear a faint voice coming from the other side. She knocked, waited until she heard the voice shout, 'come in' and entered.

There was a large, oval-shaped conference table occupying the centre; at least Wendy assumed that it was because it was so full of differing heaps of documents, it was hard to tell. A tall, thin man with silver hair and rimless spectacles, looked at her. He continued to converse on the telephone on a desk in the recess behind the fireplace.

'Yes?' he said to Wendy, while holding his hand over the mouthpiece of the telephone.

'I've come about the job for a secretary receptionist.'

'Oh I am sorry, you are far too young,' he said and as a dismissive gesture returned to his telephone conversation.

Wendy was heartbroken and felt like a good cry. She locked herself in the toilet and wept, releasing all the pent up frustrations of being grief-stricken, homesick, homeless and jobless.

Moments later she heard somebody try the door. She hastily pulled herself together and with new determination charged out of the toilet, almost bumping into a gentleman on the landing.

'My name is Fred Hough,' he said, 'I have an appointment with Mr Grant.'

Wendy was about to explain her circumstances to him when this sudden urge swept over her to act like the receptionist she was obviously being mistaken for. 'I'm not sure if Mr Grant is on the telephone,' she said politely, 'but I'll just check.'

She moved to the door and not hearing any conversation, she knocked, entered and announced to a flabbergasted Henry Grant that Mr Hough was here to see him. He reached the door to demand an explanation when he noticed the client standing behind her. Mr Hough smiled, shook hands and thanked Wendy.

'I'll bring you both some coffee.'

The offensive smell when she entered the kitchen was from sour milk in bottles in varying degrees of ageing, the worst of which was solidifying. It all went down the sink followed by some disinfectant before she sniffed the contents of an almost full bottle that was fresh enough for consumption. She set about washing crockery and utensils to serve the two men coffee, after which an impressed Henry Grant came to find her adding the finishing touches to a transformed kitchen.

'Would you mind waiting until my client has gone, I think we need to talk.'

'I would like you to give me a proper interview,' Wendy said before he returned to his office after a little grunt, but not before she noticed a hint of a smile on his face.

It seemed an age before Wendy sat at the oval table by his side, with a gas fire set in a large Victorian fireplace warming her back. He had made some exploratory notes, looked at her educational certificate and read her reference. 'Can you do shorthand?'

'I'm afraid not; Mr Palmer used a Dictaphone for his letters.'

'I think I have one somewhere.' He looked behind at the files and paperwork littering his desk. 'Never mind,' he continued, 'what about salary? How much were you getting at Palmer and Moore?'

'I think you should tell me what you were paying your previous secretary.'

He grunted, re-read the letter and looked at his notes again. 'You have only been working for six months and you are only sixteen, although I must confess you do look older; what if I were to pay you three pounds per week for a trial period of one month?'

This was the same as she had been earning at Palmer and Moore, who had offered her more to stay. She was finding the courage to mention this when there was a knock at the door that preceded an obviously pregnant young lady entering the room.

'Sorry to interrupt,' she said sarcastically, threw a small bunch of keys on to the end of the table and went as quickly as she came.

He grunted again before observing Wendy's curious look. 'She used to work for me and is getting married this afternoon at the registry office. Now that I have a vacant flat upstairs you will have to remind me to put an advertisement in the Leicester Mercury.'

A vacant flat! Was she dreaming or was this sweet music to her ears? She tried to suppress her excitement, 'Three pounds per week and the flat thrown in.'

'I thought you were living in Scott Street?'

'Only temporarily, it's a friend house, I have to find somewhere else.'

'Two pounds, fifteen shillings and the flat,' said Mr Grant.

Wendy could contain herself no longer and smiled radiantly in her happiness as she accepted. 'May I see the flat?'

It was perfect, the third floor of the Victorian building consisting of a bedroom, kitchen, bathroom and lounge, all with chalet-style ceilings, crammed beneath the eaves. Lady Luck had come from behind the dark black clouds and was positively beaming on her. It was unfurnished apart from the kitchen that had built in cupboards and a grime covered gas stove. She pulled open a drawer to find a full set of cutlery.

'The kitchen should be fully equipped; I used to have my lunches up here.'

'When can I move in?'

'Anytime you like.' He stepped towards her and placed the keys into her hand.

The only thing in the lounge was a telephone that started to ring. While he spoke to the caller, Wendy visualized her furnished flat; flowery curtains in the lounge, plain velvet in the bedroom and a light pastel shade in the kitchen. Using secondhand shops to furnish it would knock a huge dent in her precious Post Office savings, even clean it right out, but earning two pounds and fifteen shillings each week without any board or bus fares to pay, she could soon start saving again.

She heard Mr Grant finish on the telephone and went into the lounge. 'Why haven't the telephones got any dials?' she said, noticing the oblong instrument had two rows of buttons but no dial.

'Because we are on the Granby exchange and it is manually operated,' he replied, before showing Wendy how her extension, with internal as well as external facilities, functioned.

He moved across the empty room in readiness to leave. 'I'll leave you to have a look round,' he said from the doorway, 'but if you could possibly spare fifteen minutes I do have an urgent letter that needs typing.'

Wendy excitedly explored. The bedroom; two floors above Henry Grant's office, overlooked a small rear garden and cobblestone passage servicing the backs of all the neighbouring properties. The kitchen also overlooked the back and was slightly smaller than the one in Norwich. It was above the office kitchen with a door leading on to a metal fire escape. The bathroom was tiny and everything was white; bath, washbasin, toilet and tiles that reached halfway up the walls. The lounge, overlooking University Road, was the largest room and two floors above the reception office that would become Wendy's place of work.

A stimulated Wendy typed the letter to the Tax Inspector to appeal against Mr Hough's estimated tax assessment and two others that were urgent.

As he read and signed them Mr Grant said, 'If it will be of any use I have a bedroom suite that you can have. It belonged to my mother so I did not want to part with it for sentimental reasons but it is only collecting dust in my garage.'

Wendy was beside herself, totally amazed by the man that had caused her to cry in despair at nine o'clock and weep for joy at eleven o'clock.

That afternoon an elated Wendy spent most of her available cash on things for her new flat. She bought curtain material for the lounge and bedroom off a stall on the market, bed linen from Lewis's and two thick blankets and two bath towels from the Army and Navy store.

True to his word, Henry Grant arranged delivery of the bedroom furniture on Sunday morning, consisting of a double bed with springs and mattress, a kidney-shaped dressing table, a wardrobe and a chest of drawers, all manually carried up the metal fire escape. Having checked out of the YWCA, Wendy spent her first night in her new home but was too excited to sleep.

CHAPTER FOURTEEN

Wendy stirred from her drowsiness when she heard a metallic clunk. Her first thought was that somebody was on the metal steps of the fire escape, but in the murky morning light she could see through the lounge window that it was a man changing the alternate street waiting signs in University Road. Today parking would be allowed on the south side of the road.

There was an eerie strangeness; no boys snoring in the next room or her mother shouting for her to get up. This was a new dawn in her life. Feeling cold, she warmed the flat by lighting the gas fires in each room and two burners on the now gleaming cooker, thanks to half a drum of Vim and a lot of elbow grease.

She felt warm and refreshed after a bath but on opening a drawer for her underwear, she noticed her naked image reflected in the dressing table mirror. Vivid recollections flashed briefly before she realized that Sid was over a hundred miles away.

She liked her office, the larger side of the segregated reception area that was bright and airy with a large bay window overlooking University Road.

Henry Grant employed four clerks and she met them all that morning. They worked in the two offices on the second floor; one directly above and the other over Mr Grant's. They had been made into one by knocking out a section of the adjoining wall. Robin

Wootton-Smith, the senior at twenty-one, introduced himself before leaving with Kevin Jennings, the sixteen-year-old junior, to work on an audit at clients' premises in East Park Road. Nineteen-year-old Brian Holt and eighteen-year-old Clive Burston were working in the office all day and she learned from them that the clerks referred to their boss as HG. She felt he had shown her too much kindness to be reduced to mere initials. She liked the name Henry so he would be Henry out of his presence and Mr Grant to his face.

It was an exhausting day. Apart from a dash to the Post Office to withdraw money from her savings and do a minimum of food shopping she had worked non-stop typing three sets of accounts and numerous letters. Evidently the temp Mr Grant had engaged the previous week was a one finger stop and search typist that could not spell and had created such a backlog it would take ages to clear.

That evening, while her pork chop roasted in the oven, she wrote to Michael pleading with him not to divulge her whereabouts to Sid and enclosed the letter in one that she wrote to Mrs Bellamy. After dinner she completed her letter writing with a short explanatory note to Anne, one to Graham with the same request for address anonymity and a difficult one to Derek. She collapsed on her bed at ten o'clock and slept like a log.

Anne was her first visitor when she called on Thursday evening. 'It's fantastic!' she said with total amazement written all over her face. 'Michael told me you'd gone away for good when I called round to your old house on Sunday after the wedding but I'd never have imagined you would have turned up here in Leicester.'

Wendy showed her round the flat while Anne talked about her sister's wedding. They finished in the kitchen where Wendy began to brew a pot of tea. 'It's a lovely flat,' said Anne, 'but aren't you a bit scared being here all on your own? It's not like your old house with lots of neighbours.'

'I've have got neighbours. Most of this block are offices with flats at the top. Mr and Mrs Poole live next door and sometimes I can hear them slamming a door or arguing, but they're a nice old couple.'

They chatted all evening and they were both thrilled to rekindle the bond of friendship they had both missed for nineteen months. Although Anne was still courting, they agreed to have a weekly girlie night out and arranged to meet in town on Saturday afternoon for a long overdue shopping trip.

Wendy soon transformed her flat. All the things that she could not bring with her, she had left at Mrs Bellamy's where they filled two chests. She had arranged for the British Road Services depot, where Stan had worked, to transport them and when they arrived in the middle of the second week Mrs Bellamy had generously sent the table, chair and bookshelves from the study, two Axminster carpets, a standard lamp, more clothes from her wardrobe and a chest full of other bits that she claimed would be thrown away when she moved to Wisbech.

It was as well that Wendy did not have a television to distract her because most of her evenings were spent making curtains. She did not have the same skilful dexterity as her mother in the sewing department but she had undoubtedly learnt from watching throughout the years.

With everybody being so benevolent she had hardly used any of her savings, only buying a cottage settee and armchair from a second-hand shop in Conduit Street; a wall clock when she got fed up with running downstairs to see the grandfather clock and a trio of picture frames. They stood proudly on the kidney dressing table containing a picture of Graham in Army uniform, a school photograph of Michael and the wedding picture of her mother and father.

Wendy had made quite a transformation in the office as well. Doing things methodically and orderly was a skill mastered in her waitress days when serving customers out of rotation could lead to pandemonium. It made the messy heaps of documents on Henry's table an abomination to her. The morning Henry got frustrated searching for a client's tax computation was the day Wendy suggested he buy a storage cabinet. When it arrived it was an expensive mahogany, one that blended perfectly with the other furniture, which she cunningly claimed the suppliers had sent by mistake. She transferred the documents on to the cabinet shelves, labelling each with the client's name, leaving the oval table clearer than it had been for years.

Having caught up with all the typing in the first week, her night school classes at Norwich were put to the test when Henry consigned the custody of the petty cash to her. As soon as she had that work caught up and under control, the salary records with the incumbent tax tables and National Insurance cards quickly followed. She took the extra responsibility in her stride, which gave Henry time to negotiate for an agency with a Building Society.

It was a typical showery April day as Wendy typed the date on a letter, jogging her memory to the fact that it was four weeks to the day since she had travelled to Leicester.

Clive came into her office wafting a schedule he wanted typing. 'What would you say if I asked you?'

'Yes,' Wendy interrupted, jubilant on the news of a five shillings pay rise although she was warned that income tax would absorb most of it, as it was the beginning of a new tax year.

'But you don't know what I was going to ask.'

'You were going to ask me out on a date as you have been suggesting ever since I got here. Where are you going to take me?'

A rapturous Clive proposed going to the Savoy but Wendy liked to go to the cinema with Anne on their girlie night out. She felt like something more active and suggested going to the Palais. As Clive lived at Great Glen that was not very practical so they settled on going to a dance at the village hall at Kibworth on Saturday night.

'We can almost stay till the end,' Clive said, 'because there is a late bus we can catch.' Wendy wondered if it was the same late bus that she and Anne had used at Christmas because she could recall somebody talking about Kibworth.

It was eleven o'clock before Wendy stirred the next morning. She had enjoyed the dance and as she hummed and jived to the tune of "Tutti Fruitti" she realized how quiet her apartment was without a radio. She slipped on a jumper and jeans, grabbed an apple and left to go over the road for a newspaper.

"Almost new gramophone for sale", Wendy read the small ad in the newsagents and raced to the nearby Gotham Street address.

'We're emigrating to Australia,' the young husband said as his wife nursed their crying baby; 'taking advantage of the assisted passage scheme.'

Wendy soon became the proud owner of a gramophone that would play the new small vinyl records and a radio at a bargain price, but the baby, a little girl born last October, had seriously disturbed her emotions.

Henry was in a foul mood when he barged into Wendy's office the next morning. 'Where have you put the Clients' Ledger?'

'It's in the cabinet.'

'No it's not, I have looked,' Henry grumbled as he followed a calm Wendy back to his office. 'I had a shock when I looked at the bank statements that came in this morning. How many bills have you sent out since you started?'

'I haven't done any,' Wendy said as she spotted the reason for Henry not having found the ledgers. He had buried them beneath the Building Society agency literature. 'Here they are,' she said and handed over the two books.

Henry grunted before muttering his thanks but Wendy was stopped from leaving his office when she reached the door. 'And just where are you going? I want you here to help me.'

They worked as a team, bringing the records to date, with Henry showing Wendy how to keep the time ledger that recorded all the hours each member of staff spent on each client. It was to become another responsibility passed to her and, like the petty cash and wages, she was determined she would do it each week rather than let it mount up as Henry had done.

By the end of the day Wendy had typed nine invoices and seven account rendered reminders to clients who had already been billed but had not paid. Henry was in a far more cheerful mood when he said goodnight to her.

'What would you like?'

Wendy was hesitant as Henry waited for an answer. The Angel Hotel menu was alien to her with so much choice and so many dishes that she had never eaten before. She did not want to cause any embarrassment so decided to order the same as Henry. 'You've been here before what are you having?'

'The paté is usually very good so I am starting with that and then having the roast beef.'

'I'll have the same,' said Wendy without having the faintest idea what paté was.

It was turning out to be a very special day for Wendy. She had been very surprised and also very apprehensive when Henry had told her that he was bringing her to Peterborough.

Standing in his office the previous evening she had said, 'I didn't realize you were taking me when you asked me to book lunch at the Angel hotel.'

He had smiled and grunted. 'There is a great deal of typing to be done including all the monthly statements and I do not think there is anybody better qualified in the office to do that than you.'

During the journey to Peterborough in Henry's Armstrong Siddeley car, which was a luxury in itself that she could get used to, Wendy began to worry about her past associations with the place. 'Why Peterborough? We don't have any other clients that far from Leicester.'

'That's down to William Richards. I only deal with his tax and investment dividend income now but up to three years ago he had a very successful upholstery business that was bought out by a Birmingham company. He helped get Thomas Hollins started, lent him some money and had all the retail contacts.'

During the remainder of the journey Henry had explained all about their client Hollins Cane Ltd. Thomas Hollins was quite young when he started his cane furniture manufacturing business and was only forty-two when he suffered a heart attack. He was advised to take things easy that led him to decide to live in Spain, where the property was cheaper and the climate healthier. The problem had been money. The only way he could withdraw his capital was to sell the business but unfortunately a buyer could not be found. In the end Henry had proposed a deal whereby his existing management take over the everyday running of the business in rented premises and the old factory, which was a valuable freehold, was sold, raising enough cash for Mr Hollins to retire to Spain. As he still had a tidy sum invested in the company's plant and machinery, Henry had to do quarterly reports, the first of which Wendy had typed that morning.

The paté arrived and the first delicate nibble satisfied Wendy's taste buds. It tasted like a rich meat paste and she liked it. She also liked the wine that Henry had ordered.

She was in the middle of her main course when she was visibly jolted. Mrs Newman, the woman from the back street abortion clinic, was walking towards her. When they had first arrived in Peterborough Wendy had feared the remote possibility of meeting Aunt Ethel, particularly if the Hollins Cane factory was anywhere near Lincoln Road. The premises turned out to be in Stanground on the opposite side of town from Aunt Ethel's. Not for one second did she think she would ever see Mrs Newman again. She averted her gaze to the window to avoid facial contact, her heart thumping ten to the dozen as she dreaded she might talk to her, even ask about the baby. Relief swept over her when the woman walked past to sit at a table further behind.

'Is everything all right?' Henry asked.

'A hot flush, I think it's the wine,' she fibbed and acted out the pretence by removing her double-breasted navy jacket.

178

The sun was climbing into a clear sky and, being mid-June, the trees were in full leaf, housing chirping birds but New Walk was deserted of human life at seven fifteen on a Sunday morning as Wendy hurried towards the bus station in Southgate Street.

Wearing a calf-length sleeveless, summer dress she had a cardigan slung over her bulging shoulder bag that contained two gifts for Mrs Bellamy. The previous day she had bought some peppermint creams with soft centres before wandering about the bookshops around Silver Street where she had found a copy of David Copperfield by Charles Dickens.

She made the bus station with eight minutes to spare before the Midland Red coach departed on time. It was ten fifteen when Ralph greeted her as she stepped from the central doorway of the vehicle in Wisbech and ten minutes later when she bent down to kiss Mrs Bellamy on the cheek.

'You look lovely,' she said, 'you are blossoming into a beautiful young woman and you will make a wonderful wife for somebody. Why you want to visit an old crony like me when you could be on the arm of a dashing young man I cannot imagine.'

'You are not an old crony but a dear sweet lady that has been really kind to me, like a Granny in fact. Anyway, I wanted to see how you've settled in your new home.'

After lunch Wendy took Mrs Bellamy out in the glorious sunshine, pushing her wheelchair along North Brink by the bank of the River Nene.

'Ralph will be forty this year and if they do not have a child soon I fear they never will.'

'I think they both seem to enjoy teaching too much.' Wendy stopped pushing so that Mrs Bellamy could observe a pair of swans and a cygnet gliding peacefully on the river. 'Anyway, Veronica's younger isn't she?'

'She is thirty-four and you are right about the teaching; she loves it.'

Wendy released the brake, crossed the road and continued but had only gone a few yards when Mrs Bellamy raised her arm and pointed, 'See that lovely Georgian building over there? That is Peckover House. I have never been inside because of all those steps but Ralph is a member of the Wisbech Society and says it contains some truly beautiful decorations.'

They walked, they talked, they had tea and the day whizzed by. New Walk was not deserted when she made her way back to her flat. She practically bumped into the priest outside the Holy Bones Church, passed people strolling in the failing light of sunset and was wolf-whistled by three youths sitting on the base of one of the pillars outside the museum.

'This is Granby one three seven three,' Wendy said before holding her hand over the mouthpiece of the telephone to address somebody who had entered the reception area. 'I won't be a minute,' she called without turning. 'Thank you I'll try later,' she replied to the operator after being told the number was engaged.

'Happy birthday,' said Graham and Michael in unison to an astonished Wendy. Tears of joy filled her eyes as she hugged them dearly, first Michael and then Graham.

Henry popped his head round the door and said, 'Wendy could you get,' then stopped when he saw the two strapping youths.

'Mr Grant, these are my brothers,' said Wendy as she introduced them. 'Mr Adamson's phone was engaged but I'll try again in a minute.'

Both were unprepared for the exquisite homeliness that greeted them when Wendy took them up to the flat. She made them a cup of tea, foot tapping to her favourite music, *Last Train to San Fernando,* and left them playing her Paul Anka's *Diana* record to return to her work. Henry had said he wanted one urgent letter typing, which turned out to be four, before allowing her to take the rest of the day off as a birthday treat.

'I'm making some cheese cobs,' Wendy called from the kitchen when she finally returned to the flat.

'What are they?' asked Michael.

'They're round bread rolls,' Wendy answered, having just bought them when she posted the letters, 'but they're called cobs in Leicester.'

'You certainly look better than your last birthday,' said Graham after devouring his first cob. 'Do you remember you spent all day in bed?'

Wendy blushed when she recalled feigning illness to hide her pregnant bump, but then felt the emotional twist of the knife thinking about the baby that she had never seen. Did he look like her or did he look like Sid? Was he in a good home with loving, doting parents? Was he happy? Her need to have answers was becoming stronger and her desire to see him becoming more frequent.

'Mind you,' Graham continued when Wendy remained silent, 'it was hot then but I think it's even hotter today.'

Wendy stopped dwelling on the past. 'So what would you like to do this afternoon?'

The stifling heat swayed them to Wendy's suggestion of swimming at Kenwood lido, which meant a quick visit to the market to buy two costumes, quite cheaply as it turned out. The last part of their journey was slow, following a number twenty-seven bus because that was the only way Wendy knew how to get there.

Michael was the first to be changed and looked round as he waited for the others. It was like Yarmouth beach at the height of the summer holiday season with the raucous sound of people enjoying themselves. Grass areas surrounding the pool were full of people, like the beach but, unlike the sea, the pool had added attractions of two diving boards, one high diving board and two springboards, all at the deep end furthest away from him. Decorating either side of the diving tower were two semi-circular fountains, cascading water over a series of steps. A narrow bracket-shaped platform across the middle of the lido divided the deep from the shallow water, where young and old were using it for diving and jumping into the pool. Either side of where he was standing, children were queuing to use two chutes to slide into the shallower water.

'We'll find a spot to spread the towels and then you can go swimming,' said Wendy as she emerged from the ladies' changing room.

They found a space on the lawn behind the refreshment room. Michael quickly dumped his towel and ran towards the pool, jumping in at the deep end, followed by Graham using a springboard to dive into the water.

Wendy was wearing her new pink and white check bathing costume that she had bought for her previous visit to the lido with Clive, Anne and Trevor at the beginning of the month. She moved to the edge where she dipped her toe to gauge the temperature of the water; it was cold. She failed to see Graham creep up on her and uttered a playful scream when he pushed her into the pool.

Eating ice-cream, drinking lemonade, having fun with her brothers made Wendy realize how much she missed them. It was a memorable birthday but like all good things it had to come to an end. Raving hunger was satisfied with steak and chips at the Court Cafeteria in Charles Street, then she embraced and kissed them both before watching them disappear eastwards along Humberstone Road with heaviness of heart.

CHAPTER FIFTEEN

'A registered letter for me?'

An amazed Wendy repeated the postman's words as she signed the receipt slip. It was the first one that she had ever received but when she saw the sender was Mrs Bellamy she guessed it was a birthday present arriving a day late. It was no ordinary gift. The package contained the three-tier imitation pearl choker along with a birthday card and brief note that read, "I was going to give you this on your twenty-first but it seemed a shame to wait until then when you could be wearing it".

A second item of mail addressed to her contained a provisional driving licence that she had applied for. The miles she had travelled in a lorry with Stan had given her the yearning to want to be able to drive. She immediately rang Carling and Brown, a driving school she had often walked by on the London Road to enquire about a first lesson. 'Next Wednesday at one o'clock,' Wendy confirmed into the mouthpiece.

She had started her work when she heard the grandfather clock strike nine as Henry waltzed into her office.

'Good morning, Wendy,' he said jauntily, 'I expect you want to know about your rise?' By keeping the wages records Wendy knew that Henry generally gave his staff salary increases on their birthdays. 'As you have reached the ripe old age of seventeen I am going to pay you an extra ten shillings a week.'

She thanked him appreciatively in the few seconds before he went back to his office. 'Just remind me to alter your charge out rate in the ledger,' she heard him call out from the landing. It was like her birthday was stretching into a second day.

By mid-morning Wendy was still in high spirits and humming, while mundanely checking the clean linen that had just been returned by the Wigston Laundry delivery van.

'Am I looking at a common slut or the super-efficient Miss Marshall or both?' asked a prudish, expensively dressed lady that had charged through the waist-high door that separated her office from the reception area.

'Excuse me?' Wendy said abruptly as she looked up and frowned.

'Is Henry in?'

Wendy assumed the discourteously rude lady was a client. 'I believe Mr Grant is in the office. Who shall I say is calling?'

'Don't you get stroppy with me, I'm his wife,' she bellowed and quickly left the office.

Since starting her job in Leicester, Wendy had learned on the office grapevine about her boss and the difficulties he was having with his wife Eleanor, particularly during the last five years. Aged fifty-two, he lived with her at Countesthorpe in an unhappy marriage, ruined by her contemptible jealously and by their two children not just fleeing the nest so much as completely abandoning it.

Their twenty-seven-year-old son, Dudley, had followed in his father's footsteps and qualified as an incorporated accountant but then took on a three-year contract to work in Singapore. In the letters that followed came news of his meeting the girl of his dreams so he had married and settled in the colony. Henry was bitterly disappointed that his expectation of his son working and ultimately taking over the practice had failed.

In a matter of weeks their daughter Felicity departed the family home in acrimonious circumstances. She had fallen madly in love with the young window cleaner when she was only sixteen. When her mother found out she was outraged, immediately dispensing with his services, forbidding her daughter from seeing him and moved heaven and earth to stop their romance. Unable to tolerate her mother's interference in her life any longer she ran off a week before her eighteenth birthday and had not spoken to her since. Henry was devastated that his piggy-in-the-middle reconciling efforts had failed, along with his dream of walking proudly down the aisle with his daughter on her wedding day.

Henry heard from her twelve months later when she telephoned the office after he had pleaded with the window cleaner's parents for contact. In the intervening four years Henry did get the odd letter mailed to his office, always with an Inverness postmark and always without a return address.

It seemed like the middle of a dark September night but in fact Wendy had only been asleep for forty minutes when she was woken by the constant ringing of the doorbell. She reluctantly left the warmth of her bed and tentatively looked out of the lounge window to see Graham, dripping wet in the rain, waving to her.

'I got a lift as far as Grantham,' he explained taking off his wet uniform. 'Then I saw this bus that was coming to Leicester so I got on it just as it started to rain. The trouble was I got lost between here and the bus station.'

The most direct way from Southgate Street Bus Station was by using New Walk. As she listened to Graham shouting his explanation from the lounge while she was in the kitchen making a drink, she realized he had gone on a very circular route passing the Royal Hotel in Horsefair Street and the Police Station in Northampton Square.

'How long are you here for?' she asked when she returned to the lounge and handed him a steaming hot mug of cocoa.

Graham, stripped down to his Y-fronts with a towel draped over his shoulders like a cape, was sitting in the easy chair. 'It's only a forty-eight hour pass.'

The lounge was warming quickly in response to Wendy lighting the gas fire. 'I'm worried about where you're going to sleep.' She sat cross-legged on the settee and pulled her nightdress over her knees and watched Graham light a cigarette.

'Don't you worry about me; I'll kip down in here.'

'It's Saturday tomorrow. I'll go into town and buy a foldaway camp bed, I think they sell them at Millets.' As she sipped her own cocoa she could not help but notice how bereft of hair his chest was, unlike his father Sid whose mass of body hair made him look like a gorilla.

The silence was broken by the sound of twelve chimes of the grandfather clock from the landing two floors below them. 'Bloody hell, is that thing going to bong all night?'

'Every hour and half hour, but I've got used to it.'

Wendy left the fire on low to provide some extra warmth with the one blanket that she had available. She soon went back to sleep in the comfort of her bed but Graham was tossing and turning as he tried to sleep on the floor using the settee cushions as a mattress.

The next night Wendy was tossing and turning as she had a bad dream, reliving her ordeal of the previous year. She was in agony in the delivery room of the maternity hospital with the nurses urging her to push.

'I am sodding pushing,' she howled.

Graham was sleeping soundly on the new camp bed but became awakened by the screaming noises. He rubbed his eyes, saw that it was two forty-five by his luminous watch and slipped his underpants over his naked body.

'It's a boy,' said the smiling nurse in Wendy's horrific dream.

Her whole body was perspiring, now as it was then, but all she could see was mucous and blood that covered her newly born child.

'Take it away I don't want to see him,' she yelled, but the nurse moved closer and placed the bundle on her lap.

She gingerly pulled back the shawl but there was no baby, instead she saw Sid's face with lecherous eyes and a leering smile that caused her to utter a deafening scream.

Graham rushed into her room, 'What the hell's the matter?'

She was awake in an instant and sat bolt upright. 'I had a bad dream,' she cried and felt the comfort of his arms around her when he squatted on the edge of the bed.

Graham felt her body trembling against his like a pulsating heartbeat as he tried to calm her. 'It must have been bloody scary, your screams were loud enough to wake the dead. What was it about?'

Locked in his embrace with her head leaning reassuringly on his shoulder she felt a desire to confide in him. Tell him about the baby, about the evil bastard that his father was and liberate herself from all the lies in her life. 'I dreamt I was having,' she stopped abruptly, unable to go any further with her confession.

'Having what?' asked Graham after a few moments silence.

'Having to escape this evil monster that was chasing me,' Wendy lied, saying the first thing that came into her head. 'Like that Quatermass thing that was on the television that time,' she added trying to sound convincing.

It seemed a very childish dream to have caused so much distress thought Graham as he felt Wendy's shaking ease. He yawned, reminding him how tired he was and relaxed his hold in readiness to return to the lounge.

'Please don't go, at least not just yet.' Her voice was imploring, her eyes were inviting and her action was to move across the double bed to provide space for Graham to lie beside her.

He was too tired to refuse and the comfort on offer beat the camp bed by a mile. He lay on his back at her side and within minutes was fast asleep. Wendy turned to face him and then inched herself closer until she was touching him. It did not seem to disturb him when she put her hand across his chest but it consoled her as she drifted to sleep.

She was clinging to him like a limpet when she woke shortly before nine o'clock. Graham was still sleeping so she quickly dressed and went to the kitchen. To show her appreciation she cooked eggs and bacon for breakfast and served it to him while he was still in bed.

Wendy altered the calendar in her office to read December the ninth when the postman arrived with the mail. The official looking envelope bearing Michael's redirecting scribble from her old Norwich address baffled her. She opened it with some trepidation but then anxiety turned to delight when she discovered she had won two hundred and fifty pounds on the premium bonds.

'Why not buy some shares with it,' Henry suggested later on hearing her good news.

'I don't know anything about shares or how to buy them.'

'Through a stockbroker but I can arrange that. As a matter of fact I bought some yesterday in an engineering company called Ernest Goodson and I am hoping to make a handsome profit. You could do the same and the dividend yield is higher than your average interest.'

Wendy soon accounted for her winnings, buying four hundred and seventy shares, each of which would cost ten shillings and seven pence.

The next day it was overcast and Wendy's nerves were on a ragged edge, yet she accomplished a faultless hill start in University Road at the beginning of her driving test. At the junction with Welford Road she moved out slowly when the road was clear but then had to stop abruptly when a car suddenly appeared from her right travelling very fast towards her.

She could have cried. 'I'm sorry,' she said to the examiner then continued, more relaxed, being convinced she had already failed. Other manoeuvres were performed to perfection in the Clarendon Park back streets before Wendy finally brought the Morris Minor to a halt outside the YWCA hostel where she answered questions on the Highway Code.

'Congratulations, Miss Marshall, you have passed.'

Wendy was flabbergasted. 'I thought I messed it up at Welford Road.'

'That was fine,' said the examiner. 'You stopped, you proceeded when the road was clear and then stopped again when that car appeared, driving well above the speed limit I might add. It is a difficult junction because the cemetery wall and the gradient of the hill restrict your vision.'

Hearing the single chime of the Grandfather clock, Wendy knew it was Christmas Day. She had been alone for an hour since coming to bed at midnight and sleep was not coming easy.

It had been Friday the thirteenth when the postman delivered a Christmas card from Mrs Bellamy and a letter from Graham. Virtually all of the four pages had been filled with ravings about Millie, his new girlfriend of three weeks and suggesting it would be nice if they could come and stay with her at Christmas when he had some leave. Nothing like waiting for an invite thought Wendy.

The arrival of Graham's letter had deeply exercised her conscience about allowing them the use of her bedroom but at the risk of appearing a prude she had decided against it. She would sleep with Millie, and Graham would have to make do with the camp bed. If they wanted to sleep together then they could go to a sleazy hotel as Mr and Mrs Smith. As each day had passed she had kept telling herself that she was not jealous, trying to convince herself that she no longer had any feelings for him.

For Graham's sake she had really wanted to like Millie, but her first impressions had not been good that windy Christmas Eve afternoon when she had met them at the Great Central Station. The distasteful smell of her cheap perfume had been overpowering, like lavender-scented disinfectant. She was buxom, 36D cup at least, with peroxide blonde hair covering black roots. Her face was plastered with make-up and her lips pouted with too much poppy red lipstick, almost the identical colour to her varnished fingernails.

Through the unbuttoned front of her raincoat Wendy had noticed her hand-knitted fawn jumper was a tight fit, as was her chocolate-brown pleated skirt. Common as muck and tarty with it she thought, but for the sake of her besotted brother she had attempted to show kind hospitality.

Sleep should have been easy for they had spent the evening in the crowded bar of the Marquis of Wellington, where she had downed three glasses of port. She was tipsy but not sleepy. She was too concerned about what was going on in her lounge, listening to every sound and squeak, willing and waiting for Millie to come to bed.

The bedroom door finally opened a few minutes later and flooded the room with light from the landing. It made it easier for Wendy to see, squinting as she feigned sleep. Millie tiptoed into the room wearing a short nightdress. Graham, naked apart from his bulging Y-fronts, stood at the door observing his girlfriend's every move as she placed her clothes and handbag on top of the chest of drawers. It was after she turned to move towards the bed that calamity struck. Her handbag fell to the floor with a thud, spilling some of its contents. The sound panicked Graham. He closed the door plunging the bedroom into darkness before scurrying back to the lounge. Millie cursed as she bent down to feel her way to recover her belongings while Wendy continued her pretence of sleeping.

Six unearthly hours later Wendy was awakened by a recognizable noise coming from the bathroom. Millie returned to the bedroom within a few moments looking ghostly pale.

'Are you all right?'

'I'm sorry, I didn't mean to wake yer,' she apologized with a gravelly voice. 'I must have had too much booze yesterday. I'll be okay soon.'

A likely story but Wendy recognized the signs and sounds of morning sickness. She helped Millie into bed without saying another word. Her concern was for Graham. Did he know? Did he have any idea? Why could he not have been more careful? What a Christmas this was turning out to be.

'I need you to drive me to Bishop Street, that last phone call has made me late for my appointment at the bank.'

For an instant Wendy wondered what Henry was talking about after he charged into her office on a cold January morning until he handed her the keys to the Armstrong Siddeley. 'But I've never driven your car.'

'It's the same as that Morris you passed your test in, only bigger.'

She remembered one occasion when Robin, the only clerk that could drive, had chauffeured Henry to an appointment, but he was out of the office. Having nervously completed the first quarter of a mile or so she waited at the traffic lights at the top of Granby Street.

'How will you get back?'

'I'll ring when I am ready and then you can come and fetch me.'

Having comfortable seats and a polished veneered dashboard, Henry's Armstrong Siddeley was a car that she had come to appreciate on the long trips to Peterborough. Never in her wildest imaginations did she ever think it would be the first car that she would drive solo. Nor did she know then that it would be the first of many trips into the city centre that she would chauffeur her boss to avoid the problems of parking. She was still quivering with excitement that night when she switched off the bedroom light in readiness to sleep. Wednesday the fifteenth of January would not be a day she would forget in a hurry and neither would the next.

CHAPTER SIXTEEN

The day started normally enough. It was a bitter cold morning and the windows were misted over with frost. It made it hard for Wendy to leave the warmth of her bed and when she did she raced around the flat lighting the gas fires. After a cup of tea she dashed downstairs to do the same in the offices. Thirty minutes later the chill had gone and she was warmed inside by a bowl of hot porridge. She heard Henry arrive at twenty minutes past eight and went downstairs ten minutes later, a full half hour before the office opened for business.

He greeted her jovially from her office doorway. 'There's a letter for you in the post and I've left it on your desk.' He walked towards his office and stopped by the grandfather clock. 'Thanks for lighting the fire, very thoughtful of you.'

In her office she stood close to the fire, warming the back of her legs as she opened her letter, knowing it was from Graham by the postmark and his writing. It contained the news she had been dreading since Christmas; that he and Millie were going to get married.

She should be deliriously happy for him but she felt dejectedly sad. No matter how she tried she could not get it out of her mind that it would be wrong. Whether it was instinct, intuition or something else, it did not seem right. She felt it at Christmas and nothing had made her change her mind. She presumed Millie had told Graham she was pregnant and that was the reason for the haste, although he did not mention it in the letter.

These thoughts made it hard for her to concentrate on her work. After serving Henry's mid-morning coffee she set about changing her typewriter ribbon. It was a small tedious task that she had completed successfully many times so she was annoyed when she smudged the cuff of her blouse. 'Stupid sod,' she cursed and went up to the flat to change.

She cursed again when she was undoing the button on the offending cuff. It came off at her touch, fell to the floor and rolled beneath the chest of drawers. The drawers were on short, stubby claw legs, giving Wendy just enough room to feel for it with her hand.

It was not the button that she pulled out but a letter with Millie's name and address on the envelope. Crouched on her knees she stared at it while she tried to think. She recalled Millie creeping into the room in the early hours and putting her handbag on the drawers. She remembered it falling, the door closing and Millie fumbling in the dark to retrieve it and the contents. That was when the letter must have fallen out and slid beneath the drawers.

Still clutching the envelope she got up and sat on the bed. Normally she would not pry but this was somebody that she disliked and mistrusted, a wicked witch that had cast a spell on Graham. She pulled out the two sheets of notepaper to find it was difficult to read. The writing was bordering on scribble, there was no punctuation, no capital letters and the spelling was often phonetic. She read it three times before she was confident she had fully understood it. It was signed "love June" that was obviously a friend that Millie had confided in about her pregnancy.

Wendy was stirred into action. She raced down the stairs, still wearing the soiled blouse and knocked on Henry's door. 'Mr Grant, I've got to go up north very urgently,' she said hurriedly, after entering his office. 'Would you mind if I went straight away?'

Henry looked up from his work, peering over his rimless spectacles at Wendy. 'I'll be back tomorrow,' she continued, 'and I'll work all day Saturday if you like.'

'Was the letter bad news about your brother?'

'Well sort of, but he's all right.' She paused for a second, 'there's something I've got to sort out.'

Henry had come to appreciate her candid sincerity, always truthful and straight to the point. He had also come to trust her implicitly and knew she was good for her word. He did not think for one moment that it would be necessary for her to work on Saturday but he knew she would if he needed her to. 'Then you had better go and sort it out, young lady. I think I shall manage to cope for just one day without you.'

Wendy arrived at the station at a quarter past twelve, ten minutes before the express train was due out. It had been a rush; ringing the rail inquiry office, racing to the Post Office to withdraw ten pounds from her savings bank, running to catch a bus to the city centre and waiting impatiently for a number fifteen to bring her to the station in Great Central Street. Her only luggage was a shoulder bag that doubled as a handbag, with a nightdress, change of underwear and toothbrush crammed into it.

She arrived at Richmond, a town close to Catterick, at ten minutes to six having changed trains at York and Darlington. The address turned out to be a flat above a hardware shop but there was no reply to her pounding on the door. She walked across the road to a café, ordered tea and a toasted teacake and sat by the window to wait. The teacake reminded her how famished she was, having not eaten anything since breakfast, so she ordered another.

'Is there a hotel in Richmond?' she asked the proprietor when he cleared her empty plate.

'Aye lass, if thou want accommodation thou'll best get thee self over to the Kings Head in the Market Square.'

While she was pondering what to do a light flashed on above the hardware shop. She raced across the street, banged on the door and shouted for two minutes before it opened a whisker. Millie peered through the aperture wearing her raincoat and holding it together at the chest. 'What do yer want?'

Wendy put her shoulder to the door and pushed. The door flew open and she barged past an astounded Millie into an untidily furnished room where a bare-footed man wearing navy blue trousers ran into another room. Cigarette smoke and stale sweat whiffed in her nostrils, reminding her of a railway station waiting room.

'Ow dare yer,' Millie shouted as she closed the door.

Wendy sat on the edge of a green lounge chair with wooden arms. Opposite was a badly stained upholstered armchair and separating them was a scratched coffee table containing an ashtray overflowing with butt ends. A blazing coal fire heated the room and there was some underwear strewn across the hearth.

'You'd better sit down, I've come a long way to talk to you,' Wendy said, noticing a pair of stockings, a suspender belt and a fern green dress hanging over the armchair.

'Yer ain't come to congratulate me then?' Millie said sarcastically without moving from her spot close to the fire.

The man re-emerged from the bedroom fully dressed. He did not speak or acknowledge either Wendy or Millie. He walked quickly to the door and closed it violently as he left.

'Why didn't you introduce me to Tony?'

Millie was shaken at the mention of the man's name. She looked at Wendy with eyes that could turn water into ice. 'How do yer know 'im?'

'You left this at my flat,' said Wendy, taking the envelope from her bag and throwing it on the armchair.

For a moment Millie just stared at it with a puzzled face until she realized what it was then she rushed to the chair and picked it up with her right hand while still clutching the raincoat together with the other. 'I suppose yer've read it, yer nosy cow.'

Wendy ignored the accusation. 'You've got to break up with Graham.'

'Why should I? He's in luv with me.'

'He's infatuated by you.'

'I ain't going to. He thinks it's 'is baby.'

'Then you'll have to put him right by telling him the truth. If not I will show him the letter before I give it to Tony's wife.'

The threat stunned Millie for a moment as she tried to remember the contents. She recalled her friend warning her not to marry a soldier boy just to provide the baby with a father. There was caution about spending the rest of her life with a man she did not love. There was a "told you so" about expecting a married man to leave his wife and children. Tony was mentioned by name but was his address?

She smiled smugly at Wendy, 'I don't think so.' She tapped her hand over the pocket where she had put the envelope.

'I promise you I will,' said Wendy, returning the smug smile. 'Then we will have to see what sort of storm it causes, but there's no way I would want to be in your shoes.'

Millie's confidence ebbed away. She turned away from Wendy to use both hands to take the envelope from her pocket and then took out the two sheets of notepaper it contained. Two empty sheets of writing paper.

'Did you really think I would give it back to you?'

Millie threw the paper to the lino-covered floor and rushed towards Wendy. 'Yer fucking cow,' she shrieked loudly.

Wendy reeled back in her seat as Millie lunged and grabbed her hair with both hands. Wincing with the sudden pain, Wendy put her left arm on the top of her head in an effort to parry Millie's tugging. Concentrating on her two-handed grip, Millie's raincoat came apart and she was only wearing panties underneath, confirming Wendy's suspicion as to what had been going on before her unexpected arrival.

Millie's whole body was leaning over a pained Wendy who could only think of one way to stop this mad woman from scalping her with her bare hands. 'You sodding bitch!' she yelled, as she slid her right hand into the top of Millie's panties to clutch her pubic hair and pulled for all she was worth.

Millie's scream sounded like the wail of a tom cat on the tiles at night and relaxed her grip by putting one hand on Wendy's wrist to counter the pulling and alleviate the pain. Wendy seized the opportunity of catching her off guard by raising her knee and then pushed with all her might. It sent Millie reeling backwards, upending the coffee table, scattering the ashtray and cigarette ends until she fell into the opposite armchair. Wendy jumped up, grabbed her bag and ran to the door. She stood in the doorway, half in half out.

'You've got a week to tell him,' she screamed before she slammed the door and went down the stairs.

The next morning Wendy could hardly believe her eyes as she approached the railway station. Parked in the goods yard was a Fordson van with Tony Earnshaw, Carpenter painted on the side and a Richmond address and telephone number painted in smaller letters on the door. The letter never revealed the surname. The address was not in the letter as she had bluffed last night hoping that Millie would not remember. As she was making a note, any last doubt or coincidence was resolved when she spotted a man that ambled to the back of the van and picked up a tool bag. Last night the very same man had been wearing navy blue trousers in Millie's flat. Armed with all this priceless information Wendy continued walking for her train. Today fortune was smiling on her.

She arrived in Leicester in the middle of the afternoon and was about to go into her office when she changed her mind. Turning quickly to go towards her flat she bumped into Clive, causing him to drop a file that resulted in a mass of papers straying over the floor.

She apologized and stooped down to help him pick them up.

'Do you fancy going out tomorrow night?'

Caught on the hop, Wendy was rescued from an immediate response by the chimes of the Grandfather clock striking three o'clock. Her first thought was to say no but after her recent experiences the attraction of going to a dance was too tempting to turn down. She said yes just as Henry came on to the landing.

'Wendy how nice to see you,' he said. 'Had a nice trip?' His beaming smile was genuine because a huge problem was solved by her presence. A client had received an offer for his business and accounts for three years urgently needed typing for the prospective buyer.

It was on a chauffeuring errand on Monday the third of February that a cheerful Henry got into the car after a meeting with his stockbroker. 'Guess what?' He sounded pleased as Wendy pulled away from the kerb. 'There has been a takeover bid for Ernest Goodson. Those shares we bought are now worth thirteen shillings and six pence.'

'That's thanks to you, does that mean we should sell them?'

At that moment Wendy had to brake sharply when a van pulled in front of her. 'Did you see that, Henry?' she shouted irately, 'that sodding maniac pulled out in front of me.'

'I did.'

She was puzzled that he was smiling when she had come within inches of crashing his beloved Armstrong Siddeley. 'What's so funny?'

'You calling me Henry,' he said as he removed his spectacles to clean them.

Wendy blushed, 'I'm so sorry, Mr Grant, it just slipped out because I was angry.'

'I don't mind,' he said quickly. 'In fact I prefer it when we are together, but for the sake of protocol we will stick to formality in front of clients and the other staff.'

The second post had arrived by the time Wendy settled back in her office and with it a letter from Graham. She had spent the weekend wondering if Millie was calling her bluff. If that was the case then the girl was seriously underestimating her resolve. She ripped it open.

She was shocked.

"We're getting married at the Registry Office as soon as Millie can make the arrangements," Graham had written. The cunning bitch! The letter was calling her bluff. "I'm going to be away for three weeks on some army exercise so it will be as soon as I get back." Wendy could sense what a manipulative sod Millie was. Everything would be arranged while Graham was away and nobody would be told. No doubt she would be waiting at the barrack gates to whisk him straight to the Registry Office the moment he returned.

Wendy never expected anything like this. Even if she did carry out her threats it was now impossible to expose the letter to Graham. She could send it to Mrs Earnshaw and while that could well break up the marriage it was hardly likely to thwart Millie's schemes.

"I'm going to be a dad, isn't that wonderful news?" It was awful news and Wendy was sinking into despair. What could she do? Should she be waiting outside his barracks? It might be possible if she knew exactly when the exercises were to finish. Surely there must be a solution and she had three weeks in which to find it.

She was no nearer finding a solution eighteen days later when she made her first trip back to Norwich for the first anniversary of her mother's death. She caught the seven thirty-five train from Leicester and, as arranged, Michael was waiting to meet her at the city station. They hugged in a warm friendly greeting before setting off in solemn mood to the cemetery, only stopping to buy some flowers in Dereham Road.

'Miss you, Mam,' Michael sobbed, unashamedly loudly and placed his flowers against the headstone.

In contrast, Wendy spoke in a hushed voice. 'I shall never forget you, Mam'. She placed her own flowers besides Michael's with tears streaming down her cheeks.

They stood for a few minutes, each lost in their own thoughts and memories, staring at the grave. The only sound was their weeping and the whispering of the wind.

The solemn and sorrow mood lifted when Wendy returned to the market café where she used to work, to treat Michael to lunch. It was the usual Saturday pandemonium so she did not get much time with Sandra, barely enough for more than a catch-up chat.

It was a short visit, for in no time at all she was back at the station. They hugged a lamentable farewell before she boarded the three fifteen train to return. In the past they had argued, squabbled and fought yet she had a lump in her throat when the train pulled away. Her eyes watched the diminishing figure of her brother until he was completely out of sight. Thankfully there had been no sign of Sid. The only person she had recognized was Brenda Frost who had been pushing a pram down Pitt Street, but neither had spoken.

By the end of the month she was totally despondent and had asked Henry for the day off. Her plan was to travel to Darlington and find the Registry Office to see if she could discover anything about the marriage. She had reasoned on a Saturday wedding and the next day would be the first Saturday after Graham's exercises. It was very much a gamble and even if she did strike lucky she had no idea if she could stop it. She remembered a bit at her mother's wedding to Sid when the vicar said something about lawful objections or forever holding their peace. She would certainly object and she would certainly not hold her peace.

She had just set off and had reached the Park Hotel when she heard Brian Holt shouting her name.

'There's an urgent phone call for you from Catterick.'

She raced back to her office to discover the caller was Dennis, a close mate of Graham's.

The wedding was off!

Wendy was crazy with happiness. She hugged Brian because he was still in the room but he soon retreated upstairs to the safety of the clerk's office.

A lot had happened in Richmond during the last two days. Mrs Earnshaw had found out about her husband's philandering and had thrown him out. That was a mystery. Wendy had not sent the letter as she had threatened so how had she found out? Perhaps she had smelled Millie's sodding awful perfume on her husband. Perhaps she had sat in the café and seen her husband go to her flat. Probably Wendy would never know.

An infuriated Tony, who knew nothing of Millie's plans to marry Graham, had gone straight to her flat accusing her of telling his wife. His temper flared at her denial and his actions got physical. The beating Millie received landed her in hospital and she miscarried early on Thursday morning.

It was Thursday when Graham's company got back to the barracks. When he discovered Millie was in hospital he asked Dennis to go with him to visit. It was afternoon visiting hours before they saw her and it was not for long. Millie's language was evidently too fruity for Matron and they had soon been ordered to leave. She had shouted obscenities at Graham that Dennis, after first apologizing, had repeated word for word: "Fuck off, I never want to fucking see yer again" and "tell that cow of a sister I'll rip her cunt out". A vindictive Millie was obviously blaming Wendy for informing Mrs Earnshaw.

In trying to console Graham, Dennis had told him about Millie's affair and that he was probably not the father. He had also quoted "half the men in the billet have shagged her and anyone of them could have been the father". The only consolation Graham had found was in getting drunk. That very morning he was nursing a massive hangover, which is why Dennis had telephoned and not Graham.

Wendy had just got into bed when the bell sounded. It was after eleven so who could it be? From her lounge window and with the aid of the street lights she was surprised to see Graham. Without bothering with her dressing gown she raced down the stairs and opened the doors. She threw her arms around him in a consoling hug and then the stench hit her. He was drunk and he had been sick all over his uniform.

'You're a sodding disgrace,' she scolded as he flopped on to the settee. He ranted on about not being drunk but he had been no help while she had dragged him up all the stairs. Remembering a previous occasion when he was intoxicated, Wendy fetched a bucket before attempting to remove his stinking sick-soiled clothes. She had struggled to get him down to his underwear when he threw up but fortunately some of it over himself and the remainder in the bucket.

He mumbled an apology.

He was more trouble than a baby. She could not leave him to sleep in sick-soiled underwear but as she was removing his Y-fronts her hand brushed against his scrotum and she felt something odd.

'Leave me alone, you naughty girl,' muttered Graham as she fondled his testicles by way of physical examination.

She looked worried and was very perturbed. 'You've got a lump on one of your balls.'

'And I'll get horny if you don't leave me alone.'

CHAPTER SEVENTEEN

'Sid's dead!'

At ten past one on Good Friday morning Michael's hollow words mesmerized Wendy who had been sleeping deeply before being woken by the telephone.

'It were an accident; he fell out of the bedroom window and smashed his head on the mangle.' Although she had wished him dead on many occasions she still winced when she heard the sordid details.

She did not sleep much after that. She established Michael was all right and spending the night at Gregory's house. She managed to find a telephone number for Graham and spoke to a duty officer who assured her that he would deliver the message as soon as possible. Her travel plans were easy, she would catch the same early train as she had used when visiting her mother's grave. She placed an explanatory note on Henry's table before striding out for the station.

The house in Rosewood Road looked the same as it always had except the windows needed a good clean and there was a pint of milk on the front doorstep.

'We were having this argument and then he went to wallop me with that belt of his but I grabbed the end of it,' Michael explained as they stood in the back bedroom where the window was boarded up and the curtains were ripped. Typical of the period, it was low to the floor, at the end of Michael's bed and by the side of the door that led to Wendy's old room. 'He was pulling one way and I was pulling the other,' Michael continued. 'It was like a tug-of-war. I knew I could not win so when I thought I could make a dash for the stairs and escape, I let go. He had been pulling so hard that he reeled backwards; he fell against the window that gave way under his weight and out he went. The ambulance men thought his death was instant and the police reckon the wood on the window frame was as rotten as hell. I'm glad that Mrs Cunliffe saw it or else they might have thought I'd pushed the old bugger out deliberately.'

The name mystified Wendy. 'Who's Mrs Cunliffe?'

'She was his latest lady friend.'

Why didn't that surprise her?

'What was the argument about?'

'He got angry when he found me in here kissing Liz and then ranted on about you and went into a raging temper when I let it slip that I knew.'

'Knew what?'

'Knew about you and him. I saw you once when I came home from carol singing. I was only twelve and I didn't know what you were doing. It's only now as I've got older that I realized he was fucking you.'

It was the second time in twelve hours that Michael had shocked Wendy, who could not stop the tears from flowing. She did not know if she was crying because she was happy or crying because she was sad. She was not angry with Michael who she embraced tightly in her feeling of utter relief that her wretched persecution was known.

'It all makes sense why you hated him so much and why you had to run away when Mam died. I'm really sorry I didn't understand earlier, then I could have told Mam what a sick bugger he was.'

Wendy pulled herself together and decided the best way of keeping her mind off these new revelations was to keep busy so she set about cleaning the house. By the time Graham arrived at teatime it had started to resemble how it used to look when they all lived together as a family.

'Have you been to the doctor's?' she asked at the first opportunity when she was alone with him.

He shook his head. 'In the army we have to see a medical officer and if you're not half dead they think you're skiving.'

In Leicester she had been to the reference library in Bishop Street to try to discover more about Graham's lump without success but by the time Michael arrived with fish and chips for tea she had decided on a more positive course of action.

He had brought company with him. 'I met Liz off the bus from work.'

'Hiya!' she greeted with a bubbly infectious smile despite the circumstances.

Wendy was amazed that the freckle-faced little girl she remembered running on to the football pitch had blossomed into an attractive young woman. Her red hair hung halfway down her back, the freckles were less prominent and a touch of lipstick graced her lips. Like Michael, she had left school this Easter and had just completed her first week's work at Woolworth's. Wendy wondered if her brother realized he would not be able to continue with his new job at the Eastern Counties bus garage now that Sid was dead.

'If all my patients looked as healthy and vibrant as you, Miss Marshall, I could spend a lot more time in my garden.'

Wendy was Doctor Myers' last patient at the end of a busy Wednesday morning surgery. 'I haven't come about myself,' she said fidgeting in the chair. 'I've got this friend whose boyfriend has something wrong down there.' She pointed in the direction of her midriff.

Despite Wendy's reticence he soon established the truth of her visit regarding Graham's lump. 'I will have to examine him.'

'I'll never be able to get him to come to the surgery.'

'Then if Mohammed will not come to the mountain I fear the mountain will have to come to Mohammed. Will he be in at around four o'clock this afternoon if I call at the end of my rounds?'

'I'll make sure of it,' said a happier Wendy.

'No way,' insisted Graham when Wendy and the doctor confronted him, but he eventually succumbed to persuasion and allowed an examination in his bedroom.

'I am sure it is a tumour,' said the doctor.

'Then why doesn't it hurt?'

'It will if you do nothing about it. A malignant tumour will spread and suffocate healthy tissue as it goes. Imagine it as a small garden weed that if it is not pulled out it will spread and choke the life out of the other flowers in the garden.'

'What will happen to me? Am I going to die?'

'Good heavens no!' Doctor Myers smiled reassuringly at Graham. 'We have caught this very early. You will have to have surgery to remove the lump, after which you will be able to live a perfectly normal life. If it has started to spread the worst that can happen is the removal of the testicle but that will not be the end of the world. You will still have the other one, which will be completely adequate, if you intend to get married and have children.'

The funeral was at the crematorium. Aunt Ethel was the only one that was weeping, sitting on her own on the front row. Behind her were a traffic inspector and two drivers representing the bus company.

Across the aisle from Aunt Ethel was Graham looking sad but impassively indifferent in the morbid atmosphere. Wendy was stone-faced, sitting beside him as the vicar read a passage from the gospel of St John. She felt like a hypocrite and only came in response to Graham's pleading. As it was Thursday afternoon and early closing day Liz was able to be there, remaining hand in hand with Michael, sitting by Wendy's right hand side.

The only other people from Rosewood Road were Len and his wife sitting behind Wendy, whose mind wandered as the service continued towards the committal. If Len had not come to ask her mother to help behind the bar that Christmastime, then Sid would not have abused her that night he got her pregnant. Then Michael would not have witnessed the vile act and they would not have argued. And if they had not argued then Sid would not have crashed through the window. She almost wanted to laugh out loud. His evil ways had ultimately brought about his death and Wendy had gained her revenge.

As the coffin moved and the curtain closed she hoped he was going to burn in hell. Good riddance to the bastard! There would be no headstone and no memorial plaque. Unlike her Mam he would be quickly forgotten.

Later that day she went with Aunt Ethel to the bus station out of a sense of obligation. 'Sidney wasn't all that bad you know.'

Wendy could not think of anything good about the man but she held her tongue as they waited, hoping it would not be long before she could get back to pack for her train journey the next morning.

'I remember once when I was at school,' her aunt continued, 'the teacher telling us about the cuckoo. How it would lay an egg in another bird's nest so it didn't have to build one of its own and then when the cuckoo chick hatched it would throw everything else out so it had the entire nest and all the food for itself. It made one girl cry and the teacher explained that it wasn't cruel but nature, inbred into the cuckoo as its means of survival.'

'Why do you remember that?'

'Because Sidney was like the cuckoo; he did what he did seeing that it was inbred in him. Our father worked on a farm as a cowman and we lived in this little cottage in the middle of nowhere with just two tiny bedrooms. Sid and I had to sleep together in one and Mam and Dad in the other but Dad thought nothing of shoving Sid in with Mam so he could sleep with me, like I was one of his cows needing the service of the bull. If we complained or misbehaved he would thrash us with his belt. He treated us like cattle and that's why I know you can't hate Sid more than I hated my old man. The hate doesn't stop at death, it stays with you forever.'

Her memories were painful, for Wendy could see the tears in her aunt's eyes.

'We had to sleep as brother and sister until I was seventeen when I got a live-in service job, so when the old man wasn't at me, Sid was because we thought it was the normal way of life. Now can you see why we're like the cuckoo? I haven't dared get married nor have kids because I was frightened what might happen if I turned out like them. I'm sorry for what happened to you, I really am but it was the way Sidney and I was brought up, he hardly knew any different. I wouldn't wish our childhood on my worst enemy.'

The Kings Lynn bus squeaked to a halt in front of them and as she stood on the platform Aunt Ethel clasped Wendy tightly by the wrist. 'You must promise not to breathe a word about this to anyone.'

Wendy could see the sadness and the imploring look in her eyes. 'No I won't.'

Back at the house she found Graham busy clearing out his father's clothes. 'I'm going to give all this lot to that rag and bone man that comes round with his horse and cart.'

'It's not for that van parked outside then?'

'That's Harry Chadwick's. He's lent it to me so that I can take you and Michael back to Leicester tomorrow.'

'That's very nice of him,' Wendy said, grateful for the special relationship that Graham had built over the years with his former boss.

'Michael wants you to take the telly to your flat and have anything else you want.'

'Where is he by the way?'

'Where do you think? He's gone to be with Liz. Incidentally, did you know she was from such a large family?'

Wendy knew she had two sisters and five brothers but before she could answer she noticed something fall to the floor from an old coat as Graham tossed it towards the heap of other clothes. 'What's that?'

Graham picked up an envelope from the floor and frowned with curiosity. 'It's a letter addressed to my mother.' He looked at the document inside. 'It's something about tax. You have a look, you might understand it.'

She was more intrigued with the envelope that had the sender's details printed in the top left-hand corner; The Angel Hotel, Peterborough. 'It's a P45 form giving details of her code number, wages and tax,' she said as she looked at the document, 'but it's very old, look at the postmark, it was sent on the eighteenth of October, 1946.

'That was after she died. I expect that's why Dad had it but why keep it for so long?'

'Probably forgot about it, when did your mam die?'

'October the third, I remember it because it was three days after my eighth birthday.'

From her working lunches with Henry when they went to Peterborough, she had become aware that the head waiter had been at the Angel Hotel for many years so it was quite likely that he knew Graham's mother. 'Do you mind if I keep it? I'll show it to Henry, see if he can throw any light on it.'

'Hurry up,' Graham called as he started the engine of Harry Chadwick's van. 'I've got to get back this afternoon.' With the choke out and the engine running, he wound down his misted window in an effort to clear the early morning condensation.

Michael was hugging and kissing Lizzie. 'All right keep your shirt on!' He was almost tearful as he moved into the back of the Commer van, squashed up among his clothes and belongings like a sardine in a can.

Wendy glanced at the empty house as Graham pulled away. It would probably be the last time she would ever see it but at least the windows were clean and there was no milk on the doorstep.

They arrived in Leicester just before midday, having stopped for breakfast at the Coronation Café, after which Wendy drove to give Graham a break on the long journey. She parked in the cobblestone passage at the back of her flat and was carrying a second lot of baggage up the fire escape when she heard the screeching sound of a sash cord window being opened.

'Hello, Wendy, how are you?' Henry called out.

'I'm fine, Mr Grant, I was going to see if you wanted me to work.'

'Well I was wondering about this afternoon,' he smiled with relief, 'there are some urgent things.'

Henry's urgent things kept Wendy working frantically from two until seven o'clock. Graham left before she started, promising to ring as soon as he had seen the medical officer.

Michael surprised her yet again, for while she had been slaving over her typewriter he had been out and found employment with the Midland Red Bus Company starting on Monday at the Wigston garage. He had also cooked tea, something that was very alien to him a year ago when she lived at Norwich.

Wendy, burning with curiosity, waited almost two long impatient weeks before the next visit to Peterborough on the twenty-third of April.

'Yes, Mr Grant, I have worked here for over thirty years,' the head waiter of the Angel Hotel responded to Henry's question at the end of their lunch.

'My secretary wondered if you might remember a former employee.'

'Her name was Hannah Rawlins,' Wendy added, looking at him with eager eyes.

'Yes that name rings a bell,' he paused and rubbed his forehead.

'It was at the end of the war nearly twelve years ago,' Wendy prompted.

'I remember her now, she was a receptionist here, an excellent worker and very good with people.' His memory had clicked into gear and now there was no stopping him. 'She started just before the American airmen began to come from a base at Kings Cliffe. Extremely popular with them she was, she could be very discreet you see.'

'I expect the accident came as a shock.'

The headwaiter was puzzled by Wendy's remark. 'Accident? What accident do you mean, Miss?'

'When she was killed here in Peterborough.'

'I am sorry I cannot remember that. It must have been after she left here but I thought she moved to Wales. Are you sure we are talking about the same person?'

'I think so, Hannah was killed with her daughter in a road traffic accident on the third of October 1946.'

'I cannot be sure about the precise date but the person that worked here left very suddenly about that time but she went to Wales, something about looking after her sick uncle I believe.'

Wendy was speechless. Surely there could not be two people of the same name working at the same place at the same time. The head waiter must be getting her confused with somebody else.

'If we get time later we can go to the library and look at the copies of the local newspapers for that time,' Henry suggested. 'A road accident causing the death of a mother and her daughter would have been headline news.'

Moments later, as the head waiter removed the empty wine bottle from the table, he thought of something else. 'It must be a different Hannah Rawlins because her friend Barbara Lynwood kept in touch. It is unfortunate that she moved to Kettering two years ago or you could have spoken to her, but I think she may still be in the trade for I remember a request for a reference for her from the George Hotel.'

In order to try to get Wendy to concentrate on her work during the afternoon Henry took her to the library straight from the Angel Hotel. Twenty minutes of extensive research in the back copies of the Evening Telegraph failed to find any news of the road traffic accident. Was the waiter right? Could Graham's mother still be alive?

The drive home was not direct, even Henry's curiosity was aroused. He pulled up outside the George Hotel in Kettering. Once inside he ordered a scotch and a glass of port for Wendy at the bar.

'Does Barbara Lynwood still work here?' he asked as he received his change.

'She's working on reception, at least she was.' The barman looked at his watch. 'She may have gone by now.'

They caught her just in time with her coat on ready to leave. She was very wary of Henry's approach, but had to be civil, being in the place of her employment. 'I must dash, my bus goes at twenty to seven.'

Henry looked at his watch. 'You will be doing us a great service if you could just talk to us for five minutes, then I will take you home in my car.'

Barbara Lynwood's options were limited by the fact that the hotel manager was lingering behind the shoulder of the obviously wealthy customer. 'Five minutes, but I'll catch the later bus if you don't mind.'

Henry bought a gin and tonic before they settled in a quiet corner in the lounge. 'We understand you know Hannah Rawlins?'

'I don't think so,' was the guarded reply.

'We were told you have kept in touch with her ever since she left Peterborough.'

'I would just like to contact her,' said Wendy.

Barbara Lynwood jumped to her feet. 'I bet you would,' she said venomously then leaned over the table towards Henry. 'Look, Mister, the game is over for you and your bit of stuff. You might be all dressed up in fancy clothes, but I know you're her miserable old bugger of a husband, so you'll get nothing out of me.' With that she turned and hurried towards the door.

Impulsively, Wendy grabbed her handbag and followed. Outside, Barbara hurried across Sheep Street towards the library and her waiting bus with Wendy in pursuit. Taking off her shoes for speed she ran and boarded the single deck vehicle in her stockinged feet just as it was pulling away.

'I'm not going to say another word.'

'I don't want you to, I want you to listen,' said Wendy as she fiddled to put her shoes back on, sitting in a seat across the aisle from Barbara. 'That gentleman you just insulted was my boss and his name is Henry Grant. My name is Wendy Marshall and I'm his secretary not his bit of stuff. Sidney Rawlins is dead and he can't still have been your friend's husband because he was married to my mother. My stepbrother is Graham Rawlins who believes both his mother and sister are dead, as I did until lunch time today.' Passengers passing between them when the bus stopped at Dalkeith Place interrupted Wendy momentarily as she gave Graham's version of events as he had been told and still believed to be true. 'I'm sorry that you mistook us, but you, and only you, have the opportunity to reunite a mother with her son and a sister with her brother. Would your friend ever forgive you if you were wrong about us?'

Wendy stood in readiness to get off but was forced back into her seat by the momentum of the bus making a right turn into Montagu Street. Barbara reached over and touched her arm. 'Okay, I'm sorry but you did seem very suspicious.'

Sitting in the car, Wendy was extremely thankful that Henry had followed them. 'I've got the address,' she smiled, 'she lives in Benllech.'

CHAPTER EIGHTEEN

Wendy arrived back at her flat at half past seven to find Michael in a very jubilant mood. With the call-up ending he was going to miss National Service and the manager had told him he would be allowed to become a conductor when he became eighteen. He had also been selected for the depot football team that played at Saffron Lane recreation ground in the Leicester Thursday League. It seemed to Wendy that his good news was never ending, for in three weeks' time he was going to be moving into lodgings in South Wigston with a middle-aged couple who both worked for the Midland Red.

'Isn't it great,' he babbled excitedly, 'they live in Timber Street, which is ever so close to the garage so I can start going out on all the routes. It wouldn't be possible living here, as the first crew go out at four twenty-five in the morning on a service to Kibworth and Fleckney.'

The telephone rang five minutes later with some more good news. Graham had seen the medical officer and they were going to arrange some tests. 'If Doctor Myers' diagnosis is confirmed then I shall have to have a minor operation to remove the lump. The MO said it was probably malignant but unlikely to have spread.'

She started several letters to Hannah Rawlins but each one finished screwed up in the waste paper basket, unlike Michael who wrote a flowing five-page letter to Liz with all his news. His friendship with her must be strong, for at least five letters had changed hands in the twelve days he had been staying at the flat. In the end she had given up on writing and decided she would take a couple of days' holiday to visit her as soon as she could discreetly fit it in. She thought it best not to say anything to her two brothers for the last thing Graham wanted was false hope should it turn out to be a glorious hoax.

Misty rain heralded the first of May and Wendy was typing the investment portfolio of Miss Tobin, an elderly spinster, when the telephone rang. 'Good morning, Henry Grant and Co.'

'Can I speak to Mr Grant?'

'I'm afraid he is out of the office, who is it calling?'

There was no immediate response before Wendy gathered from the noise that the call was being made from a telephone box. 'Who is that?' she repeated. There was no response, other than the sound of a baby crying. Suddenly Wendy had this intuition, 'Is that Felicity?'

'I'll call back later.'

'No wait,' Wendy urged, 'your father will be heartbroken when he knows he's missed you.'

'I bet he will.' Wendy heard the barbed sarcasm in her voice.

The only thing that might prevent Henry's daughter from hanging up was to tell her about her own life. 'I ran away from home when I was only sixteen, but that didn't mean I left people behind that I didn't care for, or that didn't care about me. I had brothers that I loved and found a way to keep in touch without my stepfather knowing. Your father loves you dearly, Felicity. He has been very good to me in my hour of need, why won't you trust him?'

'He would tell my despicable mother.'

'Are you sure about that?' Wendy was aware that the three-minute call was close to ending. 'Let me have that telephone box number and I'll get your father to ring at three o'clock this afternoon. If you want to talk be waiting at the kiosk, if you don't then he'll get no reply.'

'Inverness two nine two,' Felicity said quickly after a thoughtful pause.

'She has invited me to go and see her,' said an emotionally charged Henry as he sat on the cottage settee in Wendy's lounge. Ever since Wendy informed him of Felicity's phone call he had been as jumpy as a cat on a hot tin roof. 'But I had to make a solemn promise not to say anything to her mother.'

Wendy had brewed tea in her flat to allow him some solitude to reflect, something he might have lacked in his own room with all the clerks working in the office. She was relieved having spent a few hours on tenterhooks, wondering, waiting and hoping. 'That's really wonderful, Henry.'

'I don't know what I am going to say to Eleanor.' He thought for a moment while he swallowed some tea. 'Probably tell her I'm going on a business trip.'

Wendy made all the travel arrangements for next Tuesday the sixth of May, which would involve her having to drive Henry to Rugby to catch a sleeper service to Inverness. Making the most of the opportunity of the office being quiet while he was away she had made her own arrangements to travel to Anglesey the next day.

'What old school friend are you going to see?' asked a curious Michael.

'Nobody you know, so you can just keep your nose out,' said Wendy. 'I'll only be gone for one night so keep the place nice and tidy.'

Wendy marvelled at the scenery as the train hugged the North Wales coastline after leaving Flint, giving her picture postcard views of golden beaches edging a calm green sea, stretching out to a cloud-decked sky. An hour later the train seemed to thread its way through the very walls of the ancient castle at Conway before steaming westwards towards Bangor. On the final leg of her journey the scenery took second place to her jingling nerves. Was she doing the right thing? Was her impetuous spirit steamrollering her into a situation she may regret? Her heart seemed to beat faster with every click-clack of the train racing over the rails but there was no turning back.

'There's a bus to Benllech at ten past three.' The Crosville traffic inspector's Welsh accent sounded like pure prose in response to her enquiry. 'It goes from that stop over there, see,' he pointed, 'number 520 to Amlwch.'

At four o'clock there was the salty aroma of the sea in her nostrils from the onshore breeze and two seagulls squawked noisily on the roof of the big bay-fronted house that Wendy stood outside. It was the right number and the right road so why was she looking at a sign displaying Simmons Hotel? Perplexed, she entered and felt a little relieved when she saw a smaller sign indicating the proprietor was Mrs Hannah Owen.

'Can I help you?' said a slender lady in her mid-forties wearing a holly green skirt and a crisp white blouse.

'I wonder if you have a room for the night,' Wendy replied, noting her beautifully permed hair was the same colour as Graham's.

'Just the one night?'

'Yes please, I'm looking for someone that lives in Benllech.' Wendy hoped it would arouse her curiosity and it did.

'Anyone I can help you with? I've lived here for six years.'

'Hannah Rawlins.' Wendy noticed the transforming reaction the name caused, which produced a noticeable pause.

'Who is it that is looking for her?'

Wendy took a photograph from her handbag. 'My stepbrother,' she said as she showed the lady the picture of Graham in his army uniform, 'Graham Rawlins.'

It ended the polite pretence. The eyes of Hannah Owen, as she now called herself, filled with tears quicker than a tap could fill a cup with water. 'You know Graham?' It seemed too incredible to be true. 'My Graham?' she emphasized.

After overcoming the shock the first thing Hannah did was to try to telephone Gwyneth, who was married and living in a flat above her hairdressing business in Bangor, but with no reply, she remembered it was early closing day and her daughter had planned to go to Caernarvon.

They talked all evening and well into the night, it being twenty minutes to one before Wendy got to her bed, tipsy from drinking too much port. Hannah had an insatiable appetite for hearing about her son but the conversation was not all one way, as after dinner Wendy learned about Graham's mother.

Hannah Simmons was born in August 1913 and shared a similar fate to Wendy in that her father was killed three years later, a casualty of the war on the Somme battlefield. Her mother, eight months pregnant at the time, was distraught and went into immediate labour only to lose the son they both wanted. Deeply depressed, she drowned two months later in the River Dee with no evidence as to whether she fell or committed suicide.

A straight-laced aunt brought up Hannah until she was fourteen, when she left school and got a job as a live-in maid at the Wynnstay Arms Hotel in Wrexham.

She was only sixteen when she fell in love with George Owen, a strapping handsome miner, but his mother disapproved, thought she was far too young and wanted someone from a mining family. By the time she was twenty she was two months pregnant. They married that September, which further aggravated his mother, who believed it was deliberate on her part to trap her son. George found this little cottage for them to live in and Gwyneth was born on the twenty-third of March 1934. Hannah was living every girl's idealistic dream; a gorgeous baby, a doting husband and a beautiful home.

The dream was shattered six months later when there was this disaster at the pit that killed George, together with his father and brother.

Perturbed at this point, Hannah had been rescued from continuing her story by an employee's Welsh accent calling from outside the lounge.

'I'm off now, Mrs Owen, and everything's ready for tomorrow's breakfasts.'

'Thank you, Dilys, goodnight.'

'Goodnight.' A moment later they heard the closing slam of the front door.

The break had recharged Hannah and she turned to face an attentive Wendy. 'I can understand why your mother had to remarry. After George's death I could not afford the rent for the cottage, I certainly could not live with my mother-in-law and I was pretty sure my aunt that raised me would be very reluctant to take me back.'

'So what did you do?'

She answered while she replenished the drinks. 'I tried to get my old live-in job back at the Wynnstay, but they could not accommodate me with the baby. Then the assistant manager, who I always thought was a bit keen on me, told me to try the Great Northern Hotel in Peterborough where his brother worked as a banqueting manager. So I decided to give it a go and if it failed it would be the workhouse or begging on my aunt's doorstep for sympathy.'

'That's how you came to Peterborough,' said Wendy as Hannah stopped to drink some gin. 'I presume you got the job?'

'No, I was at my wits end. I remember Gwyneth was crying for a feed and this manager let me use his office. I think he was horrified I might put her to my breast in the middle of his guest lounge. He must have felt sorry for my plight, seeing that he told me about a family looking for someone to live-in to look after a senile old lady who had recently lost her husband. I was interviewed by her two eldest sons and given the job of looking after Mrs Harding in this big house in Farcet. She was a cantankerous old bag that threw a tantrum at the least little thing, or would cry for hours grieving over her husband. She had seen off three live-in domestics in as many weeks, I think that is why I was given the job; they thought I might stick at it seeing as I had a baby.'

A bell sounded somewhere in the hotel and Hannah excused herself to attend to the demands of a guest. Wendy felt very comfortable, it was like chatting with Anne. All the needless anxiety she had put herself through over the visit was for nothing. She had warmed to Hannah. They had warmed to each other like bosom friends.

'I've found this photograph of Graham,' Hannah said on returning to the lounge. 'It was taken when he was nearly three,' she explained as Wendy studied the picture of an angelic looking boy standing by a tree.

'Now where was I?'

Wendy handed back the photograph. 'About to meet Sid, I presume.'

'No, at least not yet, I was about to meet Clifford, Mary Harding's youngest son. It was that first Christmas; he was good looking and kind, talking to me as a person, unlike the rest of the family who always treated me as a servant. His wife was an idle, stuck up bag who would ring the bell just to get me to come and blow the noses of their two horribly spoilt children.' Hannah stopped talking and took a large gulp of gin.

Wendy sensed her memories were painful because she had felt the same earlier. When you talk about your life you relive it, each and every happy and sad moment. Telling Hannah about her mother's death had brought tears to her eyes.

Hannah put her glass down and continued. 'I'm going to tell you things I have never spoken about before.'

'You don't have to.'

'I do. These skeletons have been in the cupboard for far too long. Not even Gwyneth knows. The thing was, I fell in love with Clifford and started an affair that lasted for nearly three years. I got a day off when the brothers took it in turn to look after their mother. So about every three weeks we spent the whole day together. The other times I would catch the bus into Peterborough, which is how I met Sid. He was a bus conductor in those days and always seemed to be on that route. Our first date as I remember was a walk along the riverbank, just after Gwyneth had started to walk.'

It was close to midnight when Hannah stopped to replenish the drinks. 'It was just after Christmas in 1937 when Mrs Harding became ill and it was New Year's Day when I called the doctor. It was a very bad bout of influenza, but the brothers decided to take it in turn to stay overnight, seeing that the doctor warned that it could turn to pneumonia. It was a heaven-sent opportunity for Clifford and me to actually spend a whole night together, but it had its consequences. By the time February arrived I knew I was pregnant. All of a sudden, being homeless was staring me in the face. I could not ruin Clifford's life by telling him and I would not be able to stay with Mrs Harding once I started to show. I thought of trying to get rid of it and was on my way to Peterborough to make some enquiries when Sid showed up as the bus conductor. That evening I smuggled him into the house and deliberately encouraged him to go too far. We married in the May and Graham was born, supposedly four weeks premature, at the end of September.'

'So Sid wasn't Graham's father?' Wendy could not stop herself from interrupting. Her face slowly transformed into a huge smile and her eyes shimmered like moonlight on a mountain lake. It felt like a huge burden had been lifted from her.

'No, I know it was deceitful but it was a solution. I suppose you think that's terrible?'

'No! Really, I can understand.'

'Can you? I tried hard to get on with Sid and did all my wifely duties but I didn't love him. I got a part-time job at the Angel Hotel as a receptionist during the war, which is where I met Clifford again. All the old feelings were still there, like a fire waiting to be lit and a blaze started as soon as I set eyes on him. Meeting discreetly was easier during the war.'

Wendy noticed the longing smile on Hannah's face; obviously her memories were pleasant and she wondered if she still had feelings for Clifford.

'I shall never forget the day I left Peterborough, it was horrendous.' Hannah's body suddenly shook and her smiles turned to tears. 'I suppose it started the day before when they asked me to do an extra stint at the hotel. Sid had become a bus driver by then and was working early shifts that week, so I knew he would be home for the children if I stayed on till late. The next morning I overslept and was woken by Graham asking me if it was time to go to school, so I got him ready at lightning speed and went to get Gwyneth out of bed. She looked ghostly pale and her eyes were red, which made me think she had a headache, so I left her in bed. When I got back from taking Graham she was very distressed and crying, which made me realize it was something more than a headache. She became very agitated and described how Sid had abused her.'

'The sodding monster did it to her!'

Hannah took in the implication of Wendy's outburst. 'I was furious and wanted to kill him, I'm sure I would have if he had been in the house that morning. When I calmed down I knew we had to get away. I rang Clifford out of desperation and he agreed to help me. By the time I had packed and left a note for Sid it was early afternoon. I met him at the old town hall, where, to my utter relief, he gave me twenty-five pounds and an address of a widower in Bangor, who was looking for live-in help. I then rushed to Graham's school, only to find that Sid was waiting outside for him. Gwyneth started to shout and scream as soon as she saw him, so I had to dash down a side street before he could see us. It was an absolute mess. I didn't know what to do for the best. Gwyneth was shaking like she was having convulsions, frightened by the very sight of Sid, so in the end I had to leave Graham and dash for the train.'

'I can understand your dilemma, it must have been awful.'

'It was. I got the job in Bangor and decided that once I got settled I would go back and collect Graham. That took much longer than I planned. For a start Gwyneth refused to go with me for fear of meeting Sid, and then there was the big freeze-up that winter, so it was spring before I had my first opportunity. When I got to Peterborough I found that Sid had moved to Norwich and, despite begging Ethel for the address, the stony old bag refused to give it me.'

Despite the lateness of the hour Wendy's mind was far too active to sleep. The parallels in their lives were quite remarkable; none more so than they had both ran off to escape the same man. Wendy had found employment with Henry, who had been kindness itself to her, while Hannah's widower had shown his gratitude for years of dedicated service and care by leaving a sizeable bequest when he died in 1952. With the help of Clifford arranging a bank loan she had used the money to purchase a bed and breakfast business in Benllech, which had been so successful she had converted it into a hotel in 1955.

The elation she felt knowing that Sid was not Graham's father was phenomenal as she drifted to sleep, picturing herself telling Graham all the wonderful news.

CHAPTER NINETEEN

Hannah was made-up and smartly dressed when she entered Wendy's room with a cup of tea. 'Good morning, sleep all right?'

Wendy moved herself up to a sitting position and rubbed her eyes. 'The bed was lovely and comfortable.'

'But you were like me,' Hannah cut in, 'had too much on your mind to sleep.' She placed the cup on the bedside cabinet and sat on the edge of the bed facing Wendy. She took an old photograph from her dress pocket and handed it to Wendy. 'I dug this out this morning. It's the only picture I have of Clifford and I had to steal it from Mrs Harding.'

Wendy studied the sepia photograph with attentive eyes. 'Doesn't he look like Graham?' It was an observation that gave rise to a sudden thought. She popped the photo on the bed, reached for her handbag in the bedside cabinet and took out Graham's photo.

Hannah nodded, looking at both pictures side by side on the eiderdown. 'You can see they have the same pinned back ears and the same high cheekbones.'

'And they're both very handsome,' Wendy said before drinking some tea.

Hannah smiled. Yesterday afternoon this bright young girl was a complete stranger, yet within a few hours she had confided in her. Revealed intimate details that she had never told anybody else in the world, but nobody else in the world had brought her news about her long lost son.

'There were two other things I should have told you last night. One is that I never ever said anything to Clifford, so he has never known I was pregnant with his child.'

'Why not?' Wendy frowned inquisitively

'I did not want to wreck, or run the risk of wrecking, his marriage and when Sid was accepting I was having his child, it did not seem to matter.'

Wendy drank some more of her tea then said, 'What was the other thing?'

'I never got divorced from Sid. It was impossible because I didn't know where he lived and I certainly didn't want to divulge my whereabouts.' She could see Wendy understanding the implication of her words. 'That's right,' she nodded, 'Sid became a bigamist when he married your mother.'

'It's a good job he's dead because I would have reported him. It would have given me a lot of pleasure to see that sod put behind bars.'

'Revenge for abusing you?'

It was a statement, not a question and Wendy was mortified. She sat tight-lipped, her whole body as still as a wax model staring at the forget-me-not flower pattern on the eiderdown.

'I'm sorry, I didn't mean to shock you.'

Wendy was perplexed. 'How did you know?'

Hannah reached up and put her hand comfortingly on Wendy's arm. 'You virtually told me last night, but I see the anger in your eyes every time his name is mentioned, the same anger that I used to see in Gwyneth.'

Wendy started very tentatively by telling Hannah about the first abuse, but after a fair amount of hesitation it brought a sense of uplifting, like a sink plug being pulled, releasing a lot of dirty murky water, after which she was able to continue quite openly. Many times she had wished she could have talked as freely with her mother, many moments when she wanted to chat with Anne and many occasions when she dreamed of confiding in Graham. Even when Michael admitted witnessing an abuse they had not talked about it. So this was the first time and she felt strangely at ease as she poured her heart out, yet not quite all her heart, she stopped short of saying anything about the baby.

'I wasn't as courageous as Gwyneth. Perhaps if I had have spoken out, things might have been different, but I was too scared of being belted by Sid.'

'Well he can't hurt anybody from the grave,' Hannah smiled as she stood up just as a heavy shower erupted outside and rain pelted against the window like grains of rice.

The rain had stopped by the time Wendy stood at the bus stop with Hannah to wait for the eleven o'clock bus to Bangor, on the first stage of her journey home.

'I've a favour to ask, I wonder if you would mind not saying anything to Graham.'

'Why not?'

'I've missed so much of his growing up I would give anything to be there when he finds out I'm alive. It gets me so excited just imagining it. I've decided not to tell Gwyneth, so that she can share in the surprise. Do you think you would mind keeping it to ourselves for just a little longer?'

Wendy understood and had no hesitation in agreeing, but where? The practicality of the task was not going to be easy. A meeting in Catterick was right out. It was a long way for Hannah and she had no wish to return there and risk bumping into Millie. It was difficult to see how she could get Graham to Benllech without telling him the reason why. So Leicester seemed the most practical.

'He's expecting to get some leave if he has to have an operation, but it may only be forty-eight hours. Would you be able to get away from the hotel to come to Leicester?'

'Between you and me I've sold the hotel and I'm just waiting for the solicitors to agree a completion date.'

'Oh,' uttered Wendy in her surprise, 'what are you going to do then?'

'Buy another one! This is far too seasonable for my liking. You let me know the moment you have any news and I'll be there.'

'I'll ring you as soon as I know.'

'I will have to tell Gwyneth that Sid's dead or she might not want to travel with me. I'll tell her my friend Barbara told me in a letter after seeing it in the paper,' Hannah said to give voice to her thoughts.

'I only hope I don't let the cat out of the bag,' said Wendy giggling like a schoolgirl. 'It's so exciting, I can't wait to see how thrilled he'll be.'

'You love him don't you?'

'Of course, he's my brother.'

'You know this emotion of love has a mind of its own without sense or decency, without morals or scruples. Don't you think I tried hard not to fall in love with Clifford? I agonized at night; long sleepless nights, fighting my conscience. The trouble was my heart would not listen to my head. Your love for Graham is more than brotherly love. I see the twinkle in your eyes whenever you talk about him, sparkle like sapphires they do.' Hannah paused, aware that she was making Wendy blush uncomfortably. 'You may have lived as brother and sister for the last few years but there is no blood relationship.' She put her hand comfortingly on Wendy's arm. 'Gwyneth is his blood sister and you're no more related to him than she is to her husband David. Listen to your heart and be happy.'

Wendy did not know what to say but fortunately the sight of the approaching green double deck bus rescued her. It was an emotional farewell with a light embrace. 'Don't fight your feelings,' were Hannah's parting whispered words.

'Where have you two been?' bawled Henry's wife from the doorway of the office kitchen on the second floor.

Henry was at the opposite end of the landing with Wendy who was unlocking the door to her flat. His hugely successful trip to Inverness and the reunion with his daughter had been an unforgettable experience but now a jealously suspicious wife who could not be told the truth confronted him. He dearly wished he could tell her that Felicity and Colin were married and that they were grandparents to a two-month-old little girl named Paula. He lowered his overnight bag to the floor.

'Wait a minute, Eleanor, this is not what you think.'

'Lies, all lies,' she shrieked. Her face was red with rage and her piercing eyes locked on to Henry like poisonous darts. 'You can't get out of it this time. I've as good as caught you in the act.'

'You've got it all wrong. You know I've been on a business trip and Wendy met me at the station,' Henry said calmly, directing his hand towards Wendy who stood silently at his side.

'A likely story! I've been telephoning for two days and some boy said you were both away.'

'That's right,' intervened Wendy, 'I've been to see an old school friend while Mr Grant was away on business.'

'Listen to that,' Eleanor screamed at Henry like a mad woman completely ignoring Wendy. 'Your little slut speaks as well as dropping her knickers.'

'Eleanor that is enough,' bellowed Henry. 'I think you should apologize,' but already Wendy was marching towards her.

'I'm not a slut,' she seethed, clenching her fist in an effort to control her temper, as she stood within inches of Eleanor staring eyeball to eyeball.

'Apologize? I'll show you an apology,' Eleanor fumed and slapped Wendy's face.

Stunned for a second Wendy put her hand to the mark left by the slap as Eleanor stormed away and started to go down the stairs. 'You sodding bitch,' Wendy roared over the banister, the volume of her voice increasing as Eleanor descended further down the stairway. 'You don't deserve the love of a man like Henry, you jealous sod.'

Wendy listened to the sound of fading footsteps before moving to find Henry sitting on the stairs leading to her flat with his crestfallen face resting on his hands. She was suddenly filled with remorse. 'I'm sorry, Henry, I shouldn't have lost my temper.'

'It's not your fault, you had every right after the things she said about you. It was the same with Carol, my previous secretary.'

'Was she the one leaving the flat the day you interviewed me?'

'Yes, Eleanor was so jealous of her she was continually making wild accusations, at one time she even suggested I was responsible for her pregnancy, although she did relent after she met her boyfriend. That is why I was so rude to you when we first met.'

Wendy remembered his hurtful dismissive words, "you are far too young", when she first enquired about the job. Then another thought flashed to her mind, 'If she's so jealous it's a wonder that she's let you take me to Peterborough.'

'I have always insisted that she does not interfere in the business,' Henry replied sternly. 'You may have noticed we always go on a Wednesday because it is ladies' day at her golf club and she spends all day and half the night there.'

Their conversation was halted by the sound of screeching brakes, quickly followed by a thud and some screaming. They hurried to the window that overlooked University Road, colourfully decorated with bunting in preparation for a visit by the Queen, to see Eleanor, half-hidden beneath a Trojan van, lying in an ever-increasing pool of blood.

'Oh my God!' cried Henry as he rushed downstairs while a shocked Wendy hurried to the telephone to call for an ambulance.

Henry went with the ambulance to the Royal Infirmary where his wife was pronounced dead on arrival. Ashamed for losing her temper, grief stricken for Henry and overcome by the tragedy, Wendy moped aimlessly around the flat but failed to see a badly scribbled note that Michael had left, "Graham rang, in hospital next Thursday the fifteenth".

It was Wendy's third funeral in less than fifteen months and the second that she felt discomfort at attending. If only Henry's train had not arrived an hour late at Rugby. If the driver of the van that Eleanor ran in front of had been one minute earlier or one minute later then the funeral at Gilroes cemetery on Thursday the fifteenth of May would not be taking place. Sixty minutes or sixty seconds; the difference between life and death.

Similar discomfort was felt by Felicity who openly admitted to Wendy that she hated her mother. 'She was always trying to run my life, inviting sons of her golfing cronies for dinner in her futile attempts of matchmaking. There was one occasion when she locked my bedroom while I was in the bath to stop me going out to see Colin.'

'What did you do?'

'I ran off to meet him wearing my slippers and a fur coat that was kept in the hall.' Although outraged at the time, the memory of her audacity brought a smile to her face. 'I only hope she can see me now, see how happy I am and what a lovely baby we have had together. She always called Colin a "no-hoper" but he has proved her wrong.'

'Your Dad told me that he has a very successful window cleaning business and helps in a garage as a motor mechanic.'

'That's because he loves tinkering with engines. The man at the garage has been trying to persuade him to work full time, but his window cleaning rounds are very compact, which makes it very easy to earn a lot of money in a little time. My mother could not be more wrong about him; he's hard working and ambitious.'

As Felicity related other despicable incidences involving her mother, it became crystal clear to Wendy that she had travelled out of loyalty to her father and had boosted his grieving deflated spirit, as had the return telegram from his son Dudley in Singapore. She hoped the tragedy would pull the family back together; it was certainly no less than Henry deserved.

Graham deserved a successful operation and it was, but at the cost of the removal of one testicle. Wendy was given this information during a telephone conversation with the Duchess of Kent Hospital at Catterick Garrison. Having never seen his original note it was a chance remark by Michael that made her aware that Graham's operation had taken place while she attended the funeral.

She was fighting back the tears as she relayed this information to Hannah during a subsequent telephone call. 'At least they're going to discharge him from the army,' she said trying to give comfort and cheer to herself and Hannah. 'He'll be at least a week in hospital before they remove the stitches and then another week of convalescence.'

Hannah's voice was quiet and a little garbled over the poor telephone connection. 'I would have liked to have gone up to his camp but the handover is in full swing, which makes it difficult to get away.' There was a pause and a mumbling sound before her voice continued. 'That will be the twenty-ninth, is that date definite?'

'I think so,' Wendy answered, 'as long as he's well enough.'

'I have a meeting with the buyer's surveyors on that date that I can't put off. I'll arrange to come over to Leicester the next day. Is it easy to get to you on the train?'

Wendy explained her own travel experience, 'I had to change at Rugby and wait forty minutes for the train to Leicester. Will Gwyneth be coming?'

'I doubt it; Friday and Saturday are her busiest days in the salon. Is there a hotel nearby where I can stay?'

'There is but you're quite welcome to stay with me as long as you don't mind sharing. I only have one bedroom.'

Graham arrived on Friday the thirtieth of May looking pale and dejected and walked with a wide gait as if he had been riding a horse. Wendy had waited twenty impatient minutes for his train to arrive at the Central Station on a hot and humid day, wearing a beige summer dress with a bay coloured belt pulled tight around her slim waist.

She embraced him tentatively, not wishing to cause him any pain, and kissed him gently on the cheek. 'Come on,' she said as she took his bulging kitbag, 'Henry's lent me his car so we don't have to mess around with buses.'

Wendy had received a three-minute phone call from him last Tuesday when he told her his stitches were out and everything was fine. His discharge from the army was completed yesterday. He had spurned her offer of travelling up to accompany him. 'I'm not an invalid and I don't want to be treated like one.'

She was overjoyed to see him but realised he was feeling very low as they moved into the lounge of her flat. 'Look on the bright side,' she said in an effort to change his mood, 'you're very much alive with your whole life in front of you.'

'Some life, I might as well become a bloody monk.'

'That's ridiculous it's only one testicle, you still have the other one. You can live a perfectly normal life, get married and have kids.'

'Who would want to marry a bloody freak like me knowing I couldn't fuck properly?'

Wendy embraced him again, more tightly this time and felt a tingle of excitement when she pressed her bust against his chest.

She leaned her head on his shoulder. 'I would,' she whispered softly in his ear.

He did not want her consoling pity and pushed her away. 'That's a bloody stupid thing to say, you're my sister.'

It's not that stupid; we have different mothers and different fathers, is what she intended to say but her lips remained sealed as she watched him sit on the settee with an unmistakable lack of interest in the topic. The distant sound of the grandfather clock striking five o'clock broke the stony silence that followed, reminding Wendy of her commitment. She had arranged to meet Hannah at the station and the arrival time of her train was rapidly approaching. 'I'll make you a nice cup of tea and then I've got to pop out for half an hour.'

Graham lit a cigarette and sauntered over to the window. He saw Henry and Wendy get into the Armstrong Siddeley and wondered where they were going. He mulled through Wendy's record collection and passed the time away listening to them playing on the gramophone. With the volume on loud and listening intently he neither saw nor heard Wendy return until she stood at the door.

'Graham, there's somebody here to see you.'

'Too bad because I don't want to see anybody,' he said putting another record on the turntable and, thinking it could only be his brother, he added, 'not even Michael.'

Wendy moved to his side and switched off the gramophone.

'I was listening to that,' he protested and was about to put the music back on when the door opened.

'Hello, Graham.'

He turned towards the doorway in an instant and became as motionless as a piece of stone.

Wendy looked quickly at Hannah whose eyes were wet with tears and took Graham's hand comfortingly as he bit his bottom lip to fight his emotions. 'It is your mother,' she reassured him softly, 'she was not killed in a road accident. That was a wicked evil lie that Sid made you believe.'

Hannah moved towards him, drawn like metal to a magnet and threw her arms around him. 'My son, my wonderful son, never has a day gone by when I haven't thought about you,' she sobbed, her eyes swimming in tears. 'What a fine handsome man you've grown in to.'

Bemused, bewildered, Graham's glazed eyes still stared towards the doorway as though a bright, blinding light had dazzled him. 'Mum, is it really you?' he stuttered as he put his arms around her back to complete the embrace.

Wendy gently stroked the back of Graham's head before quietly leaving him with Hannah to catch up on twelve missing years of their lives.

Henry was drafting a report when Wendy entered his office with a cup of tea a few moments later. It had been virtually a normal week, the first since Eleanor's death and he was catching up on a backlog of work. The morbid atmosphere that had previously hung over the office like a fog had lifted eight days ago, when he received a letter from Felicity with news that they had decided to leave Inverness to return to Leicester.

'Thank you, how is it going upstairs?'

'All right, Graham was very depressed, but I'm sure meeting his mother again will stop him wallowing in self-pity.'

'You cannot blame him,' said Henry. 'He must feel he has lost his manhood. Have you told him about tonight?'

'No, I'll leave that to Hannah, are you sure you don't mind?' The previous day Wendy had accepted Henry's kind offer to take them out for a celebratory dinner at the Bell Hotel in Humberstone Gate.

'It's my pleasure and it certainly beats going home to an empty house.'

It was during dinner that Henry made another kind offer. 'Why don't we all go to Anglesey in my car?'

Wendy and Hannah spoke in unison in thanking him but both thought it was far too generous to accept.

'I would not offer if I did not mean it.' He turned to look at Hannah who was sitting beside him. 'To start with, if Graham is going to stay with you for a while it will be better for him to travel in the comfort of my car, rather than the bone shaking carriages of British Railways.' Without giving her a chance to respond he looked across the table at a wide-eyed Wendy. 'And I know how much you have been looking forward to this reunion and it will give you a chance to meet Gwyneth and see the final piece of the jigsaw put into place. Besides,' he grinned broadly, 'it has been years since I have been to the seaside so I am sure it will do me good, particularly after all the upheaval I've had recently.'

Wendy knew that Henry would not be dissuaded from such a generous offer when all the logic was on his side. 'What about that urgent report for Mr Hough?' she reminded. 'I'll type it first thing in the morning if you want it in the post.'

'You must put your work before us,' Hannah intervened. 'Moreover it will give me time to have a look around Leicester, see if there are any nice hotels for sale. We can go anytime and I insist that you stay with me overnight at the very least.'

CHAPTER TWENTY

Gwyneth Roberts sighed as she began to sweep the floor of her hair salon, thankful that it was the final task of her busy day. Normally her husband David helped her close up but, with her blessing, he had gone ahead to Benllech to take advantage of the unusually hot weather. When she had Mrs Evans under the hairdryer she imagined and envied the man she was so deeply in love with swimming in the bay with his Building Society colleague.

David had been very patient, very understanding and very gentle with her during their entire relationship in her battle to overcome the trauma of being sexually abused when she was twelve. But overcome it she had, the nightmares were very infrequent and the desire for her husband to touch her body had overtaken the fear. She pictured herself sharing a bath before making love and visualized how absolutely wonderful it would be if she conceived. It would satisfy her desire to become a mother, a desire that seemed to grow stronger day by day.

She rested her hands on top of the broom handle and smiled at her image in one of the mirrors as she continued to daydream, picturing herself cuddling her very own baby. How broody she became when customers talked about babies. She would miss the salon when the sale went through in four weeks' time, not so much the work but the people; her clients who had become almost like close friends.

Suddenly her peace was shattered when the doorbell sounded as loud as a fire alarm. Overcoming the surprise of finding her mother on her doorstep she exchanged greetings before meeting her mysterious friends.

'This is Henry Grant, an accountant from Leicester,' said Hannah, indicating with her hand as she made the introductions, 'and this is Wendy his secretary.'

Gwyneth frowned, puzzled by the way Mr Grant was deliberately shielding someone standing directly behind him.

'Now I want you to meet someone very, very special.' Hannah paused for a moment, her eyes joyfully moist in a face radiantly happy. 'Your brother Graham!'

He stepped out from behind Henry and the long lost brother and sister stared at each other. It seemed like an age before Graham spoke. 'How are you, Gwyneth, still as bossy as ever?'

Gwyneth darted forward and threw her arms around him, 'I gave up hoping I would ever see you again.'

Wendy thought how pretty Gwyneth looked, even though she was wearing an unbecoming white overall, contrasting with her jet black hair, worn shoulder length and inherited from the Celtic origins of her father. Her deep brown eyes were waterlogged with tears, which was no surprise because she felt like a good cry.

After more seconds that seemed like minutes Gwyneth broke off the embrace but held her outstretched hands on his shoulders. 'How you've grown up,' she sniffed to abate the tears. 'You've grown as well,' Graham responded. 'I seem to remember you as a skinny little thing with your hair down your back in a long plait.'

Wendy was brushing her hair, having slipped into her thigh length shirt style nightdress that she had recently bought at Morley's, when she heard a tap at the door.

'Are you awake?' She recognized Gwyneth's whispering Welsh accent and opened the door.

'I hope I'm not keeping you up,' she said, seeing Wendy in her nightshirt.

'You're not,' Wendy said as she beckoned Gwyneth to sit with her on the bed. 'I'm really not the least bit sleepy.'

'I never got the chance to thank you properly for making it such a wonderful day. Fulfilled my dreams proper you have.'

'I haven't done anything that you wouldn't have done, given the same circumstances.'

'You have and you mustn't be so modest. I've had countless nightmares about Graham ever since we left Peterborough. I felt guilty you see that my poor brother was left behind.'

'You weren't to blame, it really wasn't your fault.'

'But it was you see. If I hadn't have kicked up such a rumpus when we went to collect him from school he would have been with us. So I shall never ever be able to thank you enough for reuniting us.'

'I really haven't done that much. I just wish that I could have found the letter sooner.'

'You couldn't have found it before you did and your timing's perfect. I know mother was thinking of buying a hotel in Norwich in the hope of finding Graham and I had persuaded David to have a holiday there once the hairdressing business was sold. Now we are both free to do exactly what we like.'

'I'm really pleased that you are so happy.'

'Aren't I just and it's all thanks to you. David and I are going to start trying for a baby and I'm sure now the time is right. Anyway I mustn't keep you up any longer.' Gwyneth got up and Wendy automatically followed her to the door.

'Thank you ever so much and if there is ever anything I can do for you, you only have to ask.'

Wendy closed the door and was about to get into bed when there was another faint knocking. Thinking Gwyneth had returned she called for her to come in but when the door opened it was Graham that entered with an ear-to-ear smile. She pulled her nightshirt down as far as she could but it still only covered half her thighs.

'This has been an unforgettable twenty-four hours and it's all thanks to you. It's incredible how you worked out how to contact Mum from that letter.'

'I thought it odd a letter should be sent to her after she was dead.'

'Why didn't you talk to me about it?'

'Because there was a danger it might all be a hoax and you didn't deserve that.'

'I don't deserve to have such a bloody good sister like you.'

'No you don't,' Wendy joked. More seriously she added, 'Neither did you deserve to have to go through that operation, nor be lied to so cruelly by that sodding monster that you thought was your father.'

She detected joyous tears in Graham's eyes. Instinctively she stepped forward and put her arms around him. 'It'll be all right Graham,' she said consolingly, 'it's all in the past. You've got a whole new future ahead of you with your mother and your real sister who both love you.'

'All thanks to you,' Graham whispered as he moved his hands gently over her back, sensually stirred by the absence of any bra straps. Through the thin cotton of his shirt he could feel Wendy's laboured breathing and feel her breasts pulsating against his chest.

They kissed lips to lips until he suddenly broke free from their embrace, said goodbye and hurriedly left, embarrassed by his erection the mood and emotions had caused.

Wendy could not understand why he rushed off so suddenly. Had she gone too far by kissing him? Was Hannah right? Did she love Graham more than just a brother? What did he feel towards her? Was he too self-conscious about his operation? These questions plagued her mind as she tossed and turned in her bed trying to sleep.

The next day they hardly spoke or looked at each other so the unanswered questions returned, bouncing around in her head like tennis balls, as Henry drove as fast as traffic permitted homewards along the A5 road.

'Penny for your thoughts?'

Wendy looked across at Henry and smiled. 'I was thinking about Graham.'

'That young man has gone through a lot these last two weeks. He loses part of his manhood and is then reunited with a mother and a sister he believed to be dead. In time he will appreciate he has gained more than he has lost.'

'I'm sure he will,' Wendy replied confidently. 'I'm glad he decided to stay with Hannah for a while, it will give them time to get to know each other.'

Having driven through Corwen, Henry eased off the accelerator in readiness to turn into a Regent garage. Wendy was fascinated, as she always was, when Henry paid the attendant with ten shilling notes that he kept in a special hip pocket at the front of his trousers.

'That report I typed yesterday for the bank about Mr Hough's garage seemed quite serious,' said Wendy when they were back on the road.

'It is I'm afraid,' Henry answered. 'Fred Hough's problem is that he was under-capitalized from the start and his business acumen has done nothing to improve matters. Good mechanic he undoubtedly is but his administrative skills are something else. Put a piece of paper in front of him and ask him to make out an invoice and he thinks you are speaking a foreign language.'

'Will the report help him?'

'We can only hope. The bank wants to withdraw his overdraft facility but he needs it increasing to keep going. If the bank decide they want to pull out it will force an auction sale that will raise far less money than the business is worth and poor Fred will be finished.'

'That's really awful.' Wendy winced as if she felt physical pain. 'I have a deep affection for Mr Hough because if it hadn't been for him I don't know where I'd be today.' Wendy could see the bewildered look on Henry's face. 'That first day,' she prompted, 'if he hadn't mistaken me for your receptionist I would have left and got a job somewhere else.'

Henry smiled when he recalled the incident and his own total amazement and admiration at Wendy's ingenuity. Fred Hough's singing of her praises, "your receptionist is very good, such a lovely sweet girl."

'We are both deeply indebted to Fred Hough.'

'Surely there must be something we can do to help him.'

'We can only hope the bank accepts my proposal that we take charge of his accounting. Getting his bills out promptly and his money in quicker may help temporarily and buy us some time but I suppose the real solution would be for him to find a partner.'

Wendy continued to think about Mr Hough's problems as Henry accelerated past three dawdling cars. She did not know whether it was within one mile or ten but suddenly an idea flashed into her mind like a bolt of lightning.

'Colin!' she almost shouted in her excitement. 'He loves tinkering with engines and he'll be looking for something when they move from Inverness.'

'You're right, Felicity said that Colin did not want to start from scratch building up another window cleaning round but I'm sure he would be delighted with an opportunity to have a share in an established garage repair business. I could inject some cash to buy Colin a partnership, which would get the bank off Fred Hough's back.'

'I don't think you should do that,' Wendy said softly bringing an askance look from Henry. 'I feel Colin and Felicity value their independence and might see that as interference,' she explained. 'I'm sure he will be interested in becoming a partner but I think you'll have to let him find his own money and only help if you're asked.'

Henry understood and nodded his agreement. 'You're not just a pretty face, are you?' he smiled. 'In fact you're extremely mature considering you are only seventeen.'

Wendy's eighteenth birthday fell on a Thursday and she received six cards, all with Leicester postmarks except one from Wisbech. Feeling guilty that she had not visited Mrs Bellamy for a long time, she was opening her card when she heard a faint knocking at her office door.

'I'm Barry Roach,' the young man said politely, 'I have an appointment with Mr Grant.'

Robin had passed his part two final examinations to become qualified but was forced to leave to do his deferred national service with the Royal Air Force, leaving Henry with a vacancy for a clerk. The shy nervous school-leaver in front of Wendy was almost fifty minutes early for his interview for the junior post.

After seating him in the waiting area, Wendy continued to open her cards, instantly recognizing one from Anne with a note that she was planning to marry Trevor next March after her nineteenth birthday and did she know of anyone that would like to be her bridesmaid?

Wendy smiled at the thought of being a bridesmaid as she opened a card from Hannah. Beneath the well-chosen words Hannah had written, "I shall never be able to repay you for bringing back my son. One day you may know the special bond that exists between a mother and a son." The words stirred Wendy. She had never felt any bond with the son she gave birth to, neither then nor since, but she still had cravings to see the child she had never seen.

After being separated for twelve years, mother and son were now living as a family unit in a large house on London Road. Having taken over occupancy during July, Hannah was well advanced with plans to convert it into a ten-room hotel in the first instance and ultimately fourteen rooms after some extension work.

Graham had decided to work with his mother and would in due course take on the role of hotel manager once the house stopped resembling a builder's workshop.

The next card she opened was from David and Gwyneth who had also moved to Leicester following the sale of the hairdressing business. He had continued his career by finding immediate employment with the Leicester Temperance Building Society and they were living with Hannah while they waited for the purchase of a house in Highway Road to be completed. She liked David; he was a relaxed and easy-going type of guy, yet he had persuaded her to open a share account with the Building Society by withdrawing forty pounds from her Post office savings account.

A cuddly teddy bear greeted Wendy from the front of the card from Colin, Felicity and baby Paula. Staying with Henry, they had moved in mid-June and Colin had jumped at the chance of a partnership in Fred Hough's garage. The sale proceeds of his Inverness window cleaning business provided him with some of the cash requirement, the remainder Henry had been asked to lend them. Felicity helped by keeping on top of the office work and, with the financial strains lifted, the business was already starting to prosper.

Michael's handwriting was getting worse and Wendy could only just decipher a note that he would call and see her on Friday before going to Norwich for the weekend to see Lizzie.

The serenity was shattered when everybody descended on her office. First Clive entered with a chirpy greeting and a stock certificate he wanted typing, then Brian with a petty cash voucher for bus fares followed by Kevin with a card signed by them all. They all took the opportunity to look at their possible new work colleague. Immediately after Kevin left, Henry came in with a cutting from the Financial Times.

'If you would care to fill in this Norton Lovell prospectus for two hundred shares we can get it in tonight's post.' Without waiting for a response he returned to the waiting area, introduced himself to Barry Roach and led the young man back to his office for an interview.

Since Henry advised Wendy to sell her shares in Ernest Goodson at a profit of nearly seventy pounds he had regularly brought in prospectus forms for her to apply for shares in companies starting a flotation on the stock market that he judged would be over-subscribed and thus rise quickly in price. All in all her original premium bond win of two hundred and fifty pounds had grown to over three hundred and eighty pounds.

She was looking in her ready reckoner to see how much the shares in Norton Lovell would cost when another person entered the office with their face hidden behind a bouquet. 'I have an urgent delivery for Miss Marshall.'

She recognized Graham's disguised voice. 'Thank you,' she said as she took the flowers from him. It was sweet of him to buy a bouquet, no doubt a decision influenced by Hannah, but the sparse words on the card, "To Wendy – Happy Birthday – From Graham", were definitely his own. She kissed him gently on the lips.

'Happy birthday,' he replied and returned a friendly kiss. 'If you're not doing anything tonight I have a surprise for you.'

'I hate surprises, what is it?' she asked but, before he could answer, the telephone rang with an outside call. 'Good morning, Henry Grant and Co.'

Graham took the opportunity to escape. 'See you tonight about seven.'

What should she wear? Most likely Graham was only going to take her to a pub with a walk to the fish and chip shop in Sparkenhoe Street afterwards, in which case jeans and a casual jumper would be sufficient. She settled for a flowery summer dress, sleeveless and calf length, in the hope of going somewhere better.

'What do you think?' Graham asked with enthusiasm in his voice, rapt over the Austin Ten car he was showing Wendy. It was a pre-war model he had bought the previous day. He had spent most of the afternoon polishing it so that it gleamed in the evening sunshine in University Road.

'This is really yours?' said Wendy as he opened the door dressed in charcoal flannels with the open neck collar of his shirt turned over the collar of his grey fleck sports jacket. 'And I thought the surprise was going to be you taking me out for a nice meal.'

'It's that as well, I'm driving you to a restaurant in Newtown Linford.'

'What about taking me to Wisbech on Sunday or wouldn't this car go that far?' Wendy said light heartedly as Graham pulled out into the London Road.

'This car could go to the bloody North Pole and back. It's only had one owner who only did thirty-three thousand miles in it. There's just a bad bit of rust on the nearside running board but Colin said he could weld that for me.'

Wendy enjoyed the meal, relishing the blend of banana and poultry in her selection of Chicken Maryland; Graham was more conservative in his choice of steak. Back at the flat she made coffee and sat with Graham on the settee, tucking her legs beneath her.

'Have you ever wondered how things that are really important to us started by some small insignificant chance when we were younger?' Wendy said as Graham took out a cigarette. 'I often think I'm lucky to have such a good job and work that I really enjoy and to have such a good boss as Henry. I even thought I was lucky to get that job at Palmer and Moore in Norwich and very fortunate to be propelled forward as Mr Palmer's secretary when Doreen broke her wrist.'

'What you might call a lucky break.' Graham laughed as he pocketed his lighter.

Wendy grinned at the pun and continued, 'But if it hadn't have been for Mrs Bellamy being a customer on my paper round, none of it would have happened because I wouldn't have learnt to type. Then I might have worked in a shop or a factory or even stayed on in the market café as a full-time waitress. So if it hadn't have been for Mrs Bellamy and her typewriter I wouldn't have met Henry and have my lovely flat.'

'It's fate I suppose, like Sid keeping that letter, like us finding it and clever old you discovering my mother and sister weren't dead. But fate doesn't always bring good fortune.'

No, Wendy reflected as she thought about her father and the telegram, "missing believed killed". Thought about her mother, the hardship she had suffered before her life was snatched away by cancer. Thought about Stan, the stepfather she adored, killed because of a freak bit of ice on the road. Thought about Sid and squirmed at the evil he had done. Yes, life was not always a bed of roses as she listened to Graham giving his examples.

'Look at the disaster Millie caused me. You know I have always been puzzled by what she said in hospital, "tell that sister I'll rip her..."'

'All right, Graham,' Wendy hastily interrupted. 'I know what she said, Dennis told me.'

'But you were so nice and kind to her at Christmas, why say such a horrible thing?'

She had never told him about the visit to Richmond and she was not going to spoil the evening by doing so. 'I don't want to ruin my birthday by talking about her.'

'There was a reason then?'

'Perhaps, let's talk about it on Sunday'.

CHAPTER TWENTY-ONE

Wendy was pouring water into the teapot when she heard the clanging sound of Graham climbing the fire escape. 'You're early; I've not been up long,' she said when she opened the door and immediately put a hand down to prevent her nightshirt wafting up in the breeze. There was a mouth-watering smell of frying bacon coming from her neighbour's kitchen where Mrs Poole always did a full cooked breakfast on Sundays.

'Go in the lounge, I'll be with you in a minute.' She moved towards her bedroom to get her dressing gown and then changed her mind. Sod it! Graham had seen her in her thigh length nightshirt before.

He was relaxing in the chair and smoking by the time she joined him with two steaming mugs of tea. She sat on the settee, tucking her legs beneath her.

'You were going to tell me about Millie,' he said, stubbing the remainder of his cigarette in the ashtray. 'Was it anything to do with the baby?'

Wendy wondered if he would remember their conversation on Thursday. She put her tea on the floor and delved into her handbag. 'It wasn't yours,' she said as she handed the letter to him.

She retrieved her tea and moved across to the window to allow him time to read. She looked down on University Road where an elderly lady was strolling towards the church. Then she vanished from view when a bus passed by with one solitary passenger on the top deck.

'The conniving little shit!'

At his outburst she turned round to look at him and proceeded to explain how it came to be in her possession and how it led to the confrontation at Richmond.

Graham was only half-listening, remembering his first date with Millie. How she led him into a darkened alley and got him sexually aroused. It was the first and only time that intimacy took place, which was all she would have needed to say the baby was his. Even at Christmas they only fondled each other, cystitis being her excuse for not going further.

Hearing of his sister's audacious actions and fearless fight with Millie brought a smile to his haggard face. 'So the crude threat to rip your crotch out was because you tried to do the same thing to her!'

Wendy returned to look out of the window to hide her blushes from him. What had been his true feelings towards Millie? After all she had caused him to get blinding drunk on two nights. Then visions of his being naked with her at Christmas flashed before her mind. She needed to know. 'Did you love her?'

'No.' Graham's answer was abrupt as the bark of a dog. 'I was only going to marry her because of the baby,' he went on to explain. 'I thought I ought to do the right thing.'

'You went out with Brenda Frost for a long time, twice in fact, were you in love with her?'

'No,' he said shaking his head. 'I only went out with her so my mates could see I had a girlfriend. It was the same with Janice and

Margaret, it seemed the right thing to do but they were not right for me.'

'So have you ever met anybody that's right for you?' Did she really want to know? Yes she did!

During the last three days, or nights to be more precise, she had been mulling over whether Hannah was right. Did she love Graham in a romantic way? She had compared her feelings for Michael who she did love as a brother, well most of the time when he was not being horrid.

By Anne's definitions her love for Graham was more than sisterly. When she was with him her tummy felt it was buzzing with a swarm of bees like it was doing now. Her heart pounded like the kick of a mule as it was now. Her legs turned to jelly like they felt now. She did go hot down there, but not at the moment because she was too tense, waiting for his answer.

'Does it matter?' This conversation was becoming bizarre. He wanted to shout "you" but he held his tongue. 'Nobody is going to love me now; I'm a one ballock freak show.'

'I love you.' She spoke softly, almost whispering her words. There was no turning back. She had admitted her feelings and felt vulnerably exposed. Unable to face him she persisted in staring out of the window, watching a boy walk by with a full bag of newspapers.

He could hardly believe his ears. Was she still trying to console him? Was she talking about sibling love? 'But you are my sister.'

'Gwyneth is your sister not me.' She was full of suspense, wanting to turn round to see how serious he was taking it but too frightened to do so in case he was laughing at her. 'We are no more blood related than she is with David.'

'You're being serious aren't you?'

'Yes, so why not have a sodding good laugh about it.' Could she stand his ridicule with her anxious emotions strained to the limit?

He rose and moved silently across the carpet so that he was standing in front of her when she turned. 'I'm not laughing,' he said as he clasped her hand. 'The reason all my girlfriends have been such dismal failures is because they were not you.' His woeful bloodhound look was replaced with a smile. He had been at war with his feelings for over five years, bottling them up so that he often felt like a caged animal. But no more! She had sent his pulses racing. 'I never thought I would ever say this but I love you. I've loved you ever since the first day I saw you looking across the dinner table and mesmerizing me with your sparkling blue eyes.'

Her eyes were sparkling now as a mood of rapturous happiness swept over her, replacing doubt and uncertainty. This was beyond her wildest dreams. He loved her! They were in love!

She was excited. She squeezed his hand as she detected the emotion in his eyes. 'I've been head over heels in love with you since that first day when you wore that fair-isle pullover that was far too big. And I told Anne the very next morning that I'd met the boy I'd love to marry.' Her face was glowing with a beaming smile. 'You've always been the only person I really care about, the only person I want to be with. It's taken me all this while to admit it, to myself as well as you.'

Graham's spirits were uplifted. 'Even with half my ballocks missing?'

Wendy embraced him tightly and kissed him on the lips. 'I'd still love you with all your ballocks missing,' she whispered and opened her mouth to indulge in a passionate kiss that lasted a long time and made her body tingle from head to toe.

She felt his hands drift slowly down her back until they rested on her buttocks. His grip tightened, fusing their bodies so close that through their clothing she could feel his hardness pressed against her like a metal rod.

She broke off the kissing. 'Mind where you put your hands,' she whispered, 'I've got sod all on beneath this nightshirt.'

It was abandoned in the bedroom and Graham discarded all his clothes apart from his Y-fronts, being too self-conscious to remove them.

She thought she had reached the bounds of happiness in the lounge but the boundaries were soon extended when Graham gently caressed her breasts with his hand. It was heavenly when she felt his tongue sucking her protruding nipple and licking it gently as he would an ice cream. Ecstatically groaning, she felt his hand move slowly over her stomach, through the soft cluster of hair to feel her moist vagina that was receptive to his touch. She squeezed her own hand between their writhing bodies until it rested on top of his to encourage his continuing finger massage as her entire body convulsed with sensual pleasure.

All the time that Wendy was quivering, Graham's body rocked backwards and forwards, throbbing against her until he felt a tremendous sensation in his penis. Hazy reminiscences flooded his mind of his drunken state during the previous occasion that Wendy had allowed him to explore her body, but without reaching the same heights of pleasure as now.

Only after the palpitating tingling abated did she lift her head to kiss Graham passionately.

Only after they were exhausted of passion did they relax. Her unanswered questions were answered. She was ecstatic. Having

Graham's hands caressing her breasts and vagina had thrilled her beyond words. All the happiest, most memorable moments of her life fell a long way short of the delirious pleasure she had just experienced.

Graham went and lit a cigarette before returning to lie beside Wendy who used the bed sheet to cover her nakedness.

'You look as though you've wet yourself,' she teased seeing the patch of spent semen showing at the front of his underpants, 'but I'm glad you kept them on. I'm not sure how I would have reacted if things had have gone any further.'

She pecked him a kiss on the cheek, threw back the sheet and got up. 'I'm going to run a bath then we must get going to Wisbech,' she said and made her way out of the room.

'Do you think my mother will be mad if I tell her about us?' Graham shouted in her wake.

She returned and popped her head round the door. 'I think you'll find she knows. It was your mother that convinced me that I was in love with you.'

'What about Michael? Will he be upset when you tell him?'

Wendy smiled at Graham's assumption that she was to tell him as she turned the bathroom door handle. 'I shouldn't think so,' she called out, 'he's only interested in two things; Lizzie and the Midland Red.'

Nine days later she was proved correct.

'I always knew you two were soft on each other,' said Michael after Wendy had told him, which was the sum total of his interest in the subject. 'I was going to call in last night but I went out with a relief crew when this D5 broke down on the L36 route to Eyres

Monsell. It was right outside the gas works in the middle of the bloody rush hour.'

They were both standing in her kitchen and while she concentrated on cooking sausage and mash for their meal Michael continued to relate all the details. When she turned from the stove to face him she endeavoured to change the subject. 'How's Liz? Have you heard from her since your visit to Norwich?'

'I've got a favour to ask about her. She's coming up to Leicester this weekend and I wonder if she could stay here?'

Wendy assumed a weekend would be for one or two nights but Liz's stay lasted almost three weeks because Michael somehow omitted to say she was moving to Leicester permanently. When she did move out on the evening of Thursday August the twenty-eighth, Wendy had come to admire the young girl who had immediately found a job as a trainee machinist in a hosiery factory in King Street, where she would be on piecework rates after training. In the meantime, to ensure she had enough money to be able to afford independent lodgings in a boarding house at the bottom of Princess Road, she had taken on part-time work at the Cameo Cinema on Friday and Saturday nights and cleaning at the De Montfort pub in Wellington Street on Saturday and Sunday mornings. As if that was not enough she persuaded Wendy to teach her to type on mutually convenient spare evenings as she had future aspirations greater than working on a factory floor as a machinist.

It was during the third lesson that Liz admitted that Wendy had been her shining example in leaving home so young. 'It was knowing how well you'd done for yourself that inspired me,' she had said. 'What's more I love Michael too much to let some Leicester floozy get her claws in him while I was living in Norwich.'

During Liz's stay Wendy's relationship with Graham continued more sedately and she enjoyed the simple features of courtship like feeling his arm around her shoulder when they went to the Essoldo Cinema. The pride she felt when they walked hand in hand across Victoria Park. The pleasure of evening drives in the country and the contentment of a drink in a quaint village pub. Two delightful picnics when they visited Foxton Locks and Bradgate Park. The fun at Proctors Park at Barrow-upon-Soar, an experience shared with Lizzie and Michael. The fools they made of themselves when they tried square dancing in the Cooperative Hall.

Whatever she did, wherever she went, she was truly happy just being with Graham. His presence gave her the inner strength to conquer her apprehension and overcome her fear of courting. She felt safe with him and protected by him.

'I shall have to ask Michael to be my best man, do you think he's too young for it?' Graham said and winced when Wendy grated the gears as she stabbed her foot on the button for the headlight dip control instead of the clutch pedal.

She was driving Graham's car towards Groby Pool discussing wedding plans, finding the long gear stick very cumbersome and the performance sluggish compared to Henry's Armstrong Siddeley. It was a glorious day with high pressure ruling the weather, making it warm and sultry, ideal for their Sunday afternoon picnic.

'He'll be all right,' she answered after the noisy gear change, 'he'll be sixteen by then.'

'Who will you get to give you away?'

'Henry,' Wendy responded, looking well prepared in a sleeveless tee-shirt and pink shorts as she pushed the switch to put the traffic indicator arm out to turn in the centre of Groby. 'He's the only person I could ask.'

They decided to walk round the pool after Wendy had managed to squeeze into a parking spot.

'I'm sure it's getting hotter,' said Graham and then noticed Wendy staring trance-like at a little two-year-old boy struggling to stand in the shallow water while playing with a toy sailing boat, watched by his father.

It could be my son thought Wendy. When the little fellow nearly stumbled she felt a compelling urge to rush to his aid but his father's safe hands quickly steadied him as the shrill voice of his mother called out. Wendy sought the comfort of Graham's hand to continue their walk.

'You seemed very interested in them. Was it somebody you knew?'

'No, I thought,' Wendy hesitated trying to think of something to say. 'I thought the little boy was very cute.'

'Does he bring back memories?'

Wendy felt a stab of discomfort. 'What do you mean?'

'Come on, Wendy, it doesn't have to be a secret anymore, we're practically engaged.'

The discomfort increased and her body tensed with goose bumps. She quickly pulled her hand away from his when she felt hers starting to shake. 'I don't know what secret you're going on about.'

'About Sid abusing you and everything. I hated him even when I thought he was my father, but now I hope he's rotting in bloody hell for what he did to you.'

It seemed her secret was safe. Of course Hannah would have told him about the abuse but nobody knew about the baby. The tension drained from her like water from clothes going through her mother's old mangle as she realized that Graham knew nothing about the shameful secret of her life. In her utter relief she was about to clasp his hand again, but suddenly retracted when the alarm sounded again.

'I didn't realize it was Sid's baby until after Michael told me how he'd seen him fucking you. It's a good job he was dead or else I would have bloody killed him with my bare hands.'

The tension returned and hit her like a tornado. How could he know? 'How do you know about that?' She tried hard to sound calm, her nerves as taut as violin strings.

'I saw you when you were pregnant,' Graham answered without emotion. 'Don't you remember? It was your birthday and I came to see you at Peterborough.'

'How could you have noticed? I deliberately stayed in bed all day.'

'It was when I first arrived I came round the back and saw you dozing in the chair with your hands on a stomach that looked like it had swallowed a football.'

The humiliation, the degradation and the disgrace returned to haunt her, yet there was a glimmer of light in her dark tunnel. Graham knew and it was right that the man she was intending to marry should know.

'I didn't let on at the time because it was obvious you didn't want me to know,' Graham continued. 'I was even worried myself before I knew about Sid, although my mother seemed surprised that he was responsible.'

She stopped abruptly from their casual walking. Could she believe what she was hearing? The violin strings snapped. 'You've told your Mam about me?' She looked him in the face, her eyes as cold as steel and full of anger. 'How could you? How could you sodding betray me?'

'Telling my mother was hardly betraying you,' Graham defended calmly. 'You mustn't take it so personally, it wasn't your bloody fault.'

The emotional hurt twisted inside of her. It was as if Graham's words had ripped off all her clothes to leave her standing naked with everybody watching. A cocktail of shame, hate and anger raged within her. 'I sodding hate you,' she yelled and violently pushed him away.

He stumbled backwards over the small bank, causing him to struggle to keep his balance as he reeled backwards. He lost the battle, fell and landed sitting in the shallow water.

'You can find yourself some other poor sod to marry,' she screamed at him. 'I never want to see you again.'

She left him there, dumbfounded and bemused, and stormed off towards Linford Lane, unaware and uninterested in the spectacle that she had caused. Walking briskly, she soon covered the short distance to the village where she had to wait ten minutes before a bus came along to take her back to Leicester.

CHAPTER TWENTY-TWO

Wendy removed the blanket as the sweltering day had given way to a sticky night. The window was open but there was no air; the net curtain hung as still as starched cloth. Sleep was impossible as her mind churned over the disastrous events of the day.

If Graham had told his mother then it figured that she would have told Gwyneth and David. How could she face them again? Had Graham said anything to Michael? They had discussed her for Michael had told him about Sid so he probably had, which meant that Liz would know. How long would it be before Henry found out and she would become the laughing stock around the office?

She threw back the sheet in an effort to counter the stifling heat. Pregnant at fifteen! How could she live with the shame? How would she react to being the centre of gossip like the girl being talked about in the butcher's shop all those years ago?

'I'm a Wednesday's child all right,' she cried, 'and full of woe.' The tears welled in her eyes. 'Oh, Mam, why did you have to give birth to me on a Wednesday?'

She indulged in her guilt and self-pity for nearly thirty minutes and only stopped when she heard the single stroke of the grandfather clock sounding one o'clock. Still wide-awake, hot and perspiring she discarded her nightdress.

She recounted the times that Sid abused her over the two-year period before she fell pregnant. Throughout it all her greatest fear was the constant threat of being belted. She was innocent of blame for that sodding bastard getting her pregnant but she knew the tongue-wagging would find her guilty.

'Oh, Graham, how could you let the skeleton out of the cupboard,' she called out loudly in her anguish, 'you of all people.'

She would have to go away rather than face the disgrace. She had accomplished it when she came to Leicester with a lot of hope and little more than a few pounds in her savings bank. Now thanks to Henry's skilful stock market dealings she had over four hundred pounds; a lot of money, but diminished hope.

She could return to Norwich and see if Mr Palmer had meant what he said eighteen months ago about giving her a job. It had to be worth a try and better than facing the humiliation in Leicester.

She wondered how much notice she should give to Henry and whether he would be disappointed by her decision to leave. He had been so good, the last thing she wanted to do was upset him. During the rest of the night, in fitful bouts of sleep, she rehearsed what she thought she should say to him.

Dressed in her best white blouse and navy skirt she tapped lightly before apprehensively entering Henry's office at five minutes to nine.

'You must be psychic, I was just about to buzz you,' Henry said with a radiant smile on his face. He waved some blue sheets of airmail letter paper in his hand. 'I've had a letter from Dudley and he's coming home for good.'

'That's wonderful news.' She forced a smile to hide her wretchedness.

'He says he has been homesick for some time and he thinks Singapore will not be the same now it is not a British colony.' He turned from reading snippets of the letter to look at Wendy. 'It is wonderful that I shall have my family near me again and it is all thanks to you. Whatever would I do without you?'

There was no answer to that, which added to her gloom. 'I'm really very pleased for you, it's nothing more than you deserve.'

The grandfather clock outside his office heralded nine o'clock and Henry waited for it to finish striking. 'You are looking very smart this morning if I may say so. What did you come in for?'

Wendy was on the spot as her elated boss with his resplendent face looked at her for an answer. She had not the heart to risk upsetting him by giving in her notice. 'I came for the Clients Ledger,' she lied.

The next day Henry was similarly unapproachable as he was jubilant with more good news. 'Wendy,' he smiled heartily when he looked up from reading the Financial Times as she entered his office. 'We are going to make a fortune on those Megson Plastics shares. They have won a large export contract to supply badges to America. Their shares have gone up one and four pence already.'

After profitably redeeming her holding in Norton Lovell, Wendy had acquired four hundred and fifty shares in the plastics company but knew Henry had bought two and a half thousand because she had typed a confirmation letter to the stockbroker.

'There is talk of a two for one rights issue and an increased interim dividend, so we just sit tight my girl and watch our money grow,' Henry elaborated, pointing to the article in the newspaper, feeling as cheerful as a pauper that had just inherited a fortune.

Wendy could not tell him she was leaving and risk deflating the man who was floating on the clouds. She would wait until Friday and then he would have the weekend with his family to come to terms with it.

'Sod it!' It was ten to six when Wendy screwed up her second attempt of typing a letter for Brian and consigned it to the waste paper bin. Her mind was not on her work for she had made more mistakes this week than the rest of the year put together. Still it was Thursday and Liz would not be coming for a typing lesson so she decided there was time for another attempt. Her third effort was perfect and that was enough for the day. She heard the thud as the cleaner closed the outer front door on the floor below, before her own office door opened.

'Hello, Wendy,' Hannah greeted from the reception area before the first boom of the clock sounded. They stared at each other while the clock went through its striking ritual. 'Do you think you could spare me five minutes for a chat?'

Wendy hesitated as she placed the cover over her typewriter. A moral lecture was the last thing she wanted. She did not want to talk with Hannah, neither did she want to talk about Graham, but could she be rude enough to refuse? 'All right, let's go up and have a cup of tea.'

There was a very acrid silence as they climbed two flights of stairs to Wendy's flat. She turned from lighting the gas beneath the kettle to find Hannah had followed her into the kitchen. 'What did you want to talk about?'

'I think you know the answer to that.' Hannah closed the door and leaned back against the roller towel fixed on the inside, looking as though she was barring the way out. 'I know what it is like to be imprisoned by a secret. Look at the years of misery and separation from my son that it brought me? It was you that changed that. Your love and devotion to Graham that reunited my family.' She paused for a moment and pursed her lips.

Wendy looked coldly at Hannah. She wanted the talking to end and be alone in her misery.

'A week ago I was on top of the world, my daughter was delighted because she was pregnant and my son hopelessly in love with a girl any mother would be proud to have as a daughter-in-law.'

'Well I'm sorry to disappoint you but it's not my fault,' Wendy said as she put two spoons of tea in the pot before banging the caddy noisily on the worktop. 'How would you have felt if somebody had told Mrs Harding about you having Clifford's child, or even his wife?'

'Devastated, seeing that I was old enough to know better, but you were not responsible. You believed it was Sid's baby so you have absolutely nothing to be ashamed of.'

'It was Sid's baby, sod it, or did you think I slept with everybody in the street.' Wendy said vigorously as she poured the boiling water into the teapot. She turned to face Hannah and spoke in a softer tone. 'But I don't want the whole world to know I had a sodding stepfather that was having his evil way with me, or that I was too stupid to stop him getting me pregnant.'

Upsetting Wendy was the last thing Hannah wanted to do. Even though she had only known her for three months, Hannah felt strong motherly instincts and wanted to protect her from hurting. She loved her like a daughter, almost as much as she loved Gwyneth. She was searching for a way to bring about peace and reconciliation. 'Haven't you ever wondered what your baby looks like?'

'Of course I have, lots of times.' Wendy leaned back against a cupboard while she waited for the tea to brew. 'I've also wondered whether he's happy with his adopted parents and how much they love him.'

Pleased that the change in conversation was having a calming influence, it was time for new revelations. 'He wasn't adopted.'

Wendy was puzzled and frowned at her. 'What do you mean? What do you know about it?' Her mind flashed back to the days after the birth. 'Of course he was adopted, I remember signing the paper.'

Hannah gently shook her head. 'You signed a document giving guardianship to Ethel who had no intention of letting him go for adoption.'

'Then what has happened to him?' a bemused Wendy said and then trembled violently as this strange premonition swept over her. What did Hannah know? Why was she guarding the door like a jailer?

Wendy moved purposefully across the room and Hannah stood aside to let her go on to the landing. It was her flat but there was something strange and eerie about it. The door to the lounge was shut yet she thought she had left it open. With her heart pounding like a sledgehammer she glided silently towards it. She paused with her hand shaking on the handle, every muscle in her body tense with fearful apprehension. She opened the door tentatively and slowly entered the room.

A two-year-old boy was playing with a new set of building bricks on the carpet at Graham's feet. He looked at Wendy and gave her a quizzical smile.

Quivering with shock she stood at the door for a moment, her sapphire eyes soaked in tears.

'Hello, Wendy,' Graham said softly without getting up from his seat on the settee. 'This wasn't my idea,' he continued as he fidgeted uneasily. 'We came up earlier. We thought...'

Wendy heard no more of his ramblings as she dashed and swept up the little boy. She embraced him tightly before pecking a doting kiss on his cheek. 'My baby,' she whispered, 'my very own little boy.'

Enthralled, she did not see Graham stand or notice that Hannah had moved behind her as she gently rocked and showered her child with kisses.

'His name is Stuart,' Hannah said quietly.

'Stuart,' Wendy repeated, delighted he had kept the name she had given him. She wept over him, looked at him, smelled him, kissed him and stroked her hand all over his body as she bonded with her son.

As the shock of joyful, tearful exuberance subsided her mind started to drift back into thinking mode. Who did this darling little boy look like? Not Sid, that was for sure, yet there was something familiar about him.

The photograph jogged her memory. The photograph she had seen in Benllech and that Hannah was holding before her. 'Do you still think Sid is the father?'

Her one and only moment of sexual pleasure with a drunken stepbrother, fuelled by two full glasses of neat port and a generous measure of advocaat, had resulted in her conceiving, made pregnant by the young man she loved and not the sodding monster she loathed. Still clutching her son in her left arm she stretched out her right arm towards Graham, beckoning him to come and stand close to her side.

'I'm so sorry,' she apologized as she felt his arm go comfortingly around her back.

'It's me that should apologize.'

'I shouldn't have lost my temper last Sunday.'

He kissed her delicately on the lips with his head touching Stuart's as he did so.

Wendy reluctantly had to let go of her son when he started to struggle. 'Bicks,' he babbled pointing to his building bricks as he tried to wriggle free. 'Me want bicks.'

'I was certain your baby could not have been Sid's,' Hannah said as she sat in the vacant armchair opposite Graham and Wendy, who had both sat on the settee clutching hands. 'After I deceived him into marrying me and raising Graham as his son I felt I ought to do the right thing and bear him a child that was his own, but it didn't happen. I never got pregnant during the eight years I was locked into that loveless marriage and as I knew there was nothing wrong with me it had to be that Sid was infertile.'

Wendy supposed that was true for she had never missed a period following Sid's abuse of her. 'You must have despised me,' Wendy said, flatly.

Hannah shook her head. 'No of course I didn't, but I did want to find out the truth, see if it was Sid and I that were not compatible. I decided I had to see that old bag of an ex sister-in-law so I booked myself in the Angel Hotel and spent the last couple of days in Peterborough. I was waiting outside her house last evening when she came home from work with this little fellow strapped in a pushchair. I was shocked. It was like the clock had been turned back eighteen years, for there smiling at me was a little boy the very image of Graham when he was that age.' She paused to look lovingly at Stuart, innocently engrossed with his bricks.

'She denied it was your child when I challenged her,' Hannah continued as she looked directly at Wendy. 'Said she was looking after him for a friend. Then she claimed he was hers from a failed relationship. In the end she relented and admitted she believed Sid to be the father and wanted to raise him as her own. She said she could not let him be adopted for the same reason as she had never married; ranted on about being a cuckoo in a bird's nest.'

Wendy remembered Aunt Ethel telling her about the cuckoo. Her childhood must have been horrific for her to be so mentally scarred. The thought made Wendy feel pity towards her.

'I rang Graham this morning, but before I said anything I could tell something was wrong.'

'I had just opened a letter from the hospital regarding my test,' Graham explained as he turned directly to face Wendy. 'I have a low sperm count so I might not be able to father any children. I was so down about it I said it was a good job we had fallen out because I couldn't have married you.'

'I love you.' Wendy squeezed his hand affectionately. 'Whether we could have ten children or none wouldn't make any difference, the main thing is your health and that you're clear of cancer.'

Graham nodded.

'After he told me about the pathology result I did eventually manage to get him to confess to er… an indiscretion with you one Christmas,' Hannah said being as tactful as she could.

'That much I know,' uttered Wendy. 'You really must have thought I was really obscene to have been with my stepbrother and when I was underage.'

'Not at all,' Hannah replied. 'How could you possibly have any moral scruples when Sid had been forcing himself on you for two years?'

At that moment a brick that Stuart was trying to put on a stack of five fell and he threw a tantrum, knocking down the other bricks with his hand as he cried out.

Wendy immediately knelt on the floor in front of him. 'Let me play with you,' she said. 'You've got my blue eyes but I hope you haven't got my temper. You were born on a Sunday and the child that's born on the Sabbath day is fair and wise and good they say.'

He watched Wendy collect the lettered bricks and arrange them in a line to spell his name. 'Stuart,' she said slowly as she pointed to the bricks and then repeated it.

'Two at,' he mimicked.

She took some more bricks to spell mammy but there were not enough ems, so she settled for mam. Pointing to her chest with one hand and the bricks with the other she slowly kept repeating, "Mammy", until he said, 'Mam a,' bringing a huge smile to her face.

'I must get back to see what sort of mess the builders have made of my hotel while I've been away,' Hannah said, rising quietly from her armchair.

It brought an end to Graham's captivating watching of his son and Wendy. 'I'll run you home.'

'You stay here with your family, I can catch a bus.'

'Let Graham run you home,' said Wendy without taking her eyes off of Stuart, 'then he can bring back some fish and chips. I'm famished.'

Wendy wanted to spend as much time with Stuart as she could so after the meal the chest of drawers were moved out of the bedroom to make room for the cot; a brand new one that Hannah and Graham had purchased earlier at Robotham's. To settle him to sleep she told the story of "Goldilocks" but he was still awake at the end of it. She continued to speak softly as she went on to make up a story about a wicked giant keeping a little girl prisoner in his castle and treating her very badly. Wendy stopped when she saw Stuart was asleep and felt Graham's hand rest comfortingly on her shoulder.

'I expect I shall have to go home soon,' he whispered.

'Go?' Wendy repeated, 'you're not going anywhere, what if our son wakes up and cries for his daddy?'

'But where shall I sleep?'

Wendy turned her head to look at the double bed and smiled as she nodded towards it. 'We've got a lot to sort out, an engagement party, a wedding and somewhere for us all to live.' She paused to peck him a kiss. 'And you had better be careful because, low sperm count or not, I'm not having any more of your babies out of wedlock.'

CHAPTER TWENTY-THREE

Henry had just settled in his office when Wendy tapped on the door and entered. 'Good morning,' she greeted as jubilantly as a playful kitten without a care in the world. 'I wonder if you would mind coming upstairs for a moment, there's somebody I'd rather like you to meet.'

Henry was curious and abandoned opening the post. She had that radiant look in her eye that compelled him to follow her to the lounge of her flat without saying a word.

'This is my son, Stuart,' she said proudly as she scooped him off the carpet. 'Say hello to my boss,' she urged holding him with her right arm and supporting him on her hip like any natural mother.

A feather would have floored Henry. He stood staring at them both, astonished and speechless.

'I always suspected that you ran away from something when you came here, but never in a thousand years would I have thought it was a son,' Henry said after regaining sufficient composure.

'I didn't run from him,' Wendy corrected, 'I ran away because of him. Because of the scandal of being pregnant so young and the torture of his adoption.' She looked dotingly at Stuart who had his thumb in his mouth and seemed fascinated by Henry's spectacles. 'But now none of it matters, I don't care who knows or what they think of me. I'm the happiest person in the world.' She

279

affectionately kissed Stuart's forehead. 'I've got my son back and nobody will ever take him from me again.'

'He is a lovely little chap and even I can tell he has your blue eyes. You must be very proud.'

'Oh I am, Henry, I really am.'

'What's going to happen?' He gave a familiar throat-clearing grunt. 'Are you about to tell me you are leaving?'

Wendy's smile went from ear to ear. If only Henry knew this was the very day she had intended to give her notice. 'You can't get rid of me that easily. Hannah and Gwyneth are going to look after him during the day.' Still cradling Stuart, she moved to stand close to him. 'But I do have a favour to ask. I wonder if you would give me away at my wedding.'

Henry immediately nodded his response, being too emotionally overcome to speak.

'Come on, Henry, surely I'm not that bad?'

Nobody thought she was bad. All her agonizing had been in vain because nobody despised her. The entire hassle in planning to flee to Norwich had been to no avail because nobody ridiculed her.

Having just settled Stuart in his cot, Wendy started the washing up. The last three months of her life had flown by. Organizing a wedding was hard work and time consuming. There had been calm and calamity, joy and despair, order and chaos and times when she had felt like running off with Graham to the Registry Office for a simple no-fuss marriage. But it was too late for that option. Hannah had placed a notice in the *Daily Telegraph* for her forthcoming wedding on Saturday the twenty-ninth of November, a week and a day away. Her doorbell ringing like an emergency services vehicle interrupted her thoughts.

She opened the door to find a man standing at the bottom of the outside steps with a newspaper tucked under the arm of his beige raincoat. She stood nervously still and stared at him. What was so familiar about him? Why was she so apprehensive?

He politely raised his Trilby hat and handed Wendy a note; a note that was going to change her life forever.

"I am Ted Marshall and I think I am your father. I cannot talk because I was seriously wounded at Dunkirk with a head injury. That is why I have to write everything down. I saw this forthcoming wedding announcement in the *Daily Telegraph* and got a friend to trace and telephone Mrs Hannah Owen that has led me here. Is your mother with you?"

Wendy continued to stare with glazed eyes. She reeled off the brief details of her mother's death as if she was in a hypnotic trance.

But then it snapped!

Her whole body quivered as though an army of industrious ants were crawling over her. She rushed down the steps and threw herself at him. 'Dad! You're my dad! You're my lovely, lovely dad.'

The embrace was complete when his arms shot around her and the newspaper fell to the floor with a thud.

She would have stayed locked in his arms all night had it not been for the telephone ringing, fearful that if she let go he would disappear and she would wake from her dream. But it was no dream and he did not disappear. She took his hand and led him quickly up the stairs. She reached the phone just in time to find it was Hannah checking if everything was all right.

Well into the early hours of the morning, lifetimes of information passed between them, her forty-two-year-old father listening and writing, Wendy talking and reading.

On the blood-stained beaches of Dunkirk, Ted had received multiple injuries when a bomb had exploded close to his dug out. Cuts, bruises, a gashed arm and a broken leg had resulted, along with unconsciousness, following a massive blow to his head. In time everything had healed but the head. According to the doctors the blow had damaged the dominant section in the left cerebral hemisphere, which was the part of his brain that affected his speech. In simple terms, it had been explained to him that it was like having a permanent stroke that only affected his speech.

Later he discovered his identity disc had been stolen and replaced with one belonging to a criminal soldier who was wanted by the English police. Not that it had done him much good, for he was killed boarding a fishing vessel, one of the armada of small vessels that had made the perilous crossing to rescue the British forces.

It was March 1941 before he was transferred from a field hospital to a prisoner of war camp from where he wrote many letters to Doris to an address that she no longer lived at.

After the war, his search for his wife and child had been unsuccessful, hampered by his inability to talk and the fact that friends and neighbours were either dead or had moved away from Plaistow. In the aftermath of war, neither the Red Cross nor the British Legion had been successful either.

He got a job as a porter at Plaistow hospital where in time he was able to discover that he had fathered a daughter. He still worked at the hospital, he still went to see West Ham United play football and he still went to the pub at lunchtimes on Sunday for a game of dominoes. But he had never stopped searching for Doris and Wendy.

Wendy knew from her mother's overheard conversations that they had moved frequently when she was a baby, Reading; Ongar, Baldock and Harpenden being some places that she could recall. Often with her mother working as a temporary live-in barmaid and all before she met and married Michael's father. It was no wonder her father could not trace them when they had moved so frequently and her mother remarried twice.

Wendy was far too excited to sleep. Her life had been transformed from a caterpillar to a butterfly like the hundreds fluttering in her stomach. As the new day dawned she suddenly realized that the arrival of her father had caused a problem. What would she say to Henry?

He was smiling radiantly when she entered his office at eight fifteen. It was like winding the clock back to the black Monday when she was going to give her notice.

'Wendy, I've some wonderful news for you.'

'And I have some pretty startling news for you.'

'Go on then, ladies first.'

She told him but before she reached the awkward part he interrupted.

'You're trying to tell me you do not want me to take you down the aisle?'

She was mystified as to why he was still glowing like a brazier when she thought he would be devastated. Then he enlightened her with his news.

Felicity and Colin were not legally married. It made for an easier life for them to say that they were when they ran off to Inverness. They admitted it last night because they did want to get married and as soon as possible before baby number two comes along. Henry's dream of walking his own daughter down the aisle was going to be realized.

The wedding took place in the Clarendon Park Congregational Church on a day that had begun shrouded in fog, but was free of rain. Her father looked very distinguished in his hired morning suit as he slowly walked down the aisle with Wendy delicately clutching his arm.

She looked sensational, wearing a shimmering cream dress with three-quarter sleeves, figure hugging bodice and a V-neck showing a glimpse of cleavage. Beneath her veil, her eyes sparkled like diamonds and her face flushed with euphoric joy.

Anne and Liz were her bridesmaids and they looked stunning in their full-length turquoise dresses. Liz had completed most of the work in making a little navy blue velvet suit for Stuart who took his pageboy duties very seriously by clinging to Wendy's train as if his young life depended on it.

Graham twitched nervously as the organist played the wedding march but looked extremely handsome in his hired morning suit. Michael was similarly attired and had never looked smarter in his whole life.

Hannah tried hard not to cry. She took great pride in her part in getting these two people to the altar. Graham looked very handsome, so much a young Clifford, and Wendy resplendent with the same charismatic aura that Hannah recognized when she turned up at her hotel. That night was the first time she had ever talked openly about Clifford and unlocked the secrets of her life. It was that night when she realized Wendy was in love with her son.

'With this ring I thee wed.' Graham's words sounded confident after the embarrassment caused when Michael dropped the ring on the floor with a resounding ping.

Mrs Bellamy, flanked by Ralph and Veronica, cried joyously throughout the entire service, happy that Wendy was marrying a young man that was very dashing and debonair. She always thought she doted on Graham and now she knew the reason why.

Harry Chadwick recalled the first Saturday that Graham came to work for him. "What could he buy for his sister?" At the time he thought Graham's question was an excuse to buy something for his sweetheart. How could he know that they were one and the same person?

Dudley, with his Malay wife and daughter, were additional guests, having arrived back in England in October. He had fully realized his father's dreams by joining him in the practice, which had rapidly expanded by Henry acquiring new clients from an accountant selling his business in order to retire. The clerks from the office had been invited. Brian with the young lady he was hoping to marry in January, Clive with his new fiancé, Kevin with his girlfriend and Barry. They all showed a curious interest in Liz who was going to be both Henry's new tenant of the flat and an additional typist in the office.

A surprise guest that Wendy insisted on inviting was Aunt Ethel with her hair tied in a bun as it always was. Wendy had learned that a work colleague of her aunt's had a baby a month before Stuart and had become his child minder during Ethel's working hours, a mutually convenient arrangement for them both. He was at this friend's house the night Wendy and her mother spent at Peterborough immediately after the birth. Despite her peculiar motives for wanting to keep Stuart, Wendy had soon realized that she had loved and cared for her son, which is why she threw the olive branch of forgiveness by inviting her to the wedding.

At twenty minutes past two Wendy became Mrs Marshall-Owen. Mrs Rawlins she was never going to be. Owen was the name that Graham now went by, Hannah having organized the necessary legal documents to officially change his name by deed poll. It was not for a desire to be posh, as Liz had jokingly accused her that she opted for the double barrel name. It was for the sake of her son whose birth certificate read "Stuart Marshall".

An immensely proud Wendy stood outside the church with Graham on one side, her father on the other and Stuart at her feet. Three generations of males that had caused her heart to ache on many occasions. The older because she thought she would never ever see him, the younger because she thought she had given him away for good and the gorgeous handsome sweetheart she thought she would never be able to marry. The aches had gone, her heart bubbled like fine champagne and she was effervescent.

The reception was at Hannah's hotel. The honeymoon was spent in London, where she spent a day resting from love-making to visit her dad who had returned to his council flat in Plaistow. A week later Graham carried her over the threshold of their house, an amiable semi-detached in Roehampton Drive that was yards outside of the city boundary in Wigston Fields.

Every time Wendy left a shop with a pack of Tampax she felt sad. Was Graham's sperm count so low she would never conceive? Disappointed though that would make her it was something she had to face up to when all she wanted, all she longed for was for one little sperm to have the strength to start a new life within her.

Her wedding had triggered a baby boom with everybody else. Gwyneth had given birth to Fiona, a Friday child, the following April. A month before that Mrs Bellamy had written to tell her that Veronica was pregnant and her grandson Richard had been born ten days after Stuart's third birthday on the twenty-sixth of September. Anne had only been married to Trevor for ten months when she gave birth to a daughter, Lauren. Wendy had been the only bridesmaid at the wedding on a blustery March day and was due to be a godparent at the christening.

Colin and Felicity had married in January but their second baby, Ian another Friday child, had been born eighteen months later on the seventeenth of June. Wendy had been very excited when she had cuddled him for the first time because she was a week late.

It was on the morning of her twentieth birthday during their second annual holiday as a complete family that she decided to make her announcement. It was the second holiday that they had spent at Caister in Harry Chadwick's caravan and the second holiday when her father had been with them. It was ten weeks after her last menstrual cycle and following four weeks of regular bouts of morning sickness.

'I'm pregnant.'

Graham was over the moon and soon rang Hannah from a call box by the station and the news spread quicker than a blazing bush fire to family and friends. Even the unflappable Michael had been excited, particularly when he learned the baby's due date was close to his birthday in February.

Lizzie was three months older than Michael, her eighteenth birthday falling ten days before Wendy's second wedding anniversary in November 1960. It was celebrated at a recently opened Chinese restaurant in Northampton Street, where in the company of Graham, Henry, Hannah and Lizzie's parents that had travelled from Norwich for the weekend, she and Michael announced their engagement. Bulging and happily pregnant Wendy was thrilled at the news.

The snow had been falling for two hours and covered the road like a white blanket when Wendy looked out of the window of her house at twenty minutes past six. She was anxious for Graham who would normally be home by now as she watched a car struggle on the uphill slope of Roehampton Drive with the falling snow appearing to be attracted to the headlights.

'Is that Daddy's car?' Stuart asked as he sat at the table, drawing with his crayons.

It started. It was the twenty-first of February and she was already a day late, but her first mild contraction sent her quickly to the chair. She rang Graham but he had already left the hotel. He arrived home as Wendy's second contraction started twelve minutes later.

'How long will it be now?' he asked, concerned but not panicking.

'I don't know. I was nine hours with Stuart. Will you ring the midwife? Her number's on that notepad by the phone.'

The midwife arrived shortly before seven thirty, having abandoned her car as soon as she turned off the gritted main road. Wendy was relieved that everything was normal including her blood pressure.

'While your husband's putting your son to bed we'll get you shaved,' said the midwife. 'I expect you want a girl this time.'

'It would be nice but I don't mind as long as everything is all right.'

'That's what everybody says. Have you got all your names ready?'

'Rachel if it's a girl, I'm not sure if it's a boy. I like Mark and Graham likes the name John.'

'Rachel is a sweet name, let's hope you have a little girl, then there needn't be any arguments.'

Wendy's labour lasted almost six hours and she was holding Graham's hand very tightly when their baby was born. He wiped the sweat from her brow with a towel and whispered excitedly, 'It's a girl.'

A few moments later Wendy was given her daughter to hold. Her freshly washed skin was all pink and wrinkled but her bright blue eyes looked eagerly at Wendy as she leaned forward and kissed her forehead.

'I'm going to enjoy you,' she whispered then spoke to the midwife. 'When will she want a feed? My breasts feel as though they are bursting with milk.'

'Soon,' the midwife answered as she wrote her notes. 'Born on the twenty-second of February.'

'That was my Mam's birthday,' said Wendy happily until the full implication of the midwife's statement hit her. 'What time was she born?'

'Five minutes after midnight,' the midwife answered. 'If she had have come any sooner she would have missed your mother's birthday.'

'Oh no!' Wendy said softly, 'Rachel is another Wednesday's child!'